# Jen Wylie

# Broken Aro

Untold
Press

# BROKEN ARO
# BOOK ONE OF THE BROKEN ONES

An Untold Press Novel
First Printing, October 2012

Published by Untold Press LLC
114 NE Estia Lane
Port St Lucie, FL 34983

ISBN: 978-0615703367

PRODUCED IN THE UNITED STATES OF AMERICA

10 9 8 7 6 5 4 3 2 1

# Dedication

To the one who was my best friend before becoming everything else.

You've kept me strong, and you've kept me going through all the hard times. Your patience and constant encouragement not only brought me back to myself, but made this book possible.

You're my angel, too.

# Special Thanks

As with any great endeavor, there are always so many people who help you along the way. Special thanks to my parents, kids, and Sean for their continual, never ending support. To my new friends, Terri-Lynne and Kim, dealing with authors may not be the easiest thing in the world, but I owe you a debt of thanks for helping me make Aro even better. To Donna, Jackie, and Erin for those last sets of eyes to make sure it is perfect, and to Rusty and Julie for their continued support.

Jen Wylie

# Prologue

## Fifteen Years Ago

He soared high above the coast, air rippling beneath his wings. Dipping through clouds, he enjoyed the coolness of the light wind whirling around him. Sunlight sparkled on the ocean waves far below, little winking lights breaking the monotony of the empty waters.

Like a fledgling, he played amongst the wispy clouds. Snapping his giant wings open, he broke a dive, spun, and with powerful beats, rose higher once more. Even after thousands of years, the joy of flying still excited him. It was one of the few things still able to send a thrill coursing through his veins.

From the corner of his eye, a dark spot caught his attention and he turned, spiraling around it. A ship, while not uncommon along the coast, usually wasn't found this far north. He dropped lower, noting it was a large vessel capable of making the long journey across the sea. There were fewer of them now that the humans occupied the entire eastern coastline with their pathetic little cities.

He twisted, flicking his tail, and circled. There, on the secluded beach...little spots scurrying around a smaller boat. The humans of the east were mostly pirates and slavers. Few partook of practices such as legal trade or simple transport, particularly anyone with such long range ships. They were all criminals anyways, so why would someone be picked up from a beach when there were perfectly good ports available?

Even more curious, he dropped lower, expanding his senses and almost missing a wing-beat.

*Fey? It couldn't be...* He circled above, watching with his senses fully alert. Most of the little bodies below were human, but two were indeed Fey. He watched the humans fill the small boat with items from the shore and then head back to the larger ship.

He debated investigating further. If he was seen by the humans in dragon form it could prove troublesome. He couldn't help himself. This was *interesting*. Anything that could catch his attention, or give his mind something to do, was treasured. Like flight, curiosity still brought him joy.

He did take some care not to be spotted, dropping quickly, and into a cove further north. Large rocks cut the beach into small pockets and provided some cover. Once on the ground, he quickly shifted forms.

The Fey knew he was there before he emerged from the outcropping of rocks separating the coves. The only two people left on the beach, he watched their reaction to his arrival as he walked toward them. Their momentary confusion amused him.

The woman's eyes opened wide as they took in his appearance. They knew at a glance he was none of the known races. "You're not..." Shock of *what* stalked toward them spread across their faces.

A smile twisted at his lips as he drew closer. The male stood straighter, stepping in front of the woman. Their eyes glowed with an inner orange light.

*Orange...not red. Even more interesting.*

He stopped before them, extremely pleased with his decision to investigate. These Fey could easily pass for human. Young, beautiful ones, but still human. Each wore their hair long, covering their slightly pointed ears. His hair was brown, hers pale as corn silk. By the quality of their dress, he could tell they weren't wild Fey. They were not covered in scavenged rags or hides. Their clothing was handmade, clearly bought from one of the city's markets. Most importantly, they weren't raving mad. How this could be, he couldn't fathom. Since their fall centuries ago, the creatures had become red-eyed killers, locked in their fury, rarely able to escape or control it.

This pair had managed it, somehow. That they did not fall into it now, in his presence, spoke highly of them.

"Dragos," the male said stiffly. "You are not wanted here."

He smiled. As if such things would ever bother him. "I go where I wish, when I wish. You should know this, Fey." His eyes narrowed slightly. There was something familiar about them... He searched his vast memories, carefully flipping through those that involved past encounters with their kind. *Yes...there.* Almost six centuries ago, the last time he had visited their city and their queen. This male had been at court, though not introduced.

He looked to the woman. She had been. "Dalsia." He tilted his head slightly to her. "Seer's daughter."

She stiffened, her eyes widening and shifting slightly more toward red. She tilted her head, not at him, but to whisper to her mate. "He is the Dragos named Damon."

He pushed slightly at the males mind, searching for a name. *Ketheris.*

The Fey glared at him. "Stay out of my head."

He ignored the demand and stepped to the side. He'd found more than just a name, also the Fey's current most frantic thought. Behind him, tucked against Dalsia and hidden in her arms, was a young child.

"What do you want?" Dalsia stepped forward, no longer hiding, but still holding the little one tightly.

Damon regarded her a moment. His curiosity now fully piqued, he smiled slightly. "Did you not fall in the fury? Or did you somehow recover?"

"We did not," Ketheris replied tersely.

They were strong then, stronger than most. Not only for keeping their sanity, but for surviving the mindless slaughter that came after. "Why are you going west?"

They blinked at him, perhaps surprised he knew their destination, or that he would care. "We are just traveling," Ketheris said.

*Lie.* He looked to Dalsia. Her lips pressed tightly together. He slowly pushed at her mind until she spoke.

"We're searching for an artifact to heal the Fey," she snapped.

He smiled. Her words intrigued him. "Continue."

The two exchanged glances. He could see the intelligence in their eyes. That intelligence meant he would have his answers one way or another. As a race, the Fey were not telepathic and few had learned more than rudimentary methods to shield themselves. These two had decent protection for their thoughts, but their walls were only weak little barriers he could push through in the blink of an eye.

"Some of the Seer's prophecies give us hope," Dalsia finally answered.

He knew of the Seer, of her garbled prophecies. All of the races did, except the brainless humans who were concerned with nothing but themselves. Being the only mortal race, he didn't particularly blame them. He had not been aware knowledge of the prophecies had survived. Of course he never really cared or bothered to find out either. He had been occupied and amused for decades with the chaos that ensued and then went on to other pursuits.

Dalsia, he recalled, was the only daughter of the Queen's Seer. She had been the Recorder, attempting to put the prophecies into order and decipher them.

He held out a hand. "I would see them."

Her jaw trembled in anger as she glared at him. She looked to her mate and nodded once sharply. Ketheris pulled a small book from a leather bag at her side, her hands being full with her child.

He took it graciously. They were cooperating after all. "Thank you."

He flipped through pages, worn and old, the ink fading but still readable. Each page contained a garbled mess of words and underneath, her interpretations of them, sometimes going on for pages. Reading and memorizing quickly, he stopped at the prophecy they spoke of.

Damon looked at the Fey and laughed. "You're looking for some ancient, broken weapon?"

Ketheris nodded, his face grim. "We've spent centuries scouring all the eastern lands. Unless the Elves have it, it is not here. Besides..." He stopped and glanced at his wife.

She shook her head slightly.

Damon looked back down at the worn book, flipping through more pages. Suddenly he stopped. He read the short line of prophecy twice and then looked up. "I see." His gaze went from Ketheris, to Dalsia, and then to the small child in her arms. "You think you'll find it now."

Dalsia reached out and when he didn't argue, took the book back. "It is time. We didn't understand that at first..." She smiled down at her son. "But now we do."

Damon stepped closer, ignoring how the woman froze. He bent over slightly, taking a closer look at the child. "What is your name, little one?"

The boy blinked up at him with innocent golden eyes.

Damon frowned.

"Kei," his mother said quickly. She held the boy tighter to her chest. "Don't you dare go into his mind. You know what that would do to a child."

He leaned back, chuckling at the vehemence of her words. Mothers and their young.

"Will you tell him?"

"When he's old enough to understand his part," Ketheris said.

Damon nodded. "Very well. I will let you be on your way. Safe seas to you."

The Fey regarded him warily, but spoke a soft farewell.

He wandered slowly up the beach, and kept walking, lost in thought. Could the Fey be healed? If they were...yes, things would certainly become interesting again. He was curious how the other races would react.

He paused and looked out to sea at the ship waiting to take the first Fey to the west. It was not a trip he would care to make, the currents over the sea could be vicious, as would the human's reaction to a dragon in their lands. No, he would watch and wait for their return. He would mull over the prophecies he'd memorized.

With another smile he continued walking, his boredom forgotten.

Jen Wylie

# Chapter 1
## When Bells are Ringing

*My dearest Arowyn,*

*I hope this letter finds you well. Everything is mostly quiet up here. Have you heard from your brothers again? I hope the note I included in my last letter sorted out the situation with the baker. Did you apologize like I asked you to?*

*How are your studies progressing? You were supposed to include updates from your tutors in your last letter. That you did not rather concerns me. Be sure to do so this time. I heard from John Harris that you were quite helpful to his wife and daughter not long ago. She praised you greatly in a letter to him. It gave me great pride to hear of your kind and generous actions.*

*I bet you cannot guess what I found last week. Maybe I should make you guess, but you would just get cranky. I know you would never guess right either. I found a boy in the woods, close to your age, maybe a little older. He is quite wild, and feisty. Even more so than you, if you can believe that. I have him here at the fort and it is taking him a while to settle in, but I am confident a little time is all it will take. By fall I am sure he will be much quieter. I am certain you will like him. I have grown quite fond of him myself. He will certainly fit right in. I can already imagine the trouble you will all get into. I expect you to be on your best behavior when I come home then, understand?*

# Broken Aro

*Be a good girl, keep up with your studies, and please, stay away from the swords. Wait until your brothers or I are home. I love you with all my heart, my daughter, and miss you more than words can say.*

The clanging of bells jerked her attention away from the old letter. Resisting the urge to hide her head under her pillow, Arowyn winced at the noise and sat up. The dim light of early morning filtered into her small bedroom, barely enough to read by. Certainly way too early for the market bells. She carefully folded the two year old letter and set it to the side. Crawling over the bed to the window, she pushed open the shutters.

Cool, fall air greeted her face. A slight breeze between the houses ruffled her long dark hair. Bracing herself on the windowsill, she leaned out, looking down the narrow alley toward the street. People were running every which way, some still in their night clothes. She grinned at that, until the reason suddenly occurred to her.

She jerked back inside, pulling the shutters closed. A heavy lump formed in her stomach. It wasn't the market bells ringing, but the ones from within the watch towers along the city wall.

She knelt on the small bed and wrapped her arms around herself, staring straight ahead in shock. *So soon? They couldn't be attacking already!*

Thumping on the stairs caused her head to turn and relief flooded her. She'd be just fine. Her brothers had come home just the day before. Of course they'd brought an enemy army on their heels, but at least they were here and could tell her what to do. Being alone from spring to fall every year sucked rotten eggs. She survived the loneliness, but she didn't like it.

One of them banged on her door. "Aro! Wake up and get downstairs!"

"I'm coming," she told Danny, the middle brother. Springing off the bed, she didn't bother with getting dressed. Her brothers were nothing but efficient and orderly; military to the core. If they'd wanted her to get dressed first they would have said so.

Before doing anything, she returned her father's letter to its safe place. Taking the stairs two at a time, she stumbled into organized chaos. All seven of her brothers were awake, dressed in their uniforms and light armor, and moving about in all different directions. *Had they even gone to sleep?*

Ryan grabbed her by the shoulders and steered her to the dining room table. "Eat."

She blinked once and obeyed. Dirty dishes piled on the counter proved everyone else had already eaten. She shoveled fried eggs into her mouth and just watched. Paul was bent over a swath of papers at the other end of the long table. Elliott was going through the very bare pantry and tossing most of the food he found to the side. Joel quickly jammed everything into packs. She could hear the others banging around and talking in various parts of the house.

Elliott caught her attention. "Is there more? Anywhere else?"

She shook her head and swallowed a mouthful of egg. "I didn't know you'd–"

"Paul," he cut her off. "We've a problem with supplies."

Her oldest brother looked up from his papers. "Take Joel and go to Old Lady Wences. She always has extra." Elliott nodded and gathered up a few empty packs as Joel quickly finished filling the others. "Don't forget to pay her," Paul added.

Elliott snorted. "Does it matter?"

"Just do it."

# Broken Aro

Aro watched the exchange wide-eyed. Her brothers never acted like this; at least not at home. They were all so...serious. The eggs suddenly left a bad taste in her mouth. Would the Gelanians actually get past their walls? They never had before...but then they'd hardly ever breached the mountain passes either. Until this summer when they managed to take them and push into the valley. Almost every day word had come down how they kept moving forward. So many people had died, so many towns and villages fallen. Their land supply routes were quickly lost. The city's population had swelled to more than double with refugees.

She understood the basics of all of this, she'd grown up in a military family. She planned on joining the army as soon as she came of age. She paid attention to conversations. She knew more people and less food meant falling morale. She almost smiled. It hadn't, and mostly because of her brothers. The seven Mason brothers were the country's most famous soldiers, and they were *her* brothers. She knew they would do absolutely everything to keep her safe.

Sammy bounded into the room, his eyes bright and mischievous. "I think this will do." He dropped a pile of clothes on the table. "Are you finished yet?"

She nodded and took her plate to the counter. "What's all this?"

"Her hair first," Paul said absently.

Her head shot around to look at him. "What about my hair?"

Elliott and Joel left through the side door, letting in the sound of the bells. Paul paused, listening. "We don't have much time left."

"Time for what?"

"Where are the scissors?"

She blinked. "I don't know."

Sammy ran his hand over his forehead. "Sit down, Aro."

She sat, her heart pounding faster as Sammy drew his knife. "You are not cutting my hair!"

"Don't be difficult," Paul said.

Normally, she listened to Paul. At thirty-two he was the oldest. He'd easily taken over the role of leader in the family when their father died only two years ago. She fumed as Sammy grabbed a handful of hair at the base of her neck. No, she couldn't let them cut it. "Don't you dare," she said suddenly, pulling away again.

"Aro! Sit still," Sammy jerked her back into place by her hair.

"Ow! You idiot! That hurt!"

Paul slammed his fist on the table. "Stop. Now." He looked at her. "We're leaving the city. We will be traveling and it will be easier if you're a boy. Understand?"

Her mouth opened and closed again. Everything he said was too much to take in. While her mind tried to figure out what was going on, Sammy started hacking away at her waist-length hair.

Once the first locks fell she gave up. Clenching her teeth, she tried to keep the tears away.

"I'm sorry," Sammy whispered.

She raised her chin. "Go rot."

By the time he was done her head felt funny. Sammy hadn't cut it very short, some pieces fell almost to her shoulders. Others hung around her ears and over her eyes. By the way her brothers wouldn't look at her, she figured he'd done a rather terrible job. She glared at Sammy, she'd get him back. Yes, she would.

She fingered her hair and made a face. "Gah."

Paul frowned over at her. "You're not five."

He always said that, so had father. Tears stung her eyes and she blinked them away.

"Go get dressed now," Paul said quietly.

Pressing her lips tightly together, she nodded. She'd have been angrier, but knew he hadn't done it out of spite. "How long do we have?"

Paul shook his head. "I don't know yet. Don't take too long."

She looked at Sammy, but he was avoiding her. Picking up the pile of clothes she headed up the stairs without a word.

Once in her room, she tossed the pile on the bed and started rifling through it. Everything was old and smelled musty. Castoffs from when the boys had first joined the army. She slipped off her nightdress and into the old clothes. The pants were too big, but no surprise there. With a grumble she went back downstairs. "This isn't going to work."

Paul actually chuckled. Sammy had gone off somewhere, but Ryan and Danny had returned. They stared at her and then looked to Paul. "What did you do?"

She reached up to touch her hair and her pants almost fell down. The boys started laughing and she glared at them. "This wasn't my idea! Now fix it!"

Ryan ran upstairs and brought her a belt, while Danny rolled up her pants and gave her a pair of boots. By the time her clothes were mostly staying in place Sammy came back in from the side door, arms full once more.

"Now what?"

The pile he dumped on the table made her smile this time though. Armor and weapons. She ran her finger gingerly along the blade of the nearest knife and grinned up at her brothers. "I forgive you."

Danny and Ryan sorted through the pile and fitted her out, cursing under their breaths as they tried to adjust everything to fit her. She smiled over at Sammy, her hands on her knives. At least he'd brought them for her and she was allowed to wear them out.

Everyone froze at the deep resonating bell sounding through the city. She gripped her knives tightly and looked to Paul, hoping he'd have another explanation than the one in her head.

"The port is under attack," he said, answering her unasked question.

She looked down, trying to push the sudden fear away and wondering where the Gelanians had gotten boats, or who they'd allied with.

"We need to move. Sammy check on Elliott and Joel. Danny see if you can find Aaron."

"Where'd he go?"

Paul started gathering up all his papers quickly and packing them into a leather pouch.

"He went to see what the word was," Ryan answered. He lowered his voice. "We're heading out shortly. If there is anything you want to take, there's a little room."

Aro nodded and darted up the stairs to her room. *What to take?* She knew better than to try to drag down a bag full of stuff. *Little things. The most important things.* She went straight to the small carved box on her dresser. It wasn't large or heavy, but held her most valued possessions. Well other than her weapons. She glanced around the room, checking to see if there was anything else. Seeing nothing she had to have, she ran back downstairs and handed the box to Ryan.

"That's it?"

She nodded, feeling rather proud of herself, and watched him open it. He lifted the small pile of letters from Father, noted the few bits of jewelry that had belonged to a mother she didn't remember, and a few other small odds and ends. He smiled and closed the box.

"Good girl." He ruffled her hair and winced, then patted her head awkwardly.

With a scowl she tried to smooth her hair back down. She hadn't thought to look in the mirror upstairs to see how bad a job Sammy had done. Maybe that was a good thing. "Can I bring my bow?"

Ryan chuckled and shook his head. "We'll be moving fast, so no."

"What about my sword?"

"You'll do fine with your knives. There shouldn't be any fighting, if there is, keep close to us and do what you're told."

She nodded, not taking offense at his words. Disobeying could get her killed, she'd heard enough stories about such things.

Raised voices by the side door caused them both to turn. Raising her eyebrows she followed Ryan into the kitchen area.

Elliott, Joel and Sammy were back but standing off to the side. Paul stood with his hands on his hips while Aaron glared at him. Sammy stood beside him, hovering and unsure what to do.

"We don't have time," Paul snapped. "We should have left last night."

Aro looked up at Ryan in alarm. "Why didn't we?"

Everyone heard her. With a frown at Aaron, Paul answered. "Plans needed to be made, and there were..." he paused and looked at the other boys, "things that needed to be dealt with first."

Aaron's cheeks were flushed, and he only did that when someone talked about his girlfriends. Apparently all her brothers were saying goodbye to their lady friends the night before. Somehow she held in an irritated sigh. "So what's the problem now?"

Aaron shook his head, lips tight.

Paul sighed. "If she's smart she listened to you last night and left with Marin and the others."

She blinked in surprise. "They've all left? The others?"

Paul nodded. "Last night with their families."

Marin was another brother, though not of blood. Father had taken in a handful of young soldiers over the years, orphans or those otherwise abandoned by their families. Mostly they were troubled first years, just sixteen years old at the time. He brought them into their home and into their family. Each had adjusted quickly and straightened out, growing up to become wonderful young men. The last had moved out before father had died, two had died in the war, but those left still kept in touch. Her thoughts turned to her father's last letter. He had mentioned a new boy he was going to bring home. But there had been a great battle at the pass. Father had died and the new boy had disappeared.

"Grab the gear. We need to get moving."

Her brothers jumped into motion.

"Wait!" She held out her arm, her hand a fist.

A moment later her brothers joined her in a circle, tapping their fists on hers to build a tower. "Masons! Together. Always."

Suddenly laughing, they each fought to get their fist on top. She hadn't realized how tense everyone had been until she saw them relaxed and grinning like fools. Joel and Sammy accidentally bumped heads and then a friendly scuffle ensued.

Ryan swung an arm around her shoulder. "Come on, Honey Bee. Time to buzz."

The boys hustled about, pulling on packs and strapping on weapons. Before she knew what was happening they were heading out the door. She wasn't prepared for the havoc of the streets. People and riders ran every which way. The screaming made her cringe and the blighted bells were so much louder outside she wanted to stick her fingers in her ears.

A hand at her back directed her down a side street heading toward the north side of the city. It looked like they were headed beyond the mountains to Dressan. They marched through the streets, people making way for them. It was strange the way her brothers circled her, like some rotting noble surrounded by guards.

Elliott glanced over at her. "I hope we didn't make a mistake keeping her with us," he quietly said to Paul.

Her oldest brother shook his head. "The others will be slowed down by the children. We'll protect her better."

"I don't like us separating," Elliott muttered.

"We'll meet up with them in the mountains as planned."

Aro glanced up at Paul. Noting the fierceness on his face, she kept her mouth closed and pretended she hadn't heard the conversation. Her heart hammered away in her chest. She kept a hand on one of her knives. The familiar hilt brought her a little comfort.

The bells were driving her insane. When the ones at the wall suddenly stopped she almost walked into Elliott's back. Her brothers stood in silence. She didn't know what they were waiting for until she heard the ringing of the market bells above the deeper port bells.

Paul ran a hand through his short dark hair and cursed. He pointed, swinging a finger to Elliott and Ryan. "Check it out." They dropped their packs and took off at jog through the streets. Aaron grabbed their packs as Paul gestured them all into a side street.

Frantic citizens continued to run and scream. *Where were they were running to, the palace?*

Her brothers stood quiet and alert, listening and muttering amongst themselves. She heard some people shouting there were a hundred Gelanian ships in the harbor. She snorted at that. The Gelanians had hardly any ships, and those only small trading and fishing vessels.

A little later others started shouting about the Frans. Paul cursed loudly and she echoed his sentiment with more than a little alarm. Everyone knew about the Frans. They lived across the sea on the eastern continent. They were criminals and slavers who attacked not only ships at sea, but also the coastal northern countries. They would have enough ships to launch a sea attack. *Had the Gelanians allied with them?* It was hard to tell, all the people were panicked and rumors were spreading like wild fire.

Elliott and Ryan returned at a run.

Paul didn't even let them catch their breath. "What's the word?"

"The wall's being swarmed," Ryan said.

"Remember those strange soldiers we saw a few days ago?" Paul nodded at Elliott. "You were right, they aren't Gelanians. Looks like they hired mercenaries."

"How many?"

"Three or four thousand."

"The walls won't hold. We don't have enough men to cover it and the port."

"The port is under attack?"

Paul grimaced and nodded. "Looks like they're quite serious this time."

"The commander was asking about us. I told him we're at the port," Elliott said.

"Good enough," Paul answered. He didn't look happy and Aro didn't blame him.

*Were they supposed to be at the walls? Of course they were. They were the countries best soldiers.* Guilt flooded her. *They'd abandoned their posts. For her. Would the city fall because her brothers weren't on the walls?*

# Broken Aro

*Because they were helping her escape?* Emotions bubbled up inside of her and she clenched her teeth. Yes, she wanted out of the city and safe, but not at the price of others losing their lives.

Sammy cocked his head to the side. "Now what?"

Paul stared off down the street. "We still try for the north gate."

They started off again, this time moving more quickly. The city had only two walls, the main west wall, and a shorter north one that then butted up to cliffs. The southern side of the city was built up to the mountains as well, and the east held more cliffs and then the harbor. The city was naturally well protected, but the sea and cliffs made the number of escape routes a lot smaller. She assumed their current goal was the smaller north gate near the cliffs.

She found it hard to make sense of anything as they ran through the streets. Between the people and the bells everything was utter confusion. Keeping close to her brothers she tried not to panic even when shouts the wall had been breached started to echo down the streets. They would be fine. The gate they headed for was near the middle of the city, not close to the main wall under attack.

The gate finally came into view and a great sigh of relief whooshed out of her. Soon they'd be out and hopefully her heart would dislodge itself from her throat.

The arrows whizzed by, clattering on the stone of the street around her. One of her brothers cursed, but she couldn't tell which one. She dropped into a crouch. An arm pressed over her back as she glanced over at Sammy.

His eyes were wide but he tried to smile. It didn't really work. "Stay down, Aro."

She nodded and looked forward. "Wither me," she gasped. The north wall crawled with men, but not just theirs. More appeared, coming up ladders braced against the wall. She watched the fighting on the walls in fascinated horror. All of her years of lessons hadn't prepared her for the ferocity and blood of true fighting. Kingsport soldiers fought valiantly, but quickly became overwhelmed. Bodies toppled off walls as enemy archers continued to fire into the city.

She stumbled as Sammy grabbed her arm and they all took off running down another side street. Glancing back once, she saw the small north gate literally break open from mounted soldiers pouring through.

"Next plan," Paul hollered over his shoulder. "Ashton's."

She had no idea who Ashton was, but further into the city a number of nobles had land bordering the cliffs. Perhaps this Ashton had an escape route.

The streets were finally cleared of civilians. The odd soldier could be seen running by, carrying messages or other such errands. They ran, keeping close to buildings as they moved from one street to another in the direction of the harbor.

The sound of fighting ahead slowed their progress.

"We're almost there," Paul said, gesturing for them to keep following. They reached the intersection of Baker and Counter streets. The fighting had somehow gotten ahead of them. *Perhaps those attacking the harbor had docked and come ashore to fight.*

Paul stopped and turned, drawing his sword. "Straight through. Two by two. Watch your backs. Keep Aro in the center." He looked over at her. "You're with me."

Before she could say anything, her brothers ran out into the street in pairs, fighting to clear a path for them. She drew her knives and followed Paul, sticking as close to him as she could.

# Broken Aro

Men fought all around her, yelling, screaming, and cursing. Blood sprayed, covering the stones of the street as bodies fell. She gritted her teeth and paid attention to the living. Luckily, their soldiers all wore the same general uniform under their leather armor. More enemy ran into the intersection from another street, jumping into the fight and engaging her brothers.

The clanging of swords and sounds of fighting grew louder, almost drowning out the bells. All her years of practice with her brothers kept her alive as she ducked and dodged around friend and foe. Blood splattered her face and hands. Skipping to the side, a sword slid across her armor, cutting it but not her skin.

She tried to keep an eye on her brothers, but everything moved so quickly she kept losing track of them. Bodies littering the street and growing puddles of blood began to make fighting more difficult. Twisting around, she scanned for more enemies.

An arrow bounced off of Paul's back and she wheeled around, looking for the shooter. He was far down one of the side streets, but there were more advancing behind him. "Archers coming!"

Paul turned and grimaced. "Regroup!"

She followed, jumping over bodies as Paul led them toward the far street. Half a dozen enemies turned a corner ahead and ran toward them. Paul raised a hand and she skidded to a stop behind him.

Her brothers gathered around her and she did a quick head count. Everyone was there, and no one looked to have anything more than a few scratches.

Sammy grinned over at her. "Doing good, sister."

She blinked at him, trying to catch her breath, and then grinned back.

Paul pointed his bloody sword at the men running toward them. "Masons, forward!"

# Chapter 2
## Waking up in Fun Places

Her eyes opened to darkness.

She wasn't surprised. When bad things happened and you finally opened your eyes it was always dark wasn't it? Because otherwise when you woke up you wouldn't be scared, not right away, not until you remembered. Yet in darkness nothing else could be seen but the memories of what had happened, it didn't matter if you opened your eyes or kept them squeezed closed.

What happened...

She closed her eyes again, not against the memories, but the sudden tears and choking sobs. Still, she tried to *not* remember, but her head hurt. All of her hurt, but her head hurt the worst. She'd been hit by something, very hard. She had no trouble remembering the pain. She remembered falling to the ground, her brothers screaming her name over the insane loudness of the fighting and everything fading to nothing as darkness claimed her.

She sucked in a deep breath. The fighting. Yes, the city had been attacked. The walls had been breached. There had been fighting in the streets. *She* had been fighting. Her brothers had been trying to get her out. They had been so close. Had they?

She shifted and froze, terror creeping up her throat and choking her at the same time until nothing but a strangled gurgle came out.

They had not.

# Broken Aro

She knew because she felt the cold metal shackles around each wrist, felt the weight of the chain between them. The same fetters bound her ankles. Dirty straw prickled her cheek and the other smells of her surroundings overcame her. They overwhelmed her and made her gag. The rank scents of piss, shit and vomit almost covered the stale reek of sweat and the tang of salt.

Salt.

She'd thought her head had just been spinning, but no, everything moved, lurching and swaying. She was at sea.

At sea in chains meant only one thing. The rumors had been true. The Gelanians had allied with the Franuan Slavers. Beneath the combined attack, Kingsport had fallen and the Frans had taken their cut, citizens to sell as slaves. She was a slave.

*Well that sucks.*

The idea terrified her, and left her cold and shaking. Squeezing her eyes closed, she fought to push away the horrifying images suddenly assaulting her. Breathing slowly helped a little. The shaking stopped and finally she could breathe again.

She opened her eyes, straining them against the darkness. *Had night fallen? Could that be why it was so dark?* Her eyes slowly adjusted until she could make out vague shapes; the bars of the cell in the ships hold and darker shapes of people sitting before her in the small cell.

She concentrated, squinting her eyes and counting. Six others shared the cell. *Her brothers?* "Paul?" The creak of the ship and the murmurs, curses, and sobs of the other captives in the hold almost drowned out her small voice.

"Boy's awake," one of the shapes said. Definitely not one of her brothers.

She stiffened. They'd called her boy. Even after all she'd been through, it was quite a blow to her self-esteem.

She frowned in confusion for a moment, until she remembered. Her brothers had dressed her in their old clothes, old bits of armor that sort of fit. They'd even hacked off her long hair...

She cursed them under her breath again for that. Then she almost smiled, remembering Sammy's face when he'd done it. Her brothers were such morons. They always had been. Yet they'd been stuck with raising her, and what did they know of girls? Her mother had died when she was four, and losing her hadn't been easy on any of them.

Father had been a regiment Commander and away a lot. They'd all managed to take care of her somehow, the younger of her brothers watching over her until eventually they'd all joined the army. But she'd been twelve by the time the youngest of them had enlisted. She'd been able to take care of the house while they served their time on the border. They didn't worry about her much. The army wives had helped, keeping an eye on her for them.

However, father had died two years ago at Demet's Pass. It had been hard, losing him. Harder than when mother had died because she hadn't been old enough then to know what it meant. Not seeing him at the head of their big old table, with his gentle smile, had been tough on all of them. It still was. It had been harder this past spring when her brothers had all ridden out again. Because death had become something real, she knew they might not come back.

She was fifteen now. Not really a child anymore. So she had faked a smile and waved goodbye to them all when really fear had made her want to scream instead. They had all come home, but with an enemy army at their heels. They'd been afraid then, afraid for her. They knew things she didn't, things like what would happen to a young girl if the city fell. However, she wasn't a woman yet, not in appearance at any rate. Tall and gangly with no figure whatsoever. No wonder she could pass for a boy.

"Boy."

The man who had spoken before broke her thoughts. She must have been hit in the head hard for her mind to wander back into the past. She managed to croak an incoherent sound indicating she'd heard him.

"You alive over there?"

"Yes," she lied and waited. No one else spoke. No one came rushing to her side. Panic quickened her breath as fear sped her heart. Her brothers weren't here. If they had been they'd have harassed everyone to find out where she was. At least... they weren't on *this* boat. Unfortunately, the slavers had a whole fleet. They must be on another boat. She had to believe that. She closed her eyes tightly again. *Yes, they'd been placed on another boat.*

Because if they weren't then they were all dead.

A silent sob shook her when it sunk in she was alone. Curling into a tight ball, she covered her mouth with dirty hands, trying to stay quiet. Her brothers weren't here, quite likely they were dead. Tears slipped down her cheeks in a steady stream. Overwhelming fear shuddered through her body. Her life revolved around her family and her brothers. They were everything to her. Without them she didn't have anyone. Now, when she needed them the most, they weren't here. She would never see them again. Her heart sped up, banging against her chest so hard it hurt. Everything hurt. She couldn't breathe. Everything started spinning. Panic and hysteria overcame her, drenching her in darkness once again

The screaming wouldn't stop. She opened her gritty eyes, and brushed new tears away. The screams tore at her insides. She pulled her hands from her ears. They didn't block the sound much anyways. She sat up, wincing at the faint light. Her head throbbed painfully. Her stomach wasn't feeling too great either and the screams made it worse. People were laughing at the same time and she couldn't figure out why. It didn't make sense.

She looked up to find all the men in the cell staring at her. When she'd sat up, she'd come out of the shadows. She lowered her eyes quickly, ducking her head so her shorn hair fell around her face even more. The ship lurched suddenly and she gritted her teeth when her stomach lurched with it.

One of them sighed. She glanced up to see him jerk his head in the direction of the front of the ship. "They're just at the women again."

They must have thought she'd looked sick because of the screams. She'd been getting to that, her brain had simply been working slower than normal.

She almost did throw up when his words sank in. The women screaming, the slavers laughing, she knew what was happening. Though her brothers tried to keep her in the dark about certain things, she wasn't an idiot.

Looking around the cell again, she scuttled further back into the corner and pulled her knees up, holding them tightly when she started to tremble.

She'd been lucky. The slavers had thought she was a boy when they'd sorted out their new captives. She closed her eyes and rested her forehead on her knees. How long would her luck last before they realized she wasn't a boy? She couldn't do this. She didn't know how, she had no one to help her.

She cringed at another tormented scream.

The men started talking quietly again and she raised her head a little, peeking over her knees. Not all of them. Five of the men sat close together in the center of the small cell. Another sat over in the other corner, hiding in the shadows like her. She knew he was a man, just from what she could see of him. He looked tall and built wiry, like her brothers.

She looked back to the other men. Three were burly, broad of shoulder, and had big muscles. All were obviously fighters. Another looked thinner, but that might have been due to his youth. The last one was shorter, smaller.

She suddenly noticed one of the burly ones staring at her again and she ducked her head quickly, hoping they'd ignore her.

"Boy. Boy. Boy."

The man kept repeating himself, getting angrier each time. *Rot it.* She didn't want to talk. She peeked up again. Yes. He was glaring at her now.

"Don't frighten the young pup," one of the others muttered. She didn't know which one.

"Boy," the man said again. "What regiment were you in?"

She stared. They actually thought her old enough to be in the army? Or did they just want to see what she would say or if she could be trusted? "I'm not." She flushed, relieved the dim light hid that she did so. "Wasn't." *Gah!* She couldn't speak. If only her head would stop pounding and her stomach would stop lurching about.

They were all staring at her again, even the one in the corner. She tried to get her mind in order while wishing the cell wasn't so small. A bigger cell she could disappear in, hide in the shadows. "I'm not in the army," she finally managed, trying to keep her voice low.

One with dirty blond hair raised his eyebrows. "You're wearing army issue." He said it calmly, but she knew from the slight cock of his head he didn't like the fact.

She wasn't surprised. It was against regulation for someone not enlisted to wear army issue. She looked at her knees, at the dyed leather covering them. Her brother's pants. Her hand went to her chest and she grimaced at the absence of the leather armor. Only the thick cotton undershirt remained. The slavers had also taken her weapons. She couldn't feel the familiar weight of her knives at her sides. It seemed the only thing they'd left had been her greaves, probably because they were so small and not in very good shape.

"Boy…" The first man spoke again, clearly losing patience with her by his tone.

"My brothers," she said quickly. Saying the words brought a sudden pain to her chest. "They were trying to get me out of the city."

Silence met her comment and she looked up again. They all continued to look at her, but at least they didn't look angry.

One with black hair hanging just past his shoulders, the one who'd spoken to her first, began looking at her very intently though. She looked back at him. He looked a little familiar. Had she seen him somewhere before? It was possible. Her brothers had been popular and had a number of friends in most of the regiments.

He spoke next, a faint wry smile coming to his lips. "And we are waiting for you to tell us who they are."

She blinked rapidly. Oh. Yes, of course they were. "The Masons. Paul, Elliott…"

The blond choked. "The seven Mason brothers?"

A bit of pride welled within her and she nodded quickly. Of course, if these brutes were in the army they'd

31

know of her brothers. They'd been well known throughout the country, famous from all their exploits and successes in battles.

"You're Commander Mason's son," the smallest one said and she nodded again, wishing she could see his face. However, where he sat she could only see a shadow in the faint light.

The dark haired one stared at her, eyes wide. Before she could react he scrambled over to her side, putting his face right before hers, his hand tilting her chin up. Fear froze her in place.

"Aro?" He stared incredulously at her.

Her mouth opened in surprise and he sat back suddenly, looking like someone had punched him in the gut. He chuckled unexpectedly. The noise sounded so out of place, tears threatened again.

Yet, his laughter, she knew it. She'd heard it before at home. She struggled to remember who he was. One of her brother's friends obviously. When they had been home the house overflowed with them. She'd loved it, the laughter and the jesting and the cussing. They'd treated her like a little sister while she'd danced around serving them drinks and food. For once she was glad everyone had always called her Aro and not her given name, Arowyn. Aro was more of a boy's name than a girl's. He hadn't just given her away.

His name came to her suddenly. "Kendric?"

He began shaking his head in disbelief. She stared at him for a moment. "You shaved off your beard." She nodded to herself. That's why she hadn't recognized him right away. "You looked like a bear last time I saw you." Relief washed over her and she almost smiled. The panic of being totally alone subsided a little. Kendric wasn't one of her brothers, but at least he was someone she knew!

He chuckled again, running a hand over his eyes before dragging it down his face. His look became solemn while he regarded her thoughtfully for a moment. He turned toward the other men. "He's safe."

She rested her chin on her knees. *What did that mean? Had they thought her to be a spy or something?* Suddenly, she understood his words and sighed. He obviously didn't trust all of them if he wanted to play along with the whole boy thing.

She gathered her courage, fighting the lump in her stomach. "Are my brothers here?"

Kendric looked down at his hands and shook his head, dashing her faint hopes. Really, she'd known they weren't though. They had always been so protective of her, if they'd been on the ship she'd have heard them. They would have asked everyone if she was here.

"Aro?" She turned to look at one of the other men. His darkly tanned skin and rough looking face stood out. He certainly wasn't pretty. The long scar running down one side of his face didn't help either, but he had a happy, friendly look to him that made him not look scary at all. "How old are you?" His voice was gentle, as if talking to a young child.

Everyone started staring at her again. "Fifteen," she said quietly. Maybe she should have lied. Worry knotted her stomach. She had no idea what she should do.

"Can you fight?" The blond cocked his head to the side, waiting for an answer.

She blushed and looked at Kendric for guidance.

"Tell the truth," he said quietly, his voice very kind. A faint smile played at his lips though, because he knew the answer.

His smile returned some of her confidence. She nodded at them all. "But..." she grimaced slightly and wished they weren't all staring at her. "I've been having trouble with the sword lately." Everyone raised eyebrows at that. Her words came out in a rush. "Because I just keep growing and growing and I can't seem to do anything right."

Everyone one of them either smiled or chuckled at her admission, and of course they would. They remembered the same thing happening to them. She sucked in a breath and continued. "I'm good with a bow. I've not been having much trouble with it." What else to tell them? Were they disappointed in her lack of sword fighting skills? Obviously they were planning some sort of escape. Would they leave her behind because she couldn't fight? "I'm best with knives."

Kendric's mouth twisted slightly, as if he fought to hold in a grin. "You know, I do recall that."

She grinned but ducked her head again to hide it. Yes, her brothers had often showed her off. She could play with her knives and bow all year. Her brothers made her wait for them to be home before they let her get her sword out, but she was pretty good with a knife.

"Get some rest," Kendric said, leaning over to ruffle her hair.

She smiled a little in response to his gesture and watched him move back to the little circle of men. Their whisperings began again almost immediately. Were they talking about her? She couldn't hear what they were saying over the other noises of the ship. Part of her wanted to jump up and run over to see what was going on, to be in on the planning. The rest of her pushed for caution. She didn't know these people, and they weren't her brothers. She'd only met Kendric a few times and he'd been her brothers' friend, not hers. At least the other men knew of her family. Maybe that would help, she'd just have to wait and see. Leaning back, she closed her eyes. Surprisingly, she wasn't shaking anymore, and her heart wasn't beating like crazy.

She had a connection to these strangers now, even if a small one.

She looked over at the other man in the corner, wondering why he wasn't included. Maybe they just didn't know him. Or maybe they did.

She stared off into the shadows, her mind numb. All day she'd drifted in and out of sleep. Her head still hurt and she gingerly touched the lump on it. If only she hadn't taken that hit. She would know what happened to her brothers. She didn't know how much time she had lost. That was probably a good thing. The less she remembered the better.

It wasn't dark yet, but the ship had started rolling wildly. Kendric sat beside her, a hand on her shoulder, keeping her from lurching around. It wasn't much help. Her stomach kept cramping.

"Tea would be good right about now," she said absently.

He chuckled and nodded. "Winds picking up. We may be in for a storm."

She looked up at him. He looked tired. "So what's the word?"

His lips curved into a small smile again. The phrase had been something her brothers always said. "You're good. No worries with the men. I can vouch you're who you say you are. They all knew your father, or your brothers."

A choked sound escaped her and she looked away quickly.

His hand squeezed her shoulder slightly. "What is it?"

"You said knew," she whispered. She closed her eyes, fighting tears and pressing darkness in her heart. "I didn't see what happened to them."

"None of us did either," he said gently and she looked back up at him. "I asked the men for you. They don't remember seeing your brothers."

She sighed and fought to control her raging emotions. Though pleased he had asked for her, it still wasn't helpful. Her words came out in a panicked rush. "They could be dead. Or have gotten out of the city. Or be on another ship. Or dead."

"Aro..."

"I know…" She faltered and took a little breath. "I know they're probably dead. Right?" She looked up at him again and his brown eyes met her tearful ones. "The city fell, didn't it?"

He looked away and moved his hand off her shoulder. "Aye. It fell."

She nodded to herself and concentrated on keeping calm and taking little breaths. Things were how they were. She had to deal with it. Her brothers had taught her that. "And now we're in another mess altogether." She turned her head slightly, resting her cheek on her knees. "What happens now?"

"We're headed for Janur Port. There we'll be unloaded and taken by caravan to Franua."

"The slave capital of the world," she said blandly.

He nodded. "Aye. There we'll be stripped, sorted, and branded before we're sold on the auction blocks."

"Gah," she said with little feeling. Did he have to be so honest?

"That about sums it up," he agreed.

"Any hope of a rescue?"

He shook his head, dashing any little hopes she may have had. "No. The slave fleet may come across the Dressan Navy but they'll just sink us all."

"You're doing a wonderful job of making me feel better."

Looking over at her, he gave a little chuckle and grinned.

"What?" She regarded him warily, her comment had been serious.

"Never thought I'd be watching out for someone. Certainly not like this." He shook his head. "Aro being a boy." He glanced at her again. "Would have been easier a few years ago."

"Hmph!" She glanced over at the others who had been watching them intently. "I think they're thinking you're just insane. You shouldn't be laughing."

He chuckled again. "Well there is that, too."

She rolled her eyes and nodded in the direction of the quiet man in the corner. "I see he's not in your circle of friends. He a problem or what?"

"Observant." He made a slight face. "Not a problem really."

"Then what?"

"He was one of a number of visiting princes. Bo remembers seeing him around the castle."

She looked over at the man again, her curiosity piqued. "A prince? Prince of where?"

"No idea. We asked and he wasn't telling. Won't give his name either. So we're just calling him Prince."

"He must love that."

"He didn't look too impressed." Kendric agreed with a smirk. Soldiers and nobility never got along. "I see where he's coming from though. If the slavers knew, it could be troublesome for him or his people."

"Hmm," she replied, not really having any idea exactly what trouble that would be, but not wanting to show her ignorance. "So is he in on your plans of escape?"

He raised his eyebrows. "What makes you think I've got some?"

"Well if you don't yet then you're an idiot."

He chuckled. "You got me there. He's in. He's just not participating overly much now. In a bit of rough shape."

She looked over at the man, Prince, again. "Well, I'm in on whatever you're doing."

"Aro…"

She glared up at him. "You aren't leaving me behind!"

Her words obviously shocked him. "Of course not!" He grimaced. "I owe your brothers, if nothing else."

"You know I can fight," she said quietly. "I'll be doing so no matter what you say, so you might as well give me something to do."

He glowered at her, she glared back. He snorted. "Fine."

She grinned and sat back, tucking what remained of her hair behind her ears.

Shaking his head, Kendric looked over at her. Suddenly he lunged at her, raking his fingers through her hair until it covered her face again. "Rot it, Aro! Don't be doing that!" He shook his head again at her shocked look. "You don't look *that* much like a boy," he whispered.

Her cheeks grew warm in embarrassment. "Sorry."

"Well, back to planning. You coming?"

She looked at the group of strange men. "Do they know? About me?"

He glanced at them. "No. I'm thinking it'd be best to keep this up as long as we can. Safer that way."

His comment worried her. Did he not trust them not to hurt her? "If you think so." She looked over at Prince again. "I think I'll see what's ailing his royalness." Kendric raised his eyebrows and she made a face and leaned back again. "In a little bit. When I build up my nerve. And don't feel like throwing up."

"You'll get used to it."

"I doubt it," she muttered. "Anyone else hurt?"

"Nothing serious. How's your head? You've been out for a while."

She raised her hand and rubbed at crumbling dried blood in her matted hair. "I don't think it's too bad. It's not opened up again."

"Good. Get some rest." She nodded and he moved back to the other men she didn't know.

She grimaced. She didn't want to think about meeting them all. Their stares were bad enough. She didn't know if she could succeed in acting like a boy.

"What's with the boy?"

"He's good. Just right now he's feeling a bit shy, and sea sick. This isn't easy on a young boy." The others nodded solemnly and looked over at her.

She put her forehead on her knees again. She was definitely going to hurt him. The ship lurched again and her stomach twisted. "Uh." Yes. As soon as she didn't feel like dying.

# Chapter 3
## Meeting a Prince

The sea calmed at some point. Being trapped in a ship made it hard to tell the time of day. The cell's location at the back of the ship didn't help either. Outside the bars she could see the small hatch that let in light part of the day, and an occasional wash of sea water.

The men kept up their quiet chatter. The one in the corner remained still and quiet. She frowned as she watched him. Kendric said he was in rough shape. She assumed he'd been injured in the fighting. His wounds must not have been too severe, or the slavers wouldn't have taken him.

Often enough she'd have to patch her brothers up. In the winter, they were always getting into tavern brawls or injured during weapons practice. She could set simple breaks and stitch and wrap wounds. Her father and brothers had taught her a little, but she'd learned more from some of the army wives. She'd made an effort to learn all she could. Her plan had been to the join the army, which meant fighting. Knowing how to tend wounds could save her life.

Unfortunately she didn't have any of her supplies. Hopefully the prince's injuries were something she could help with. Her brothers always said she did a great job of tending to them. Pain curled in her chest again. Closing her eyes tightly she tried to push thoughts of her family from her mind.

She crawled over to the prince, trying not to blush when he turned his head to stare at her. She took his silence as a good sign. She'd never met a prince. She avoided nobility whenever possible. Nobles and soldiers didn't get along, or so her brothers had told her often enough.

She stopped and knelt beside him and sat very still, just looking at him for a moment while he did the same with her. Fair's fair right?

Sitting in the corner, he rested his back against the hull with his long legs stretched out. Aro could tell he was tall. She stared at his pants. They looked soft and expensive. She forced her eyes up. It surprised her he wasn't wearing silk, but a white cotton shirt, until she saw the marks and nodded faintly to herself. So he had fought, he'd had mail on at any rate. Regret spread through her that the slavers had taken it and she'd never get to see it.

She noted he had his left arm stiff across his abdomen. From the way he held it she guessed a broken arm. Her eyes went to his face last, shyly. She didn't really care what he looked like, but she wanted to make sure he wasn't glaring at her.

A little gasp escaped her lips before she clamped them shut. He was beautiful. She shouldn't have been surprised. He was a prince after all. Weren't they all handsome? She took in his long black hair, fine and straight. Hers had never looked so nice. His skin was fair, except for a purpled bruise high on his left cheek and curling over his temple. His features were angular, but somehow slightly soft, too. Gentle. His nose was impossibly straight and his eyes... his eyes were glaring at her.

She looked away quickly.

"Are you quite done?"

Even sharp with anger his voice sounded beautiful and refined, with a slight accent she of course didn't know. A visiting prince, Kendric had said. Where was he from then?

41

# Broken Aro

She looked at him again because she hadn't finished. She'd only noticed his too long dark lashes and fine sweeping dark brows before his glare had scared her. She wanted to finish the picture and see what color his eyes would be.

They were blue, of course. Perfect, brilliant blue.

They were also glaring again.

"What do you want?" His pretty voice wasn't friendly at all.

Her eyes dropped back to his arm. "It is broken?"

After what seemed like forever, he answered. Relief flooded her that he didn't sound furious anymore, just irritated. "Yes. It is."

She glanced back at him. "Will you let me look at it?"

"Can you do anything if it is?"

His attitude began to irritate her. "Actually yes," she snarled, making him start. His blue eyes opened wide. He wasn't used to people talking to him in such a way. "Well, depending on how mangled it is. I know how to set broken bones. My brothers came home with enough of them."

"Fine," he said. He looked away and held his arm out toward her as if bestowing some great gift. *No wonder no one got along with nobility, bunch of arrogant asses.*

She stared at it a moment before shifting closer, and had to move even closer to reach his arm. She gently took his wrist and slid his shirt sleeve up to his elbow.

She grimaced. His fair arm was black and blue from his wrist almost to his elbow. She looked up at him. "Shield arm?"

"Yes," he said in surprise.

She gently moved her fingers over his arm, testing the swelling, feeling for the break, or breaks. "How much does it hurt?"

"Enough," he replied curtly.

"Did you hear a snap?"

He didn't answer and she looked up at him to see him glaring at her again. She wished people would stop doing that. It was really starting to unnerve her.

His lips pressed tightly together for a moment before he finally answered. "Why all the questions?"

Anger rose within her again. Men were impossible. Truly they were. Here she was trying to help and he was not appreciating the fact at all. "Well. I'm trying to discover if you've a clean break or a shattered arm. If it's shattered, it will have to come off. If it's just a break I can actually do something about it." *Hopefully.* If she could find something to set it with, and even then, if he was really unlucky it could still go bad. If it did he wouldn't make it to port before the fevers came and killed him.

He stared at her intently, his lips a fine angry line before suddenly letting out an exasperated sigh and jerking his head away to stare at the far wall. "Yes, it snapped."

She still had her hands on his arm and let out a sigh of her own. *So then, time to find the break.* It didn't take her long, even though she worked slowly, trying not to cause him more pain. She'd seen what pain could do to people. Sometimes it made them crazy. She eyed the prince again. He was big, a lot bigger than she was. It surprised her that his arm was in no way soft. Under all the expensive clothes he was in incredibly good shape. *Especially for a prince, considering they just sat around all day doing princey things.* She felt around the area, trying to feel for splinters but it seemed to be a truly clean break.

She let go of his arm and sat back, thinking. She could set it, but it wouldn't do much good if he moved and the bones shifted. She looked around the cell, trying to find a small board or anything else she could use as a brace.

*Nothing, nothing, nothing. Rot it, how could she fix him?* She frowned, trying to think.

"Well?"

She shifted uncomfortably, knowing he was glaring at her again without even looking. She sat up straighter suddenly and looked up at him, raising a finger. "Wait, let me think."

Her greaves. They might work, if they weren't too wide. She looked at his arm. Hers was scrawny in comparison. His, while being well-muscled, wasn't bulky either. Maybe if she wrapped the arm in something...

She shifted position from her knees onto her bottom, bringing her legs forward. She undid the buckles on one of her greaves and then pulled the piece of hardened leather armor off. It wasn't like she needed her shins projected now. Thinking, she stared at the other men a moment and doubted they'd help. He was a rotting prince after all.

"Whatever are you doing?" He sounded both angry *and* irritated.

She risked a look at him as she held up the old piece of armor. "Something to brace your arm with."

He stared at her incredulously and shook his head. A faint and beautiful smile came to his lips. "Clever."

She smiled slightly at the praise, and of course was immensely happy he stopped glaring. She pulled at her shirt, un-tucking it from her pants.

"And what are you doing now?"

She looked up. "It will need to be wrapped in something."

He frowned and his good arm reached out, his hand resting on her arm. "No."

Her brows drew together in confusion. "No?"

He tugged at his own shirt, easily pulling it free from the waist of his pants. With a jerk he started a rip and then abruptly stopped.

She looked from the rip to his face and saw it had paled. Of course, he'd forgotten about the chains and the sudden motion had jerked his broken arm as well. Her hands moved to touch him, to try to sooth him...and froze when his body tensed. She yanked her hands away. "Sorry."

He jerked once again and a piece from the bottom of his shirt came away. Her eyes widened in surprise. He was a lot stronger than he looked to shred his clothing so easily.

"Will that be enough?" His lips pursed together tersely, pain still etched across his face.

"Yes." She took it from him and set it on top of the greave lying beside her. Concentrating on his arm again she let out a long breath. *Now the hard part.* She moved her hands over his arm, finding the break, and paused to look back up at him. "You want me to count off or something?"

"Just do it," he snapped.

He sounded angry again. *Just what she needed.* She sucked in a deep breath. One, two, push and pull and snap and the bones fell back into place.

She froze, hands still on his arm. The prince was *snarling.*

She squeezed her eyes closed, hoping he wouldn't hurt his arm. She didn't want to have to fix it again. On second thought, she hoped he wouldn't hit her either. At least not too hard. Yes, that's what she should have been wishing for first off, because she suddenly knew he would... just like Sammy had the one time because it had hurt too much. She should have found something for him to bite on. That would have been smart. Or maybe have

45

had one of the others hold him down. They probably would have agreed to do that. Fear tightened her stomach because the prince was strong, too.

She heard him move and gritted her teeth, tensing for the blow.

She wasn't prepared for gentle fingers cupping her cheek and tilting her face up. The first thing she noticed when her eyes flashed open at his touch was how he had suddenly become much closer. The second was the pained look on his face.

"I apologize," he said very quietly, his brilliant eyes staring straight into hers. "I did not mean to frighten you. I will not hurt you."

A ragged gasp escaped her and she swallowed over the fear in her throat. *Well then. So he was one of those noble princes.*

Unfortunately, he now stared intently at her. His fingers slid across her cheek, brushing her hair from her face. It was too tender of a motion. *So maybe he wasn't so noble. She just couldn't win could she?* Before she could move herself away she was yanked backward violently. She turned and stared in shock at Kendric.

A very, very furious Kendric.

"Touch Aro again and I'll break more than your arm." His quiet voice quivered with barely suppressed rage.

Too shocked to do anything but stare, her eyes went first to Kendric and then to Prince.

Prince chuckled suddenly and leaned close to Kendric, his voice a mere murmur, "You should tell her not to speak so much. She doesn't sound like a boy." While they both stared at him in shocked horror, Prince looked at her, a faint smile playing across his lips. He winked. "Nor does she look like one."

She grimaced at Kendric, punching him in the arm. "If your other plans are this bad you're going to get us all killed."

Kendric scowled at her.

Prince chuckled and held his broken arm out to her, catching her eyes with his own as he did so. "I will keep your secret." He looked over her shoulder to the other men. "Be quiet, and keep your face hidden and I doubt they will notice."

Kendric snorted and she looked away with a deep sigh. She picked up the strip of Prince's shirt and quickly and efficiently wrapped his arm.

"You do know what you are doing."

She could hear the surprise in his voice and it made her angry again. She scowled at him. "Go rot."

He chuckled and then winced. "Ow."

"Baby." She clamped her mouth shut. *Shouldn't have said that.*

Prince only grinned at her before looking to Kendric again. "Truly though. Aro will be just fine."

She could feel the soldier's gaze on her and ignored him as she carefully set the greave as a brace.

"I did cheat a little," Prince divulged and they both looked at him.

"What do you mean?" Kendric tensed as he waited for an answer.

Prince looked over at him. "There was much talk in court of the Mason brothers, their father, and..." he looked at her again. "Of the youngest...sibling."

Her eyebrows rose as she secured the greave. "They were talking about me at court! Why would they be doing that?"

"Many wondered what you would be doing come spring. When you came of age. If you would be joining your brothers, or not."

47

She frowned. "Why would they care what I did?" Yes, her family had become well known and respected but she was just a girl.

"Your brothers were not commenting and that had everyone wondering of course."

"Of course." She rolled her eyes. Her troublesome brothers again.

Kendric looked surprised. "You're considering it?"

"Idiot. Of course I am! They were still fighting over it. Like they'd be able to stop me."

Prince frowned. "Why would you want to join the army?"

"Why does everyone think I'd prefer to get married off? Not a chance!"

They both looked at her like she was crazy. She resisted jerking on the leather strap in her hands and clamped her mouth shut. She sat back, finished, and sucked in a deep breath trying to steady herself. Prince touched her knee lightly. "Well done. I thank you."

She nodded, sudden pain and loss choking her for a moment. "It doesn't matter anyway," she said quietly. "The city fell. The army's gone, dead, scattered, or slaves. My brothers…" Thinking of them brought the terrible hollow pain to her chest again. She truly was alone. They would not come riding back this time. She would not be protected or rescued by them. They were dead. She couldn't try to delude herself into thinking otherwise.

"Aro?"

She looked over at Kendric. "All done." She turned slightly to Prince, but didn't look at him. "Try not to move it too much. Let me know if feels wrong, or anything. Or if you start to feel feverish." Not that she could do much if anything did go wrong.

"I will."

He sounded so very serious she couldn't help a faint smile.

The ship lurched suddenly and Kendric caught her by the back of her shirt before she sprawled into Prince's lap.

"We've just turned very suddenly," Prince said quietly, a frown on his face.

They heard a lot of banging above, people running about, and loud voices yelling words she couldn't decipher. She looked in alarm to Kendric.

He was looking up, listening.

She looked at Prince. He did the same. She waited, looking from one to the other for what seemed like forever, waiting for someone to tell her something, anything.

"The Dressen Navy," Kendric said finally.

"Wither me," she muttered. "This is really not my day." She looked up again with all the others at another flurry of activity above.

The Dressen Navy. Sinkers of slave ships. How could things get much worse than that? She was likely going to be fish food very, very soon.

# Chapter 4
# The Men

She stayed with Prince when Kendric got up to stand at the bars of the cell with a few of the others, listening in tense silence to the commotion above.

Eventually she moved to put her back to the wall, sitting beside Prince, but not touching him. She didn't want to jostle his broken arm. She drew up her knees, wrapped her arms around her legs and rested her forehead on them. She sat that way for a long time, just listening, swaying as the ship rolled and occasionally lurched sharply.

Memories of her brothers came again and panic made her breath catch. Tears burned her eyes and she blinked furiously, hoping to keep them away. Trying to forget, to distract herself, she spoke, "So you're a prince."

"Yes." Short answer.

She peeked over at him to see if he was angry because of her question, but he didn't appear to be. His gaze remained raised to the continued sounds up above.

"Do you have a crown?" Immediately she regretted asking such a foolish question.

"Yes." He smiled slightly. "But I didn't bring it with me."

She smiled before she could help herself. "Do you have a white horse?"

He chuckled. She loved the sound of it. "Yes. I've a number of horses at home. My favorite is the black though."

She found herself liking him. Even if he was a prince. "Do you have a princess? I mean," she floundered, "are you married?" Not a bad question, he looked old enough he could be. Though really, she couldn't tell his age. His features seemed grown up, but at the same time she'd noticed his face wasn't covered with days' worth of stubble like the other men.

"No," he said more quietly than he'd answered before.

"Were you looking for one? Is that why you've been traveling?"

He looked down at her and though he smiled, it was a tight smile. "No. Just traveling."

She looked down at her knees and picked at a worn spot on her pants. From his tone he was done with her questions. "I always wanted to travel," she said quietly. "But not like this."

"Yes, I know," he whispered.

She wasn't sure exactly what he meant, other than he understood her. It was enough. She didn't ask any more questions. Sometimes silence was better.

Somehow she managed to fall asleep. When she woke, the sun had risen. The noise still continued loudly above.

"The Navy is still chasing us," Prince said, before she could even wake up enough to think to ask. Happily, he didn't seem to be angry with her for the questions she'd asked the day before.

"Great," she said, forcing a smile that didn't last very long.

They sat in silence as the day wore on, tensing when the ship would turn suddenly and shouts would echo from above.

Prince's voice suddenly startled her. "I think we've outrun them."

She looked over at him where he leaned against the ship's hull, his head tilted back slightly, eyes closed. "That's good right?"

"Better than getting sunk," he said wryly.

*True. Did Prince have a sense of humor? That would be strange.* "Will they catch up with us again?"

Prince shrugged.

"How long does it take to get to port?"

Prince pursed his lips slightly in thought. "Ten to fifteen days I'd think, depending on the weather and the winds."

She nodded slightly, and frowned. She had no idea how long they'd been at sea. Of course she had no idea how long she'd been unconscious either. She looked up toward the hatch. It looked like it was getting dark again. "How long have we been at sea?"

He glanced over at her. "This was the fourth day."

So it was almost night, and four days. She must have been out a while. No wonder she felt like she hadn't eaten in a month. Her stomach hurt. Water at least wasn't a problem, buckets hung by the cell door. They were filled every once in a while. There was another bucket, too. She'd embarrassingly had to use it a few times. At least the rolling sea had its advantages; she wasn't the only one who sat to use it.

She ducked her head suddenly as a few of the slavers came down the ladder with their lanterns and started peering into the cells, checking on them all.

She held herself as still as she could, arms still wrapped around her knees, trembling with both the effort to try to be invisible and in fear of those who had chained her. Her heart began pounding in her chest so hard she thought it might burst. Tears started to well in her eyes and run down her cheeks. She fought the urge to sob hysterically.

Prince's hand suddenly rested gently on her shoulder. He didn't say anything, but for some reason, after a moment, she wasn't quite so scared. She was almost...calm. Everything would turn out just fine his hand seemed to say. It allowed her to push the hysteria away, to think. She had to stay calm and hidden. She had to survive this.

She sucked in a deep breath, and regretted it a moment later. The hold wasn't smelling any nicer as the days passed. She choked on a gag and worked on taking little breaths, trying to calm her frantic heart. She kept her face hidden and eyes squeezed closed. She could hear them though as they tromped down the center of the hold taunting their prisoners. They banged on the cell bars, filled the water buckets and emptied the other less pleasant ones. Men cussed and mumbled. Men and women both sobbed. She tried to drown them all out, concentrating on her slowing heart beats, counting them.

Prince removed his hand slowly. "There. They are gone now," he said quietly.

She took another small, steadying breath before opening her eyes and peeking over her knees. It had grown darker. Hardly any light remained causing everything to be thrown into shadows. "I hate them," she said without feeling.

"I, too," Prince replied gravely.

She leaned back and turned her head to look at him. "How's your arm?"

"Well enough. How are you feeling?"

The question surprised her; that he would care. She forced a small smile. "Good, I guess. Considering the situation."

He regarded her thoughtfully.

She scowled at him. "What?"

"I think you are very brave, Aro," he answered, his voice very solemn and serious.

She stared at him for a long moment. He must have gotten knocked in the head, too. "Brave? I'm not brave. I'm just surviving...and trying not to get caught."

He shook his head slightly. "Listen."

She did. She heard the sounds of men and women crying, pleading, and screaming, even after four days. She'd cried, but not like that. Her tears had been silent and hidden in the shadows. She wasn't having hysterics. *Maybe that was what he meant? But then, he was a prince, he was used to noble ladies and tittering maids.*

"Thank you. I think," she said. She stumbled over what else to say but looked up and saw Kendric trying to get her attention.

"Aro, come over here," Kendric said quietly, motioning to a position suddenly open beside him in his circle of men.

Her stomach clenched and she swallowed quickly, trying to not look afraid or nervous. She wasn't ready to meet everyone else, not at all. But she had to, if there were only a few days left to plan their escape, she had to stop hiding and get ready. She crawled over and took the open space he'd indicated and looked up at him, mostly because she didn't want to look anywhere else.

He ruffled her hair with a little grin.

"Bastard." She scowled.

He chuckled and looked away from her. She forced herself to look at the others, wondering if any of them suspected she wasn't really a boy.

"Men, this is Aro Mason. I've known him a number of years." He looked down at her again and she clenched her teeth, fighting the urge to hit him.

*Why he was smiling so much?* Her eyes narrowed. "What's happened?"

He chuckled again and grinned at the others, as if making a point. Maybe that she wasn't a complete fool. "From what we've been able to overhear from the slavers, the navy took out four of the slave ships."

His news shocked her speechless for a moment. They'd been lucky. "And that's good?"

He stared at her like she was a moron. "Four ships worth of slavers are now at the bottom of the sea."

*Well yes, that was good. But...* "I was thinking of the four ships worth of our people down there, too."

His face sobered. "Ah, Aro…"

She shrugged and looked around the circle under lowered lashes, quickly checking facial expressions. The smiles and grins were gone. They looked at her with...was it pity? Yes, of course. They knew she hoped her brothers might be on one of those ships. She stared at the floor in front of her. "How many slave ships were there to start with?"

"Only six ships," one of the others said. "The rest had still been loading when we left."

She looked up at the one who had spoken; the one with the scar on his face. Though his face looked serious now, she still couldn't bring herself to be afraid of him. She had good instincts with that sort of thing. This man was kind.

Kendric tapped her shoulder. "Meet Bo. He was with the Palace Guard."

Bo gave her a brief nod.

"Next to you there is Cain, Jonathan Cain. With the third. Our youngsters here are Avery Brennan," The blond across from her flashed a charming smile. Youngster indeed, he had to be under twenty she'd bet. "And Kei. They were both with the fifth."

She looked at Kei, who was surprisingly even younger. Not much older than she was from the little she could see of him. Even more surprising was just how different he was from the others. The growing darkness made it difficult to see, but his dress alone set him apart. Where she and the others wore shirts of cotton or wool and leather pants in shades of browns and blues, he wore all leather in a flat black, and his clothes were *tight*. She had no idea how he could move in such clothing. He didn't even really have on a shirt, but a vest cut so short it displayed half of his torso.

Kendric elbowed her. "Don't stare."

She ducked her head quickly as her cheeks flamed. She hadn't even realized she'd been looking for so long.

"It's fine," Kei said kindly, and she peeked through her hair at him. His voice was surprisingly soft and deep. "He's never seen anyone like me before." He grinned at her, a flash of white perfect teeth.

*Gah, but she wished there was more light.* "The problem is I can't see anything at all," she muttered.

The men of course heard and their response to her complaint ranged from a chuckle to a snort.

A new sound began, or perhaps it had started earlier and she just hadn't noticed. She looked up as a strange pounding roar filled the hold.

Bo swore. "Wonder if they headed into the storm we were feeling earlier?"

"I certainly hope not," Kendric replied tartly.

The clouds now covered whatever faint light the moon and stars had given them.

"Well. Let us get some sleep then, before the wind finds us." *That was Cain. Or did they say he was supposed*

56

*to be called Jonathon? John? She should have paid more attention.*

She crawled back a little to lie down in the dirty straw and closed her eyes. She listened to the men settle and the pounding of the rain. Her thoughts spun madly in her head. *Were here brothers dead or not? What was she supposed to do now?* Eventually the thrum of the rain lulled her into sleep.

# Chapter 5
# The Fey

She woke with a start.

Someone was touching her, a feather light caress trailing down her arm. She tensed, sucking in a breath to scream. A hand clamped over her mouth.

Warm breath suddenly tickled her ear. "It's Kei. Hush."

Eyes wide, seeing nothing but pitch black, she nodded frantically

Kei's hand moved from her arm. Frozen in stunned silence, the pounding of the rain echoed through the hold around her. The sound thrummed so loudly she couldn't even hear her own ragged breaths.

"Sorry."

"You scared me." The overpowering smell of wet straw overcame her and she gagged. It registered suddenly, her clothes were wet. She grimaced and sat up, the straw squishing under her.

She heard him sigh. He sat somewhere in front of her, but she couldn't see anything.

"You were having a nightmare, I think," he said quietly.

She blinked and cursed under her breath. "Did I wake everyone?" She concentrated, trying to hear if the others were up.

"No. You weren't screaming. Just thrashing around." He laughed softly. "You kicked me in the head."

A blush crept up her cheeks, thankfully the darkness hid it. "Oh. I'm sorry."

"It's fine. I wasn't sleeping much. It's getting wet in here."

She snorted. "I noticed."

"Well. Go back to sleep."

She could hear him moving. What he was doing? "I think I'll just stay up," she said, more to herself than to him.

"Do you…would you mind if I sat with you?"

Her eyebrows went up in surprise. Why would he want to? But then again, she didn't know him. He wasn't much older than she was. Maybe he just wanted some company in the darkness. "Sure," she said finally, "If you want."

She could feel his presence suddenly closer to her, even if she still couldn't see him. He touched her arm, pulling slightly. "Come over to the hull, it's a little higher and not so wet."

She let him guide her and only bumped into him a few times. He settled next to her, back against the damp wood, staring forward in the darkness.

"I hate the dark," she murmured.

"I don't mind it so much. Usually." She could imagine him grinning, and wondered again what he looked like. "I'm glad to get a chance to talk to you," he said quickly, as if forcing out the words before he decided against saying them.

"Oh?"

"Mmmhmm. Since Kendric announced who you were."

"Why?"

He paused again for moment, before continuing in a rush, "I knew your father. He was a very…kind man."

"Oh," she said quietly. She furrowed her brow, she hadn't gotten the impression he was that old. "How did you know him?"

He became silent again for a while. "Can I tell you a story?"

"Will it answer my question?"

He chuckled. It was a very pleasant sound. "Yes."

"Go ahead then."

"First though. I've a question for you." Before she could speak, he began talking again. "In the city, did you happen to hear the gossip about the Fey who joined the army?"

She blinked. Where had the sudden change in topic come from? "Of course. About two years ago. That's all anyone talked about for long time. What's that have to do with anything?"

"I want you to look at me," he said gently.

She turned her head in his direction. "I can't see–" Shock paralyzed her voice, and fear, too. Two golden eyes stared back at her. They weren't really glowing, but more lit with an inner light. "Gah..."

The eyes went out.

She stared into the darkness, her own eyes wide. Her breath froze in her chest while she tried to comprehend what had just happened...trying to calm her suddenly frantic heart. When she could speak her voice went up an octave, or three, too high. "Do you like to scare me?"

"I didn't mean to." His voice sounded so very quiet and tinged with such sadness, she reached out a hand to him. Well two hands, since they were attached by a foot of chain. She found his, limp in his lap.

"You could have warned me." She laughed suddenly, putting her hands back in her lap. "I nearly pissed myself."

He let out a deep sigh.

"So," she continued when he didn't speak again. "I'm guessing you were showing me you are the Fey everyone was talking about."

He made a sound of agreement. "Are you frightened of me?" His words came out so quietly she barely heard him.

She took a moment to think about it. "No," she said finally. What did she know of the Fey? Nothing but children's stories really, and how much truth was in them? "Should I be?"

He laughed bitterly. "Not really," he admitted. His words came out in a rush again, "Though, I am much stronger than you. If I wasn't careful I could hurt you by accident without even meaning to. But I've been practicing a lot, being around people."

"That's good to know," she said wanly. "So is it true you can move really fast?"

"Yes."

"Huh." Her eyes narrowed. "So how did you get caught by slavers?"

"I got hit over the head," he admitted wryly.

She chuckled. "Me, too."

"That's right," he said. "You were unconscious a long time." She started as she felt his hand by her face. She froze as it moved around her hair and paused as it found the matted dried blood.

"Who cut your hair?" His voice rose in mock horror.

She choked on the memories of her and squeezed her lips together tightly to gain control. "My brothers," she finally managed to answer.

"Huh," he replied. "Have you seen it? That's about all I've seen of you, and truly, it's very bad. I could fix it for you, if you like. When we get out of here."

She blinked rapidly, trying to follow him. He talked so fast, so earnestly. Did people never listen to him? "No. I haven't seen it. If we do get out of here you can shave it off for all I care."

"Why have you been hiding?" His voice grew very quiet again. "We never see your face."

She didn't answer and they sat in silence for a few moments. "I thought you were going to tell me a story," she said finally. "You said you knew my father?"

"So I am. The story of my life. Are you ready?"

She nodded before realizing he couldn't see her. "Yes. But! You need to slow down, you talk way too fast."

"I do?" His voice sounded so innocent it made her smile.

"You do," she said firmly.

"I didn't mean to." He sounded like he actually meant it. "I don't…talk a lot. I'm not very good with people."

"I think you're doing just fine," she told him.

He grew silent again for a moment and then took a deep breath. "So. My story. It's really very short because I don't remember much of my past. I remember my parents. I remember we traveled all the time. We never stayed anywhere for long. I do remember taking a boat across the sea, but I was only a few years old."

"So you really are the first Fey to come west to our lands?"

"As far as I know, yes. Now don't interrupt."

"Sorry."

"So. I was ten when my parents were…when they died. The years after weren't easy for me. Alone so young. I had learned much of the Fey lore from my parents already, but there was so much else I hadn't learned. Humans were not kind to me." He paused and took a shaky breath. "After a while I gave up and ran wild in the forest. I stayed away from people. I was…very savage. Then your father found me."

"He found you," she exclaimed in a whisper.

"Near Demet's Pass. He and some of his men were out on a scouting patrol. I think. It was a surprise to me, to see people. It became a bit of a standoff, they had me cornered. Some of the men knew what I was from stories, I guess. They were arguing whether to run away or to fill me full of arrows then and there."

A gasp escaped her before she could stop it. "Why?"

"I guess you've not heard all the stories about us Fey," he answered, his voice subdued.

"Oh," she said quietly. She had in fact, heard a number of stories about the Fey. Everyone grew up on stories of them and Elves and other creatures of the east. The stories told of how they could fight. The wild slaughter they could cause. "You mean, they are true? Once you get into a fury you can't be stopped?"

"Yes."

"I see," she mumbled.

A small bitter laugh left him. "Yes, so. Your father stepped forward then. I don't remember what he did, or what he said. I just remember being so shocked that someone was being kind to me. He calmed me down. And then he took me back to Demet's Fort with him."

"When was this?" How had she never heard this story?

"A few weeks before he died. I don't remember a lot of those two weeks, either. Except for him being so kind and always there with me. I was so out of control, I know I must have hurt him, I can't see how I couldn't have. But he never said a word. He had such great patience."

"He's the father to all of us, of course he did," she muttered, but her thoughts began to wander, remembering…

"I suppose," Kei continued. "I remember him saying I reminded him of his children. I was your age I think, around fifteen.

"It was…a great pain to me…when they told me he had died. And then of course the pass was almost taken. They even let me out to fight. If the fifth hadn't come when they did, the pass would have fallen. The end of the story goes they absorbed me into the regiment with the rest of the survivors. I stayed up there, fighting, until it did fall and we were forced back to the city."

She stared at him, or at least at the darkness where he sat. She struggled to figure out what he meant when he said they'd even let him out to fight. *Had he been locked up? What had this boy been through?* "That is quite the story," she said finally, trying to keep her voice even.

He didn't answer.

Too many questions flew through her mind. She sat silently, trying to make some sense of them. Most of all, she was shocked at the overwhelming feeling of hope rushing through her. She never thought she'd find it in this horrible cell, yet here it was beside her. *Could it be…was he the one?* Maybe, if she was right everything wouldn't be so bad.

"You're quiet," he said. "I've upset you, talking of your father."

"No," she lied. She took a little breath and concentrated on the sound of the rain for a moment, trying to empty her head. "I'm just…remembering…things," she said lamely.

Finally she got her thoughts into some sort of order. "I think…" she said finally. "You are the one he wrote to me about. In the last letter I got from him." She paused, but he didn't speak, so she continued. "I didn't get the letter until after word had come he'd been killed, but he mentioned a boy he had found. I think he meant you." She turned her head toward him, the hope inside of her wavering, wishing to be true. "He didn't find anyone else while wandering out there did he?"

He let out a small laugh. "Not that I know of, no."

"Hmm. So it must have been you." She nodded to herself and a crazy grin split her face. She tried to keep calm, but it was hard. So hard. "I've wondered about you. I'd asked about a young boy back then. Father hadn't written how old you were, just that you were around my age. No one knew anything though, so I'd assumed you'd been killed when the fort was nearly taken, or had run off somewhere."

"I'm guessing he didn't mention I was a Fey," he said, amusement coloring his voice.

"No."

He didn't reply to that, and they sat quietly again. She wondered if she should say more or if she should just hold her knowledge of what he suddenly meant to her tight within her and hope it would be enough to make everything alright.

He shifted slightly. "I wanted to ask…that is…could I…" he floundered and stopped, a rough sound of irritation escaping.

She prodded gently, "What?"

He let out an exasperated sigh and she heard the chains clank as he moved. "Your father meant a lot to me, even if I didn't know him long. He saved my life. So…if you don't mind, I would very much like to take care of you now. Protect you for him. I know you don't have anyone, so I'd like to be there for you like he was for me."

She stared into the darkness, shocked at his words. Unwanted tears came quickly then, even though she tried to stop them. Her chains made too much noise as she brushed tears from her eyes.

"I will do it whatever you say. Even if you don't want me to," he said firmly. "But if you don't mind, it'd make it a lot easier."

He had become so very serious a strangled laugh escaped her. She struggled against the sobs that clawed at her chest. *To have someone, to not be alone in this horrible cell...*

Not only that...this Fey...this strong wild creature, had meant something to her father. Father had trusted him, had taken him in and cared for him. He'd been with Father before he died.

"I don't mind," she finally managed to whisper.

She hadn't realized how tense he had been until she felt him relax next to her. "Good," he said. "I mean..."

She smiled slightly at his floundering. He truly wasn't that great with people. "I understand."

He let out a little growl of frustration and it made her smile. It was something she would think a Fey would do. A Fey. She still couldn't quite believe they truly were real, that she was sitting next to one.

"So you'll do what I tell you," he said finally. It wasn't a question.

Her eyebrows shot up in surprise. "Hold on..."

His hand rested on her arm again. "When it comes to protecting you," he amended. "If I tell you to run, you run. If I tell to hide then you hide."

"Oh. Yes, I suppose I can do that. But..."

"No but," he said firmly. "I need to know you'll listen. I'm a Fey, you mustn't forget that. I don't want you in the way when I fight."

*Oh yes. The fury of the Fey.* "I will do my best," she said quietly. *It wouldn't be that hard, just like listening to her brothers.* She blinked, her thoughts going off once more.

He let out an irritated breath, distracting her. "Fine. I hope you do. I'd feel really bad if I killed you."

"So would I."

They both laughed quietly and sat in easy silence for a while again.

She shivered and grimaced. She hated being wet...and cold. Fall quickly approached and though the days weren't too cold yet, the nights had started to get chilly. They'd been lucky so many people in the hold had kept it relatively warm, but the wet and chill of the rain wasn't helping.

Kei shifted closer to her until his side pressed right up against her. The sudden warmth shocked her. "How can you not be cold?"

"I'm Fey," he reminded her. "We're very warm-blooded."

She chuckled, resisting the urge to turn and try to snuggle into the warmth.

"May I ask you a question?"

She nodded, forgetting the darkness again. "Yes, of course."

He paused, "Did...did your father say anything else about me? In his letter?"

His voice was so quiet, so...shy. She smiled slightly, that her father's words might mean so much to him. "Yes. He wrote nearly a whole page." Her smile faded as she remembered the letter. It was lost now. Pain pulled at her chest again. How long would she be able to remember it?

He sat quietly beside her, waiting.

She was so dense sometimes. "Not a bad word in it," she assured him. She bit her lip and then made up her mind. "Would you like me to tell you all he said?"

# Broken Aro

He sucked in a sharp breath. "You remember?"

"Of course. I have it memorized," she said quietly. "It was the last words of my father. It goes," She closed her eyes, bringing the page to mind. "I bet you cannot guess what I found last week. Maybe I should make you guess, but you would just get cranky. I know you would never guess right either. I found a boy in the woods, close to your age, maybe a little older. He is quite wild, and feisty. Even more so than you, if you can believe that. I have him here at the fort and it is taking him a while to settle in, but I am confident a little time is all it will take. By fall I am sure he will be much quieter. I am certain you will like him. I have grown quite fond of him myself. He will certainly fit right in. I can already imagine the trouble you will all get into. I expect you to be on your best behavior when I come home then, understand?" She sucked in a breath and then coughed. "That's all he wrote about you."

She could feel him shaking against her. "Kei?" He didn't answer. "Hey, are you laughing or crying?"

A choked laugh answered her. "I'm not sure."

Embarrassed she waited in silence for him to get control of himself.

"He was going to take me home, to meet you all," he whispered finally.

She blinked rapidly, as she understood his reaction. She reached a hand out to touch him. He didn't understand, not like she now did. "Not just to meet us, Kei. To live with us. To join our family." She sat back as he froze.

"Are you sure?" His whispered voice broke slightly.

"Very," she said firmly. "Father was like that. He liked helping others. I have a few foster brothers."

His words came out in a rush again, "So you'd have been like my sister?"

It became her turn to freeze. "Does everyone know?" She ground her teeth in frustration.

"That you're a girl?" He chuckled. "I've always known. You smell like a girl."

"Huh." She grunted, leaning back and crossing her arms, her chains rattling. *Smelled like a girl? What did that mean?*

"Who else knows?"

"Kendric. He's a family friend. And the prince. He heard about me at court."

A quiet growl came from beside her. "You should stay away from him."

She raised her eyebrows. "Do you know him?"

"I know his kind," he replied curtly.

Apparently he didn't like nobility either. "He's not so bad," she said quietly. "Let's not fight about it. We need him to escape all of this."

"Fine."

She sighed and again they sat in silence. She thought of her father and her brothers. Kei was one of her brothers. Or would have been, if Father hadn't died. She couldn't keep the small smile from crossing her lips. Taking ahold of the thought, she refused to let it go. Kei was family. She wasn't alone. They weren't all lost to her. Not only that, he *wanted* to take care of her, to protect her. The horrible fear that had been crushing her lessoned a little. She'd make it through all of this, she would.

"Do you believe in magic, Aro?"

"What?" His sudden question startled her. "Well, I guess." She paused, thinking. "They say the eastern lands are full of all manner of beings that aren't human. Some are...something more. Like you. Is what you do magic?"

"Sort of. You could say part of me is magic. The Were use it more, changing forms. The Elves have their powers."

She interrupted him warily, "Are you going to do something strange again?"

He was silent for a very long time. "We Fey have a special magic. A magic of the heart and soul. A magic of...binding...of promise and intent. Do you understand?"

"No idea at all," she admitted.

"I want you to know how serious I am about protecting you, and I want you to know it's not just because of your father. I like you, Aro. I want us to be friends."

"I sort of thought we were heading that way already."

"But I can make it *binding*. Forever. Forever friends. No matter what."

She considered about what he said, who'd he suddenly become to her. He was her brother, her father had believed in him, but still...she hesitated. "Would it hurt?"

"Of course not," he said incredulously. "It's words and a little magic. That's all."

"Sure," she said impulsively. "What are the words?"

Her answer seemed to have surprised him. He took a moment before answering. "In friendship I shall bind my heart and soul to yours. Forever beside you I shall stand. Together or apart always will I be with you. Eternal friends we shall ever be."

Her throat tightened as tears came to her eyes at his words. "That's beautiful," she finally managed to whisper.

His warm hand closed around hers. "I don't know really, if it would work, you being human. I don't think it's ever been done with one before. But, if you would like to, for you I would say these words and even if there was no binding, I would still mean every word."

To have a friend forever. No matter what. To not be alone through all of this...She nodded her head frantically as tears splashed down her face. "Yes."

"Yes?" He seemed startled she had accepted. "Are you sure? It's not something to be taken lightly, Aro."

She squeezed his hands. "I want to. Tell me what to do."

"Very well." He sounded immensely pleased. Again, she could almost see him grinning. He shifted himself until he sat in front of her and took her hands and placed them palm to palm to his, raised between them. "I'm doing the eye thing again," he warned her, and suddenly she could see them, glowing faintly.

A little gasp escaped her as she actually looked at them. "They're beautiful," she murmured.

He chuckled, and ducked his head for a moment, clearly embarrassed. "Thank you," he said shyly. "Now look into my eyes and repeat after me." He said the words again, and she repeated them after him. Not once did she make a mistake. It surprised even her.

Staring into his golden eyes as she spoke, his hands warm against hers, sent her heart pounding. She wasn't alone anymore. As the last word fell from her lips she smiled slightly. It hadn't been too bad...

She gasped suddenly, as his hands suddenly became warmer. Much warmer.

"Don't look away," he murmured, as she was just about to do so.

She stared into his eyes as the warmth spread from his hands into hers, and then rushed through her entire body. It didn't hurt; it didn't feel bad at all.

He was smiling softly and her eyes widened as she noticed this. She could *see*. Little lights danced around them both, like tiny fireflies. A few moments passed before the lights settled onto them both like little motes of dust and the faint light faded away.

She blinked in the darkness. His eyes had gone out, too. She took in a shaky breath. "That was so strange."

His fingers gently entwined through hers. "It didn't hurt did it?"

"No. I feel…wonderful. Warm." She paused a moment. "Does that mean it worked?"

"I would think so," he replied in amusement. "I've never done it before, but something certainly happened."

"Indeed," she agreed.

"Aro, don't tell anyone about this. Not about us being friends," he added quickly, "About what we just did, I mean."

She paused and bit her lip. Maybe she shouldn't have agreed so quickly and should have asked more questions. "Why?"

A little growl of frustration escaped his lips. "Humans wouldn't understand it. They would be afraid I did something bad to you. And people like me, well… I don't know if it's really allowed. So…"

"I understand," she said quickly, before he started his quick talking again. She grinned. "We've our first secret?"

"Aye," he said with a chuckle. He pulled her in close to him as he shifted to lean again against the hull. "Now go to sleep, little Aro. I will watch over you."

She did easily, because she suddenly felt safe. She wasn't alone anymore. He wouldn't leave her. He'd promised.

# Chapter 6
# Mother of All Storms

Faint light shone down into the cell again as she woke, nestled against Kei's side. She blinked and shifted away quickly, her cheeks coloring. Not only was Kei not one of her brothers, she was also supposed to be a boy. What would everyone think? The men of course, were all up.

Everyone stood about the hold, even Prince. Looking down, the reason became quickly apparent. The straw covering the cell floor had become a soggy mess overnight.

"Morning, Aro," Kei said quietly as he stood.

She scrambled to her feet, keeping her head down. "Morning."

She peeked up at him, catching his small smile. This was the first time she'd seen him so close, even if the light was poor. Surprisingly, he looked almost exactly as she'd imagined. He was boyishly handsome, his face round with high, defined cheekbones, and his chin slightly pointed. His skin had been tanned gold and perfect, his eyes a yellow gold and not human at all. Slightly pointed ears showed through his light brown, spiky hair. He certainly looked like she imagined a Fey should.

Kendric walked over, the straw squishing under his boots, and held out his hand. "Hey, Aro. Here. They fed us today."

She stared at his hand and the dark lump in it. Her nose wrinkled. "That's food?" She peered up at him through her hair as she took it. "What is it?"

He made a face. "Bread. A bit dirty, but no bugs at least."

She stared at it. Even as starving as she was, she didn't want to put it in her mouth.

"Eat it," he said firmly. "We all ate ours."

She looked at Kei and he nodded. She noticed how Kendric saw the exchange and raised his eyebrows, yet he didn't do anything but smile slightly. That was odd. He had seemed so protective of her before. Maybe he and Kei had already spoken before she woke up. Either way, she somehow managed to choke the hard, dry stuff down.

The day went by slowly. Kei introduced her to Avery. He was, Kei told her, a good friend of his. They had served together in the fifth since he had joined with them. She liked him and they got along well, even though they said little to each other. It came as no surprise. None of the passengers were chatty. Chains tended to have that effect on people. He didn't seem to mind how she hovered by Kei, or the Fey hovered around her. In fact, she caught Avery grinning at them both a few times as if immensely pleased. Perhaps it was because Kei had obviously found a new friend. She wasn't exactly sure, but didn't really care. As long he remained close she felt safe. He helped to keep the panic and loneliness away.

Kendric checked on her a few times before always returning to stand with Cain and Bo. The three of them together didn't really surprise her. They had to be at least a good ten years older than the rest of them. Prince remained off in the corner by himself. She noticed she had been right; he was very tall. He stood a few good inches at least over all the others.

She spent the day staring at the walls, the cell bars, the men, and the slowly rising water. It helped her to not think of where they were, where they were going, and what would happen in the days ahead. The wind and rain continued, occasionally picking up before dying down again.

The only excitement occurred when the slavers would come down. Each time Kei moved to stand in front of her, blocking her from view. Twice the slavers left, dragging bodies to toss overboard. The conditions in the hold had started taking lives already. Once they took one of the women up. She never came back down.

She went once to check on Prince. He glared at her.

She glared back at him. "What?"

His eyes narrowed and he stared at her for a long moment before answering. "Why are you with that Fey?"

The way he said the word Fey spoke volumes. He didn't seem to like them much. Anger rose up within her at the unfairness of his attitude toward Kei. As far as she knew, Kei hadn't ever done anything to him, and he had been so nice to her. "In case you hadn't noticed, I've limited company."

His jaw tightened at her flippant remark. "I meant you now seem attached to his side."

"I like him," she answered defiantly, raising her chin.

His lips tightened into a thin angry line and he looked away, shaking his head. "You're asking for trouble," he said. "The Fey can't be trusted."

"And I can trust you?"

He looked back at her, his gaze still hard. "Of course."

She snorted. "Of course," she mimicked him. "Because nobles are known for their honesty, truthfulness, and for helping others."

Judging from the look on his face, her mocking tone didn't seem to impress him.

"How's your arm?" She changed the subject quickly before she got seriously angry.

"Fine."

"Good." She turned stiffly and went back Kei and Avery.

Kei immediately took another step closer to her as she stopped beside them. "Why do you have to talk to him?" Kei kept his voice to a low snarled whisper. "He's obviously doing fine."

She shrugged, still furious about the whole thing. "He's alone. Alone isn't a nice thing to be. You're right though, his arm doesn't seem to be bothering him."

Kei growled slightly and she tried to smother a sudden grin at the sound as she glanced over at him. He saw it however, and a small smile crossed his own lips in response as he reached over and ruffled her hair.

The ship rolled suddenly and they braced themselves against the hull.

The following days played out much the same. She attempted to speak to Prince a few more times, but he became just as surly on each occasion. She did feel bad for him though, even if he was a prince. Every time he glared and snapped at her she tried to remember he was hurt and alone and pretty much ignored by everyone but her.

The slavers attempted to pump the water from the hold. They lowered a long leather hose and Aro heard the sound of billows above. It worked at first and the water level dropped. The slavers should have cleaned the hold first. Straw and filth quickly clogged the hose and once again the water began seeping in quicker than they could pump.

Sleep became almost impossible. Even though they now fed them hard rounds of bread every day, it didn't seem to help. Her stomach seemed continually cramped from hunger. The water continued to rise from a mix of rain and sea water. By their ninth day at sea it had reached almost to her knees. Her wet feet drove her crazy and her toes felt swollen in her boots. The other men grumbled about it, too. There was nothing they could do. At least they could stand and keep the rest of their bodies dry. The rain never stopped. It increased every hour, so did the wind and the rolling and pitching of ship as it rode bigger and bigger waves.

As the sun set and the hold once again sank into darkness, she braced herself against the wet hull. The filthy water swelled and splashed around her with each roll of the ship. Lack of sleep wore upon her. She was so tired she could hardly keep her eyes open. If she went down she could easily drown. Judging from the growing number of bodies the slavers kept hauling out and dumping overboard it had happened to some already. Sickness had also begun to manifest within the horrible conditions of the hold.

Wrinkling her nose, she smacked the water around her in frustration. They were trapped. There was nothing they could do. She wished she had her knives. The cell was empty of anything to use to try to escape.

"Rot it!" She fought sudden tears at the hopelessness of it all. Her body didn't want to obey and she turned away from the others. She wanted to be home. She wanted her brothers. At the very least, she wanted to know what had happened to them. Their absence was nothing new, spring to fall they'd always been away. But she'd had letters and she'd known where they were. The loneliness after the youngest had gone off had been hard. She'd hated it and had fought it constantly. Deep inside she always knew they'd be coming home though. Two years ago, her father hadn't. The hopeless feeling she felt now reminded her of that. So did the pain in her chest. Losing her father had been devastating. Now, losing all seven of her brothers at once was something she didn't even want to think about.

She glanced over at Kei. He had become something to hold on to. Taking a deep breath she pushed the pain and hysteria away. It would do no good here, now. Her family had taught her that. She needed to stay in control in case an opportunity to escape presented itself.

The storm intensified. She hadn't thought it possible until the ship rolled nearly onto its side as the waves grew even larger. The winds could be heard through the hull and had grown into an unnatural howl.

"Quite the storm they've rode into," Bo remarked with a grimace.

When darkness fully blanketed the hold Kei took her hand. She squeezed it tightly, wishing the chains didn't prevent her from wrapping her arms around him. She just wanted to hold on to something and not let go.

The rolling got worse. Eventually they all moved to the cell bars so they had something to grasp and keep them steady.

By the faint light she could see people in the other cells doing the same. She listened to the cursing and watched the gripping arms and hands for a while before it registered there seemed to be a lot more people in each of the other cells. She asked why aloud.

"We're worth more," Prince answered quietly. Even he had come to the bars so he wouldn't be thrown about the cell.

She turned to look past Kendric at him and he smiled faintly, with little amusement. Was he still mad at her or not?

Before she could ask any more questions he continued, "The cells at the front with the women are likely not as crowded either. But the others are packed in twenty to thirty to a cell."

Her mind went over this information. The fact that the only thing those in her cell had in common was that they were soldiers, left her confused. "So they want us to fight for them or something?"

Prince shook his head, his face grim. "No. Their…entertainment is the arenas. The crowds watch as slaves fight to the death."

His words turned her stomach and she clenched her hands tighter on the bars in an attempt to fight down the rising panic and fear within her. Dying in an area was what she had to look forward to? No. She didn't really, because when they arrived at port they would certainly find out she wasn't a boy and then...

A deafening crack suddenly echoed above them, followed by a groaning long creak and a boom that made the whole ship shudder.

"Tell me that wasn't the mast," Kendric grated.

"It was," Prince answered. Kendric glared over at him, as if it were his fault.

Aro shifted to hold a bar with two hands, Kei and Kendric both close to either side of her. The mast. That certainly wasn't good. Did ships come with extra? Could they fix it at sea? She had no idea.

*Gah! Somehow things had gotten even worse. How was that even possible?* She found it hard to think. Exhaustion pulled at her, but so did hunger. The cold and wet of the water only made things worse. It didn't help she had started to not feel well, she wasn't sure if it was from the rolling ship or being hungry.

She had no idea how long they held on as the ship rolled madly. She blacked out a few times, or maybe just fell asleep. Either way, it frightened her. After the first time she started awake to find Kei and Kendric holding her up, each with a grip on her upper arm.

Eventually the storm and sea began to calm. Her mind spun so much she almost didn't notice. No, not her mind. Her vision. "I don't feel so well," she whispered, before turning and collapsing into Kei's arms.

# Chapter 7
## Into the Sea

Consciousness returned slowly. Something was wrong, but she couldn't put her finger on what. Her thoughts moved sluggishly, yet were strangely calm considering the situation. She rested her cheek against the warmth that held her, content for the moment in the quiet world of being not quite awake.

Reality, in the form of screaming, finally began to penetrate the calm, quiet place she'd been in. It seemed odd the screams resounded so frantically through the hold. She had become used to the crying and cursing, even the screaming of the women when the slavers came down, but this was different.

She blinked her eyes, trying to focus her spinning head. Everything remained foggy. Had she been sick?

It took her some time before she realized someone held her, that her cheek rested against a warm chest, her hands tucked into her lap. She could feel an arm under her knees and another around her waist.

For a moment everything remained perfect. Safety and calm continued to surround her, holding her close and protecting her. She almost smiled before the sudden sense of something not right shot through her. It wasn't Kei who held her.

She stiffened as her eyes popped open and her head shot up to see the face, of all people, Prince.

"What?" The simple word was all she could manage in her state of utter confusion. *Why him?*

"We've struck something."

She blinked rapidly, her vision clearing a little. She still didn't feel well though. She was light headed and nauseous. Her eyes burned and her head hurt. Still, she didn't want to be held by the man who'd been glaring and yelling at her the past few days. Panic and worry overwhelmed her. Where was Kei? Had something happened to him? She had to find out...

"Put me down," she demanded more sharply than she intended.

He glared down at her. "Fine."

He nearly dropped her and she flailed in the water as she splashed into it. It had risen to become now higher than her waist. The cold of it shocked her into full consciousness. Prince grabbed her shirt and righted her as she struggled. She turned on him in the faint light, uncertain if it was morning or night. "Where's Kei?"

She could see his jaw clench as he looked away. "Busy."

She blinked at him stupidly.

"Aro, are you hurt?"

She turned to see the others standing around staring at her, their faces worried.

Kei suddenly popped up out of the water in front of Kendric, nearly scaring her half to death. "What happened?" She fought to think around the pain in her head.

"We've hit something, the ship's breaking up," Kendric replied. He lifted his hands showing the foot long chain that had attached them now broken. "Kei is breaking all our chains, so we'll be able to swim free."

She looked at Kei, soaking wet and gasping for breath. "Kei?"

He flashed her a tired grin. "Just you two left."

"Then what?" She tried to keep her voice calm as he splashed his way toward her.

"Kei will rip out the cell door and we'll jump ship. Hopefully we're close to shore," Cain answered.

"I'd assume so," Kendric said. "I don't know what else we could've hit. Reefs or rocks I'm guessing."

The ship lurched suddenly and the screams of the others in the hold intensified.

"We're caught up on something?" The others nodded as Kei reached her and she looked at him.

"Don't worry," he said quietly, noting her increasing panic.

"But...but I can't swim," she whispered. "Not at all...I can't..."

"We'll help you," Kendric said quickly, apparently hearing her. "The rain has stopped, and the moon is giving us some light, it shouldn't be a problem."

"There will be lots of floating debris we can hang on to," Cain added. "Just grab something and point yourself in the direction of the shore and kick."

She took a deep breath. That didn't seem hard. They made it sound so easy.

The ship lurched and seemed to swing suddenly before hitting something with a deafening crack. Before the movement could knock her off her feet, Kei sprang forward and pushed her backward so hard she crashed into Prince and sent him down as well.

She came up out of the water sputtering. Blinking water out of her eyes, she choked. A beam had broken loose collapsed where she had been standing.

It pinned Kei to the side of the cell.

"Kei!" She floundered in the water trying to get to him. Blood ran from his mouth. His eyes were squeezed closed and teeth clenched tightly in pain. His hands clawed frantically at the beam across his chest. The sight tore her breath away. *No!* This couldn't be happening.

The men reached him first, their curses loud enough to be heard over the continued screams of the other captives.

"Hold on, we should be able to move it," Kendric said quickly.

Kei shook his head. "No. Get out."

She didn't understand, but the others looked up suddenly and she followed suit. The beam angled up toward a new hole in the cell's ceiling.

"Kei," Avery groaned.

The Fey shook his head violently. "The waters coming in too fast," he said, speaking so quickly his words tumbled into each other. "You'll not get me out in time, and I…I won't be able to open the door now." He grimaced again. "Go!"

Kendric stared at him a moment before he rested his hand gently on the Fey's head. He blinked and scowled suddenly. "Let's go then."

She stood in shock as Cain and Bo both hopped up on the beam and began scurrying up. "Wait…no…" She couldn't breathe, couldn't move. They were going to leave him?

Avery took Kei's hand. "Kei, look at me. You get out of here, you hear me?" His voice cracked. "I'll see you on the beach. Agreed?"

"On the beach," Kei repeated quietly.

Avery squeezed his hand. "I'll be waiting. Understand?"

A faint, bloody smile crossed the Fey's lips and he winced. "Go already."

Avery paused a moment but Kendric reached out a hand to help him up onto the beam. Once the young solider had scrambled up, her brother's friend looked at her and held out his hand. "Let's go, Aro."

She stared up at him a moment while she tried to get her mind to work. Ignoring him, she flung herself at Kei, wrapping her arms around his head and burying her face in his wet hair.

"Go. I'll make sure she comes." She recognized Prince's voice. Why was he still down here? He would hate her for certain now, because she wasn't going...and she really didn't care.

"Aro..."

She blinked back tears and leaned back to look at Kei. "I'll stay with you. I won't leave you. I'll get you out."

He smiled so very softly it nearly broke her heart. He took her face in his trembling hands, forcing her to look at him. She looked into his eyes and saw they had lit with that strange inner light again, though this time they glowed more of an orange than a yellow. *Did the change in color mean anything? Was he dying?*

"You have to go. I'll try to get out. I promise. I'll come and find you."

"Kei..." She choked through her tears as she frantically shook her head.

He looked over her shoulder and suddenly reached out. She turned to see he'd grasped Prince's arm and they were staring at each other intently. *Men. Still fighting.*

"I'll take care of her," Prince said after a moment, shaking the Fey's hand off.

She glared at him before turning back to Kei.

"Go, Aro," he said quietly, his voice cracking in pain.

"No."

He closed his eyes in frustration. "You promised you'd listen to me."

She clenched her teeth as tears streaked down her face. "I...I can't leave you like this," she whispered, leaning forward to press her cheek against his.

A faint sad smile crossed his lips as he gently pushed her back. His fingers brushed her cheek. His eyes were wet, too. He held her gaze a moment and then looked over her shoulder and nodded.

Prince grabbed her waist from behind, tearing her away from Kei. Before she could even fight him, he tossed her up into the air. Kendric caught her flailing arms and she screamed in frustration. "No! Kei! Kei!"

She couldn't hear if Kei said anything more to her. She stood shaking on the deck. Kendric's arms wrapped around her, holding her tightly as she sobbed and tried to escape him and return to Kei. "Please," she sobbed. "We can't leave him here! You don't leave men behind!"

A moment later Prince climbed out of the hole and she glared at him for his treachery. She couldn't breathe, couldn't speak for the wreck of emotions tearing through her. They couldn't do this do her. They couldn't make her leave her brother behind. Her heart shattered and broke. She couldn't do this again. She couldn't take losing someone else. Shadows blurred her vision as pain crushed her chest.

Kendric spun her around and pointed in the faint light of the moon and stars. "There, see the dark line. That's the shore."

She shook her head, her mind locked in despair. "No. Please..."

"Look, Aro!"

The anger in his voice forced her to look up. The shore seemed so far away, and scattered in between...

"Try to avoid the rocks," he added more calmly. He took her hand, moving it up to her face. "Grab your nose, take a deep breath."

"What?" Everything was happening so quickly. Even as she numbly did as she was told he lifted her up and tossed her overboard.

# Chapter 8
## Take a Deep Breath

She hit the water with a hard, painful slap along her side. Immediately she sank, the cold, raging waters surrounding her, taking her in and holding her tightly.

Kei hadn't gotten the chance to break her chains. She panicked, struggling to move back to the surface. Twisting, turning, thrashing, and kicking, her struggles proved to be in vain. She didn't know how to swim. She didn't know what to do. Slowly, or so it seemed, she kept on sinking.

She was going to die.

Keeping her eyes squeezed closed, she held in a sob. She tried to keep the little air she had in her lungs. She didn't want it to end like this. If she was going to drown, why couldn't she have done it holding onto Kei? Why did she have to be alone?

*Why had Kei made her leave? Stupid boy.* She was so angry at him and at Kendric and Prince and the others who'd left him and hadn't let her stay with him. But it didn't matter. She'd never get to tell them, because she was still sinking. Into the dark. Maybe her brothers would be waiting for her. Maybe Kei would be, too.

Something pulled her hair suddenly and then brushed against her head, her shoulder. Her panic grew. She twisted and kicked, hysteria pulling at her throat. Had the fish come for her already? Would they try to nibble away at her when she wasn't even dead yet?

Something grasped her arm, lost its hold and then caught her tight. She wouldn't open her eyes to look, not that she'd see much. It began pulling with jerking movements, pulling her deeper, closer to death. The water became a vise around her body. Her strength ebbed out of her as exhaustion pushed aside her fear. She struggled weakly, but it didn't matter.

Cold blasted her face, startling her, a shock to her system. It struck her something had pulled her *up*, not down. Someone.

Her eyes flew open. Salt water burned her eyes. Gasping for air and choking on waves she kicked wildly, struggling to stay above water. Air. She could breath. She sucked in a great lung-full, her heart beating furiously in her chest. She grasped frantically for the one who'd saved her.

Prince.

He was saying something but she couldn't hear over the crashing of the waves.

She yelled at him, kicked him, and hit him with her hands and the chains that bound them. "It's your fault!" His fault she wasn't with Kei. His fault Kei was alone. "You left him! How could you? I hate you!" She hit him again. "I hate you!"

He grabbed the chain between her wrists and jerked. "Be still!" His bellow was so loud, so full of anger, it actually made her stop.

She started to sink and the panic came again, the fear of the crushing darkness below. She reached for him, hands grabbing at his face and shoulders as incoherent screams ripped from her mouth.

"Shhh. Hush. Do not tread the water. Be still." His voice, though still loud, had become calm.

She stopped screaming, though the sobbing would not stop. After a moment her body even listened and soon they just floated, the waves bouncing them gently about.

"There. See. Be calm, be still, and we will be fine. I've got you."

She tilted her head to look up at him and her fingers curled into his shoulders. "I'm scared. I'm scared."

"I know. Do not worry, child. I won't let you go." They were words of comfort...and probably lies. But they made her feel better.

A wave caught them suddenly and twisted them about violently. It yanked her out of Prince's arms. She screamed, the sound cutting off abruptly as he again caught hold of her. She started to shake. It wouldn't stop. She knew fear caused the most of it, however the terribly cold water didn't help any either.

"Aro. This is not working." She looked up at him again as he continued, "I won't let you sink, but you must let go for a moment. You must trust me."

She didn't. But she did release him because it didn't really matter. If he wanted her to drown she would. All he had to do was let her go.

He moved his arms. "Grab my shoulders." She did so quickly before she could go under. His arms were raised now.

"What are–"

"Now put your chain over my head."

She understood suddenly and struggled to do as he asked. As soon as she did his arms lowered around her, holding her close to him and she could feel his chain across her back.

"There. Even the waves won't part us now," he said into her hair.

She nodded and wrapped her arms around his neck. He shifted and they floated quietly, his body tilted back as she rested across him. *How could he possibly be floating?* She let the strange thought slip away. She didn't really care. She wasn't sinking, and if the waves constantly splashed her face and she choked on water more than air sometimes, she could at least breathe.

The only sound was the crashing of the waves. It frightened her. She turned her head and looked around. Though night, the moon lit the world with a soft, eerie glow. "The others?"

"I don't know."

She turned her head again and bit her lip hard. The ship, at least a small chunk of it, hung on the rocks behind them. Even as she watched it banged against the rocks, pieces falling into the water. Unable to tear her eyes away she could only stare silently until eventually the last piece fell and the waves claimed it. "Kei."

She closed her eyes to try to keep the tears away and then gave up. It didn't matter. She held on to Prince while she shook and cried.

She stopped crying sometime. She didn't know when, but the shaking continued and her teeth chattered. They kept floating on the rough waves. She could feel Prince's legs moving steadily but slowly under her as he kicked. Sometimes his arms would shift across her back as he steered them through the growing debris around them.

She looked up sharply once, when for just a moment everything became dark.

"Just a cloud," Prince assured her. She relaxed her grip on his neck, unaware she'd held him too tightly.

Her eyes scanned the starry sky. She didn't see any clouds, not anywhere near the moon anyways.

Every once and a while, wood bounced off of them, hitting her legs or shoulders. It didn't hurt. She was numb from the cold and the waves had finally started slowly growing calmer. It was almost peaceful.

# Broken Aro

"Aro."

His voice sounded distant, foggy. She opened her eyes a little. "Mmm?"

"How are you?"

What a foolish question. "Wet. Cold. Tired." That summed up the main points.

"We're coming up on the rocks. The currents there will make things a bit bumpy. Keep your head up."

At least he had good news though. The rocks had been at least halfway to shore. So they were headed in the right direction and getting closer. Maybe they would even make it...and then...what?

He twisted suddenly and she hung on as they reached a current and the waves sucked and spun them, dragging them this way and that with a growing ferocity. She held on more tightly, her numb hands in fists behind him.

She didn't see what struck her so suddenly and so painfully her vision blurred and pain shot through her head. She blinked and closed her eyes against it, but the stabbing pain didn't fade and she could feel a strange warmth sliding down one side of her forehead.

"Aro?"

"I'm fine," she whispered and turned her face so her cheek pressed against his, wanting to shield her face from whatever else floated dangerously on the waves.

They turned suddenly. His hands tightened around her. He banged up against something, jarring them both, making him stiffen. They spun away, only to hit something else, and then again.

It took her a while to figure out he kept turning them, over and over, so he would be the one who hit the rocks. He was protecting her. She didn't understand why, but silently thanked him for it.

She did not go unscathed; a few times the angle they hit caused the back of her hands to scrape along the rocks. It stung, but didn't really hurt. She knew it should have, that it would later, but her hands had just become too numb to feel anything.

They banged their way through the rocks until finally they were free and floating quietly again. Her mind was numb, everything was numb.

His face pressed against hers. "You mustn't sleep."

She made a muffled sound of agreement, too cold and too tired to speak.

"We are almost there. You can sleep on the beach, but not here," His voice grew angrier when she didn't respond and he shook her. "Don't you dare fall asleep!"

Tears came again. He was angry with her. He was always angry with her. He continued to yell at her, his voice a distant rumble in her ear. She wanted to answer him, but just couldn't. Everything felt too heavy, too cold and dark. Had he let her go and she had started sinking again?

She didn't even have the energy to care.

# Chapter 9
## Alone with a Prince

Everything hurt. She remained motionless and in pain, trying not to move, hoping the pain would go away. It didn't, and eventually she cracked open her eyes, wincing at the brightness.

Tears welled and she blinked rapidly. Her eyes felt gritty and she let the tears come, trying to blink the salt and sand from them.

They cleared after a time and she stared off to the side, vaguely noting the beach and that it ended some distance away, cut off by ragged outcrops of rock. A blurry dark shape moved by the rocks. She blinked and the strange shadowy form disappeared.

Her fingers curled. She winced at the pain the simple motion caused on the backs of her hands. She raised her head slightly as her mind started to clear and where she was sank in.

They'd made it to the beach.

She was sprawled half across Prince. Her cheek rested on his chest with her hands on either side of her head. Lowering her face again, relief flooded her as she felt his warmth and the slow rise and fall of his chest.

Was he asleep? Unconscious? She could feel his hands resting warmly low on her back, unmoving. They had survived.

She closed her eyes. Exhaustion overcame her. She let the sound of the waves lapping the shore and the *bump,*

*bump* of his steady heart beat beneath her lull her back to sleep.


She awoke again to a faint crackling sound. Light flickered against her eyelids. Hot and cold assaulted her simultaneously. She shivered and curled herself up into a tight ball.

As awareness slowly came back to her, she remembered Prince had moved her. She recalled him speaking to her quietly, carrying her gently, and later untangling their chains from each other.

Opening her eyes she saw the flickering light and the crackling sound came from the small fire a short distance from her. The fire gave her the warmth, the cold came from the stone she rested upon.

She sat up slowly, wincing as everything still hurt, and her mind seemed foggy. For a moment she sat very still as everything spun. Once she found her balance again she looked around in the light of the fire and was surprised to find herself in a cave.

Not quite a cave. It looked like water had cut sections out of rock. Prince had moved them to a ledge. She crawled forward, looking around. Erosion had left tiers throughout the cave, as well as a series of small pools and a small flowing stream. To her left she could see the rock opening to the sea, and a little to the side stretched an opening that led to the beach. To her right the rock continued, and she stood and followed the ledge until it ended and she hopped down to a lower one, it did not go far before she came to a large pool. Above it rose the forest ridge she'd seen before, a small waterfall gently falling from it.

# Broken Aro

She knelt at the pools edge. Her chains clanked and rattled in the quiet. She certainly wouldn't be sneaking up on anyone anytime soon. Cupping water with her hands, she drank deeply, wincing as her hands stung. It wasn't yet dark out, but looked to be getting close. She had more than enough light to see the backs of her hands, the skin scraped raw and weeping, cut deeply in a few places. She grimaced and stuck them in the water, swishing them around, hoping that would be enough to clean them.

"Aro!"

She looked up at the sound of her name as it echoed sharply through the stone.

"I'm here," she said, more quietly than she intended, but her voice didn't seem to want to be working.

He still heard her, as a moment later Prince came into view, a tight frown across his face. She sat back as he made his way to her side and bit her lip. Why was he frowning now? She hadn't done anything!

He crouched down when he reached her and leaned forward, pressing his cheek to her forehead.

She pushed him away. "What are you doing?"

He frowned again. "You've had a fever. I see it finally broke."

"Oh." A blush spread across her cheeks.

He stood suddenly and with more grace than she'd ever have, slipped along the ledges and around a corner by the pool. How he moved so gracefully in chains she had no idea. A moment later he came back, arms full.

She looked at him questioningly as he set down what looked like a pile of clothes and two large bowl-shaped shells. One nearly overflowed with something purple and sweet smelling.

"What's all of this?"

He held up the bowl with the sweet stuff in it. "Today I gathered roots, berries, and so forth from the woods." He smiled slightly. "This should help your wounds."

She leaned forward to look at the gooey substance. "You made that?" He nodded. "Do I eat it?"

He smiled slightly and shook his head.

*He should smile more. It certainly looks much better than his scowl.*

"I scavenged some cloth. It will likely be needed. I washed them as well as I could. I believe they are dry now."

She raised her eyebrows. "You made medicine, and you did laundry? How long have I been sick for?"

The frown came back and he looked away, adjusting the pile of cloth. "We reached shore early yesterday. You succumbed to one of the sicknesses on the ship I believe. When I woke, you had already become lost in the fever. Delirious. I did not think you would make it through the night."

She stared at him, not quite certain what to say. He looked very uncomfortable, and she wasn't quite sure why. "Thank you," she said finally. "For taking care of me."

He nodded once, sharply. A quick, fake smile crossed his face. "Well, let me look at your hands."

She put a hand in his and watched him examine it. He rinsed it in more water, dabbed at it with a piece of cloth and proceeded to carefully cover the wounds in a thin layer of the purple mixture.

"Why didn't you do this earlier?"

He frowned again. "I did clean them as best I could." He glanced up at her. "I just finished gathering the ingredients."

"Think I'd die and didn't want to waste your time?"

"Do not even think such things," he said softly.

She held in a smile as he finished her other hand. He just looked so serious, his brows drawn slightly together. She could almost picture him sticking his tongue out a little as he concentrated.

He chuckled suddenly and released her hand. "Do not get used to this."

She smiled. "I wouldn't dream of it."

He looked up and grinned at her, and it was such a boyish, sweet smile it made her breath catch. Flustered, she looked away, her gaze falling on the pile of cloth. She paled suddenly, as what they were, where they had come from finally registered.

Scavenged he had said. From dead washed up on shore. *Gah!* Her stomach twisted at the image. Why did she have to be reminded about what had happened?

"Aro? What's wrong?"

She looked away from the pile and shook her head quickly. "Nothing."

"Let me look at your head."

She tilted her head, allowing him to better see the cut she knew was on the side of her forehead. "Is it bad?"

He gave a little shrug as he cleaned it. "It is deep. Long. It should be stitched. You will have a scar, but your hair should hide most of it."

"Perfect," she muttered. She wasn't pretty to begin with, and now both her hands and face would be scarred.

He began spreading on the paste. "This will help quite a bit. It will both kill any infection already there, and prevent further ones from occurring. It will also pull the wound together somewhat as it dries."

"If you say so."

"I do." He smiled slightly. "Leave it be, until it turns almost white, and begins flaking off on its own." He sat back and looked at her hands. "I think I will wrap your hands though. It will help protect them."

She grimaced slightly, but nodded and tried not to watch as he ripped strips and carefully wrapped her hands.

"You know what you're doing, too," she commented quietly.

He smiled again slightly.

"How is your arm?"

He looked down at it. "Fine."

He had finished with her hands. "Let me see." He didn't protest as she took his arm and undid everything. The wrappings were wet and she set them aside to examine his arm. It seemed to be healing well. It hadn't become swollen or turned any strange colors. Prince handed her more ripped cloth and she carefully re-wrapped his arm and put the greave back on.

She noticed suddenly, through the rips in his shirt, purple paste streaked up the outside of his arms, from shoulder down to his elbow. Memories of the sea and the rocks, of crashing and pain skittered through her mind. Clenching her jaw tightly for a moment, she pushed the memories away.

She frowned suddenly. "How's your back?"

He opened his mouth slightly, closed it again and sighed. "Will you look at it?"

She nodded and he turned. The back of his shirt was in tatters. Brownish stains covered large areas, causing her to grimace. She gently raised the bottom of his shirt up to sit on his shoulders. She cursed the chains again. If they were gone he could have just taken the shirt off.

When she finally saw his back, curses erupted loudly from her mouth before she could stop herself.

"Is it that bad?"

Tears formed and escaped as words caught in her throat. She sat back, her hands to her mouth. He looked like he had been whipped. His back was shredded and cut into ribbons. Patches of skin hung loosely across his back. The rest had been scraped completely raw.

"Aro?"

She closed her eyes, took a deep breath, and tried to steady herself. "It's messy," she finally answered. How could he sit there so still, so quiet? "Doesn't it hurt?"

"Very much," he said calmly.

Apparently, she didn't understand men at all. Or at least not him.

She took another breath and leaned forward. He had helped her, she would help him. Her conscience left her no choice in the matter.

It took a long time to clean it, to try to put pieces back where they belonged, and keep them there while she applied the paste. Breathing slowly helped keep her stomach from heaving. It was hard to *not* think about what she was doing. Tears continued to slide down her cheeks. He was like this because of her. Because he'd protected her. Finally she finished and wrapped the worst spots. Before he could turn around she quickly brushed the tears from her cheeks. She couldn't do anything about her shaking hands.

"Aro? What's wrong?"

"Nothing." She shook her head quickly. "I'm just tired. And hungry."

He watched her for a moment before he nodded and stood, gathering up his bowls and cloth. "Let us head back to the fire and have something to eat."

Her head shot up at that. He had food? Her stomach cramped at the idea of food. How many days had it been since she had more than a few pieces of that horrible bread? She followed him eagerly, and then watched impatiently as he puttered about the fire, cooking a few small fish on sticks. What looked like clams or muscles he placed by the fire until they opened.

She stuffed her face, and licked her fingers. "Oh, that was so good!"

He smiled over at her as he continued eating, in a much neater and proper fashion.

"So you can cook, too?"

He nodded. "I travel often. There are not always inns and such to stay in."

She yawned and curled up by the fire, watching the flames flicker. "Well, you are very good at it. At least with seafood."

He laughed quietly. "Thank you." He finished eating and tidied up. She watched him leave for a moment, and when he returned and handed her a small piece of wet cloth, she smiled. She sat up, laughing at his manners and wiped her mouth and hands.

He watched her, as if making sure she did a good enough job, and then settled down to sit beside her.

"Is there a reason you're being so nice?" She struggled not to yawn. "I wouldn't think you'd care about someone like me."

He paused before answering, as if surprised at her comment. "I am actually quite fond of you."

"Mmm," she managed, not really believing him. She lied back down again. A full stomach made her so tired.

He chuckled suddenly. "I have always had a soft spot for children."

His words caused anger to shoot through her. *He thought her a child?* She frowned slightly as she wiggled against the cold stone, trying to get comfortable. Finally she closed her eyes. "So you're that kind of man are you?"

She cracked an eye open to see how he'd taken her comment and couldn't hold in a chuckle. His cheeks were absolutely flaming, his eyes wide and horrified. They narrowed quickly however, at her laugh. "Got you," she murmured.

"You are such a troublesome child," he said sternly.

"I'm not a child," she muttered.

His fingers brushed hair from her face. "Ah, but you are," he said so very softly. "Don't rush growing up. Being a child is so much better. Hold on to your innocence."

"So I should stay a boy? I don't think the others would do that."

He grew quiet for a moment, as if trying to figure out what she meant. "Ah, yes," he said finally. "That was not...quite what I was speaking of. So you are...yes of course you are."

She smiled slightly at his floundering words. "I've never even kissed a boy," she admitted quietly as sleep pulled at her more strongly.

As she drifted off she felt his hand on her shoulder. "You have lots of time, Aro. Lots of time."

# Chapter 10
# A Good Day

The next morning she couldn't see Prince anywhere. She frowned, looking around. She was certain it had been his leaving that had woken her. She could vaguely remember him brushing hair from her face, and the feeling of his cool fingers against her forehead.

Had she dreamed it?

No, if she'd dreamed of him, it wouldn't be something like that. He simply still worried about her being sick, or maybe getting sick again. That was beyond strange itself. She hadn't thought he liked her, but from what he'd said the night before, he did.

Maybe they had started to become friends after all.

Such thoughts quickly sobered her. What had happened to Kei? Had he died? Or had he somehow made it out of the ship? Even if he had, she had no idea how badly he had been hurt. He might not have made it to shore. Panic bubbled up inside of her, twisting her stomach. Had she lost him?

She sniffled and rubbed away tears that suddenly started sliding down her cheeks. He had been all she had left. She didn't want to think about him anymore. It hurt too much. She didn't want to think of everything she'd lost. Everyone.

She looked at the fire and moved to toss another small piece of wood on it. Prince had left her breakfast; a fish cooked and left on a large green leaf. The sight made her smile a little, proof he continued to think of her, to take care of her.

She tended the fire and ate slowly, one never ate fish quickly. It was a sure way to choke to death on a bone. After cleaning up she headed out toward the beach, wondering where Prince had gone off to.

She looked down its length, all the way to the next outcrop of stone, and didn't see him. He must have gone back into the woods. She also noticed the absence of bodies. Had he moved them? She didn't know, and decided she wasn't going to ask either.

Picking her way down the beach, she collected odds and ends that might be helpful. They were stuck here after all, wherever here was, and they had nothing.

She found a few pieces of rope, some netting that needed only minor repair, and another large bowl shaped shell. Holding them to her chest, she carried them along with her. When she kicked over a board she discovered her greatest find. A long, thin nail stuck out of it.

"Oh!" She grinned. It would do nicely.

When Prince finally returned to the fire a while later she struggled to contain her excitement. "Hello, my prince," she sang, bouncing up and down.

He stopped to stare at her strangely before setting down a number of items.

When his hands became free she shouted, "Catch!"

He did so with ease, and stared in shock at what lay in his hands.

She held up her hands and wiggled her fingers and laughed. Her now free hands.

"How..?"

She laughed again and ran up to him, holding out the nails she had found. "I found some nails, and freed them from their boards, and shaped them with rocks, see?" She waved them in front of his nose. "And then I picked the locks."

His eyebrows rose at that and she laughed again.

"So, my prince, how much should I charge you?" She grinned up at him sweetly. The look on his face made her laugh harder. "Just teasing. I'll take yours off, too. Come and sit."

He did so, and with only some minor cursing she was able to remove his chains as well. She watched him rub at his wrists, his head bent, dark hair falling over his face but not quite hiding his smile.

"See," she said softly. "I can be useful."

He shook his head and looked over at her, still rubbing his wrists. "I never said you couldn't be, Aro."

She shrugged and looked away. He'd spoken so very seriously her face grew warm.

They each shared the few things they had found, what she had gotten from the beach, and some food he had found in the forest. They washed up and prepared a small afternoon meal. Afterward he checked on her cuts and she checked his back, applying more medicine to a few places. They both added some to a few places on their bruised and chaffed wrists. He traded his torn shirt for one from his pile. It was too short in arm and length, but fit well enough otherwise.

They went back to the beach afterward, checking the shallows by the rocks for clams and mussels and fish stranded in little pools.

After a while she found herself staring out at the sea, her eyes searching for Kei even though she knew she wouldn't see him. Part of her didn't want to believe he was gone. Couldn't believe it, because it hurt too much. "He lied."

Prince stepped up beside her. He rested a hand on her shoulder but didn't say anything.

"He promised he'd never leave me. That we'd be friends forever."

"He was foolish to promise you such things."

She nodded, because really she knew he was right. No one knew what the future would bring. But, "He said he'd protect me. He lied."

Prince looked down at her. "He did not lie, Aro. He did protect you, from being crushed by the beam. He made sure you got off the ship."

*True.* Everything Prince said was true. It didn't make it easier. "But he died," she murmured, speaking more to herself than her companion.

Prince let out a deep sigh. "Aro, you must understand things always have a price. Did you think those who protect you will come to no harm? If you are in need of protection, it is always possible they will be hurt, or die, for your sake. Kei accepted this when he made his promises to you and in the end he died so you could live."

The words stung, hurt. More tears came and fell. Then she thought of his back, the wounds he had taken while he protected her, got her to shore. He was right. He was always right. It was getting annoying.

She looked up at him. "I didn't think you liked Kei."

He grimaced. "I do not. However, I respect the sacrifice he made for you. He did a very honorable act. It is not like the Fey to do such things. They are wild, uncaring creatures. Perhaps," he paused. "Perhaps he was different."

She wiped away tears and looked out to sea again. "Do you...do you think he might have gotten out?" She looked back up at him. "The Fey are strong right? He might have?"

Prince shook his head slightly. "I don't know. He had been very badly injured." He sighed, as the tears continued to trail down her face. "He might have, I truly don't know."

She sniffled again and managed to nod as she moved her gaze to her feet in the shallow waters, letting her hair fall to hide her face and her tears.

His arms suddenly slid around her, and she didn't fight him as he embraced her very gently, stroking her hair like she was a little child. Resting her cheek on his chest she let herself truly cry, just a little. Though she had been trying so hard to be strong, he was being nice, and she didn't want to make him angry. She didn't want him to be mad at her again, she couldn't stand it when he was. She didn't want him to go, too. That would be worse, so much worse.

"I'm sorry, Aro," he said quietly.

She didn't know what he was sorry for. Perhaps that she had lost Kei, or her brothers, or her home. He could have been sorry for her for any number of things. She'd lost everything. But it helped a little, knowing he did care, and it allowed her to calm down the tears.

He tensed suddenly and she looked up quickly as his arms tightened around her. "What–"

"Shhh," he muttered quietly and slowly turned. Keeping one arm around her, he guided her back into the rocks. She knelt when he motioned her to do so, watching as he did the same and peered around a large rock. Though he had relaxed his hold on her, his eyes darted back and forth quickly as he watched something in the direction of the other side of the long rock outcrop they called home.

She resisted the urge to look herself, or to ask what he had seen or heard. Her brothers had taught her enough about scouting, so she knew when to be still and quiet. Besides, it wasn't like they were in friendly territory. She had no idea where they had ended up, for all she knew the next beach over could be Janur Port, or another slaver city or village.

He frowned suddenly, but relaxed. She clenched her teeth to keep from asking what was going on, and her silence paid off as he finally looked down at her with a faint smile. "I believe it is Bo and Cain, making their way around the outcrop."

She grinned and clapped her hands silently at his words. Someone else had survived! She had tried not to think about it, the possibility she and Prince might have been the only ones to make it to the beach. She tried not to think about a lot of things. It helped, somewhat.

Her smile broadened as she heard them suddenly, cursing as they moved around and across the wet rocks. Yes, she could definitely identify Bo and the occasional quieter curse from Cain as well.

She leaned forward slightly and whispered, "Should we go meet them? Or at least let them see us? Is it safe?"

Prince frowned slightly but nodded, turning toward her again and ruffling her hair so it fell over her face.

"Thanks."

She peeked around the rock and waited a moment, when she saw the others come further into view she stood and waved. She tried not to hide her disappointment to see it was only Bo and Cain. Kei, Kendric, and Avery weren't with them. Of course, they were the three she knew the best. She had to be the unluckiest girl in the world.

"Hey." She walked out and greeted them as they drew closer.

Bo's grin grew. "Hey there yourself, pup. Glad to see you made it."

She smiled back. "You, too." She turned slightly, and saw that though Prince had stood and shown himself, he hadn't moved. She sighed.

Bo chuckled. "Been stuck with quite the company."

"Actually, I wouldn't have made it to shore without him," she said honestly. "I got a fever, and he took care of me, too. So," She shrugged. "He's really not so bad." She could have said more, a lot more. But she was supposed to be a boy, and boys didn't gush about how wonderful other men were.

Bo and Cain both looked over at Prince. A smile broke across Bo's face suddenly. "Good enough. We all need to stick together. This isn't the time or place for such nonsense. Cain?"

The other man nodded. "True."

She jerked her head in the direction of the cave. "Come on, there's water and a fire. And if you're good I'll take off those chains."

They suddenly noticed she didn't have any, and as they made their way carefully back she explained. She quickly gave them the very short tour of where they'd been staying. The first thing done was to remove their chains, and then both men went to the waterfall pool to wash and drink. Since she didn't want to accidentally see anything she shouldn't, she suggested to Prince they go back out to search for more dinner.

# Chapter 11
## A Not so Good Night

When she and Prince came back from searching for food she found the boys tending the fire and saw they had also brought in more wood. Prince asked her to go collect more of some large leaves he used for cooking, so she scrambled off before it got dark. She didn't have to go too far, many of the kind he liked grew just past the waterfall along the ledge walls.

When she returned she didn't miss how everyone grew quiet. She grimaced at them. What had they been talking about? There were a few huddled whispers between the three, followed by some sort of agreement as she reached the fire and tossed the pile of leaves to the side.

She frowned at them all. Should she even bother to ask? It wouldn't do much good. She'd gotten the same treatment from her brothers and other adults, too. She knew they all considered her a child, so quite possibly it wasn't anything she actually wanted to hear.

She helped Prince prepare the food while they all made small talk about the various items they'd been able to scavenge.

She turned to Bo when the food was almost ready. "So what's the word?"

He accepted a leaf full of food from Prince and she saw the two exchange quick glances. "How about we wait until we're finished eating?" He grinned at her. She thought it looked a little forced, but she didn't know him well, and it was hard to tell with the long scar on his face. "Then

110

there won't be any interruptions to the story. We can both
tell our tales. I'm interested in hearing what you two have
been up to."

She agreed and dug into her food with enthusiasm.
Bo and Cain laughed at her exuberance while Prince
frowned. She ignored them all. It wasn't her fault it seemed
she never could get enough to eat. Though she hadn't been
starving in the city, food had begun to grow scarce as the
enemy army had drawn closer and roads had slowly been
cut off. The time on the slave ship with almost no food had
been hard though. She knew she had lost weight, and her
still growing body seemed to always want more food than
they could find.

When they had all finished, they cleaned up and
Prince left to take their remains away. She settled by the
fire, holding back sudden shivers. The sun had gone down,
and the nights had become so much colder. She wondered
how far north they were, and if the winters here would be
cold and snowy like they had been at home.

Prince returned and took a spot next to her.

"Well, let's hear yours first," Bo said, before she
could say anything about them telling their tale.

She didn't know if she should do the talking or
Prince, and looked to him for guidance. The little frown of
his that annoyed her so much appeared for a moment until
he gave her a brief nod. She didn't know what he meant by
that though and bit her lip in frustration.

Bo sensed her unease and prodded her along.
"What happened when you went over, Aro? I didn't see
you."

She grimaced. "I sank." She glanced over at Prince
"He pulled me up and kept me from going under again."

To her surprise Prince then took over the story,
relating events in his refined quiet voice. She only
interjected once, telling the others about Prince protecting

her from the rocks. For some reason she really wanted them to like Prince. Seeing how he had been doing so much for her seemed to be helping with that.

He didn't seem too impressed with her efforts however, shooting an angry glance at her interruption before continuing with their story up to the present.

"So you haven't seen anyone else?" Cain looked at them both, clearly hopeful.

She shook her head and looked to Prince, who shook his as well. "Have you?"

"We've seen a few footprints on the beaches, and heard things moving in the woods. Could have been people or animals." He shrugged. "But I'm getting ahead of myself." He told of both he and Cain reaching the beach located two coves south of theirs. Much like they had, the two had dealt with searching for water and food, finding shelter and regaining their strength. "Once we began feeling a bit more alive we decided to see if we could find anyone else and started checking out the other beaches. I guess we were lucky we chose to come north."

"So you haven't seen any of the others?" She tried to keep the desperate hope from her voice. It hadn't failed her notice how they'd avoided her question previously. "Kei or Kendric or Avery? You don't know what happened to them?"

Bo and Cain both looked over at Prince, and the expressions on their faces told her that yes, they did know something. They just didn't want to tell her.

Despite the sinking feeling in her gut she wanted to know. She needed to know. "Tell me," she begged, looking from one to the other.

Bo sighed and ran a hand over his face. "We found Kendric. He didn't make it."

She stared at him as his words sunk in. "He's...dead?" Suddenly dazed, she looked off to the side.

Kendric was dead. She couldn't believe it. Didn't want to believe it. He had been so alive. He had been someone she actually knew. She lowered her head as it truly hit her he was gone. She wouldn't ever see him again. He wouldn't ever tease her again. He wouldn't...

"Aro? I'm sorry. I know he was your friend. I'll miss him, too."

Bo's words, though kind, did not help. The urge to suddenly break down into hysterical tears flooded through her. She scrambled to her feet, struggling to hold in the tears. "I...I just need..." She didn't know what she needed, so didn't bother to finish as she quickly slipped down off the ledge to the next and headed toward the waterfall.

She heard Prince say something behind her, but just walked faster, moving as quickly as she could by the faint light of the fire. The stars and moon helped after a short distance as she neared the waterfall. By the time she reached it tears had started streaming down her cheeks and she struggled to keep from sobbing.

She moved around the pool edge, trying to keep out of sight of the others and sat down quickly. Wrapping her arms around herself, she cried, trying to do so as quietly as possible.

It wasn't long before someone sat down beside her. She tried to hold in a shuddering breath but it didn't really work.

"I am so sorry, Aro," Prince said quietly.

"Me, too," she mumbled. She wiped her nose on her sleeve and kept her head down, trying to hide. She rubbed at her face, trying to wipe away the tears and keep them gone.

"You are allowed to grieve."

She choked on a laugh. "I'm supposed to be a boy, remember?"

He sighed. "Boys, and men, feel sadness as well."

She peeked over at him. "You're not crying."

The frown returned. "I did not know him."

She sniffled. "I didn't either really" she admitted. "He was more my brother's friend. But," She sighed and wiped away more tears. "He was someone I knew from home. Someone alive. He reminded me of my brothers, he had known them. And now..." She let out a shaky breath. "Now it's like everything is gone. There's nothing left."

She leaned forward and put her face in her hands. "I don't know where I am, or what I'm doing, where I'm going. I have nothing. I don't know what to do. I'm so scared."

His hand rested softly on her back. "We will figure something out," he said gently.

"Gah." She snorted and shook her head and then the rotten tears came again and she cursed around them.

He began to slowly rub her back. "Things will work out. I will admit it may take some time for things to be normal for you again. But I will stay with you and help you as much as I can."

She nodded slightly and took shallow breaths, trying to calm down. She almost laughed at his words. She knew he only wanted her to feel better, and he had been careful not to make any promises. But he was trying. That was something. She sat up a little and looked over at him. "I don't want to be any trouble."

He chuckled and shook his head. "You are fifteen, I'm quite certain you will be a great deal of trouble."

She scowled and swatted him.

He grinned back and gestured to the pool. "Wash up a little, and come back to the fire with me. We need to get some sleep."

She fidgeted a little when the others watched her come back. They didn't say anything, for that she was truly grateful. She also had her horribly cut hair to hide behind, and Prince, too. He settled her down, told her to go to sleep, and stayed close to her as she did.

She drifted quickly into that foggy almost asleep state. A strong grip on her shoulder startled her awake immediately and she awoke in a near panic. She looked around quickly and saw Cain beside her. Prince and Bo were gone.

Cain raised a finger to his lips and nodded toward the woods.

She bit her lip and sat up silently, straining to hear anything. What was going on? Whatever had happened, it likely wasn't good.

She kept glancing ahead and then back at Cain, but he didn't look like he heard anything either.

The noises came suddenly, and were barely distinguishable before they disappeared again. She looked over at Cain, wide eyed and afraid to speak. Her heart beat madly in her chest. She wished again she still had her knives. Or any kind of weapon. Even a big stick would have been nice.

After long sickening moments she heard footsteps and quiet talking. She jumped up as a figure hopped up onto the ledge.

"Avery!" She ran to his side and stopped herself from hugging him just in time, changing it into more manly shoulder and back slaps.

"Hey, Aro. Cain." The young man moved over to grasp the other's arm.

He turned quickly though, looking behind him. "Listen," he said, quietly. "There are two others with me. I don't know about them. Be careful."

She frowned but nodded, effectively also shaking more of her hair over her face.

Before he could say any more the others returned. Bo and Prince came immediately to join them, but the two strangers hung back, looking around.

One gave a low whistle. "Nice place."

She looked them over as Avery introduced them all. They were certainly rough looking, but she could say the same for her other companions right now as well. Still, she would do as Avery suggested, and be careful. She didn't know them after all.

"This is Allen and Garic," Avery said quietly. "They washed up on the same beach as I did."

Bo raised his eyebrows. "Where?"

"North." Avery grimaced. "I'm not sure how far. We saw a ship in the distance, so took to the woods."

She tugged on his sleeve and leaned forward. "No Kei?"

His face turned sad and he shook his head. "You neither?"

"No." She looked away, trying to hold in more tears. Boys didn't cry.

He sighed. "He said he'd be here."

She choked a little and covered her mouth with her hand.

"What happened to your chains?"

She blinked, noticing they still had theirs, though Avery's had at least been broken by Kei. She dug in her pocket for her nails as Bo explained how she had removed them for everyone.

She did Avery first, and glanced at Bo and then at Prince. Both nodded and she went nervously to the new men, keeping her head down and working as quickly as possible. She could feel their eyes on her and for some reason their attention made her feel uncomfortable. When she finally finished she let out a sigh of relief and moved away from them as quickly as she could.

The others all sat around the fire talking and she sat in an empty spot between Prince and Avery. Bo and Cain sat beyond them. The strangers remained together but apart from them. She wasn't sure if she should find their behavior odd or not.

She curled up and listened while the others talked. She felt safe, with Prince and her other friends around her. That was something at least.

# Chapter 12
## What We Found on the Beach

The next morning she was in a foul mood. She couldn't even really say why. Maybe from all the crying she'd done the night before. Maybe because the only person of their group not found was Kei. But even that wasn't true. He could be still pinned in the wreckage of the ship now under the sea.

She washed up quickly and joined the others, spending the morning gathering wood, and searching for food or anything else useful.

It didn't take long for Avery to join her. His presence didn't surprise her much, they were closest in age. They had both been close to Kei.

They wandered the beach together, everyone else off doing other things. "How long will we stay here do you think? On the beach I mean," she asked suddenly.

He shrugged. "I don't know. Not much longer, I don't think it's very safe. Of course, now that everyone is here..." His voice trailed off and he looked away, his gaze going to the sea.

"I miss him," she said.

His face became sad and he nodded. "I do, too." He grimaced. "I thought he would make it. He was always so strong."

"They wouldn't let me stay and help him," she said quietly. "I would have. In the ship."

Avery looked over at her and she turned away.

Avery didn't comment, but changed the subject. "So was Prince much of a problem?"

She chuckled and shook her head. "No. Other than being an arrogant ass at times, and having way too many manners. He's not that bad." She grimaced slightly. "I wouldn't be here if not for him. He got me to the beach, found shelter and water and food."

"He took care of you."

She nodded. "He did."

"Huh." He shook his head. "Though truthfully, I'm not too surprised. When you were sick on the ship he certainly was worried about you."

His tone sounded questioning and she cursed mentally. "He thinks I'm a child, that's why. It's really frustrating."

Avery laughed and punched her in the arm. "You're the youngest. You know all of us would have done the same thing."

She mumbled a few curses under her breath.

He laughed again. "I know. Being the youngest isn't easy. I was there not too long ago."

She rolled her eyes as she continued to walk along the beach, kicking at debris, stooping occasionally to look at something. She looked up suddenly as Avery urgently whispered her name and cursed.

"What is it?"

"Something moving at the end of the beach." He stepped closer to her and pointed out a shadow moving by the far rocks.

She squinted, trying to see what had caught his attention. "Slaver you think?"

He shook his head. "I don't know."

"Should we run? Tell the others?" Her voice rose slightly as panic started to flutter within her. Had they been found already? She didn't want to be in chains again. She took a step backward, ready to bolt and hide, but Avery grabbed her arm.

"Wait." He went up on his toes for a moment, a hand above his light blue eyes, blocking the sun. "I think..."

The shadow moved off the rocks onto the beach, becoming a person. She waited, her body tense. Would more people appear? One certainly wouldn't be a problem. Even without weapons there were enough of them here to handle a lone person.

But as he drew a little closer she gasped. She knew that shock of hair, those strange, dark clothes. "Kei!"

She tore her arm from Avery's hand and sprinted down the beach, stumbling through the sand in her haste to get to him. She saw Kei smile before she pounced on him, dumping him down onto the sand.

"Ow."

She sat up, unwrapping her arms from him as she blushed. "Sorry." She couldn't keep a smile from her face though. "You're alive!"

He grimaced as he sat up, brushing hair from his eyes with one hand, the other going to his ribs. "Well, I was."

"Gah! I'm sorry!"

Kei chuckled and looked back at her, his smile softening. "I'm fine. You?"

She nodded quickly, holding her hands in her lap and trying to keep from bouncing up and down like a fool girl. She couldn't keep the grin from her face no matter how hard she tried. Joy and relief at finding him alive coursed through her.

She looked him over, seeing him for the first time in sunlight. A blush crept up her cheeks as she did. He turned out to be handsomer than she'd imagined with the sunlight in his hair and him smiling at her. A flush spread across his face as well as they continued to stare at each other silently. She looked away quickly, suddenly embarrassed.

He looked past her and grinned. "Hey, Avery."

"You're late."

Kei laughed quietly and stood. She scrambled to her feet, a hand almost going out to him when he stumbled. She bit her lip slightly. He obviously wasn't fine.

"Aro's been worried about you," Avery commented, punching her in the arm.

She scowled at him.

Kei looked back at her, a frown crossing his face, his brows drawing together in worry. "I'm sorry."

She fought another blush and shrugged a shoulder as she ducked her head. She looked up quickly at him and grinned. "But you're here now."

He reached over, moving some of her hair aside. She froze, until she realized he was looking at the cut on her forehead. His eyebrows went up. "Prince?"

She didn't quite follow, until she remembered the purple paste covering the cut. She nodded.

He frowned again. "You said you weren't hurt."

She rolled her eyes and pushed his hand away. "It's not that bad."

His boyish face turned stern. "What else?"

She sighed and held out her hands, still roughly bandaged. "Just some skin scraped off. They aren't serious or anything either." His jaw clenched and she let out a deep breath. He was going be worse than her brothers. "Prince is way worse off. He kept me from hitting the rocks. His back is cut up really bad."

Kei looked over at Avery who gave him a shrug in response. She poked a finger gently at his ribs, getting his attention again, and put her hands on her hips. "You aren't fine either, are you?"

A half smile played across his lips. "A few broken ribs." He ruffled her hair. "Don't worry, Aro. I heal really fast."

"Hmph. What took you so long?"

Kei looked off to the side, his brows drawing down.

"Kei?"

"When he goes into the fury," Avery said quietly. "Sometimes it takes him a while to calm down again."

"Oh." The fury. When a Fey's eyes turned red and they went wild, and got stronger. That explained how he got out of the ship.

"Chains?"

She stared at him in confusion until she figured out he meant hers were gone. The way he talked would certainly take some getting used to. He'd been right when he'd told her he wasn't good with people. Since the wreck he seemed to have gotten even worse. Had he cracked his head on the ship?

He cocked his head to the side, waiting for an answer.

"Oh, I picked the locks," she said quickly, her hand going to her pocket for her makeshift tools. Then she remembered she hadn't put them back last night and cursed under her breath. "I can do yours, but my stuff is back at the cave."

He nodded, smiling slightly. "You come across anyone else?"

"You're the last one," Avery answered. He glanced at her. "Kendric didn't make it. But everyone else is here."

Kei sucked in a shocked breath and whirled back to face her. "Aro..."

She didn't look at him, couldn't. She didn't want to think about Kendric. Not when she had just been so happy to discover Kei alive.

"Aro," he persisted, reaching out a hand to her.

She stepped away and clenched her teeth a moment. "I'm fine. Don't worry about it." She kept her eyes to the sea, not wanting to see the look on his face. She hated pity.

She stared at the dark spot on the horizon for a few moments before her mind recognized what she saw. "Wither me," she choked out.

She pointed and the boys turned to look at the ship off in the distance.

"We need to move," Avery said, his voice firm but quiet.

She cursed and shot him an annoyed look. As if she didn't know that. She wasn't a total fool. She followed the boys with a grimace, glancing back to sea again and again as they made their way to the others.

She was getting tired of having bad days.

# Chapter 13
## Into the Deep Dark Woods

The men conversed quickly in quiet whisperings after their return and Avery told them about the ship. Kei was greeted warmly by Bo and Cain, stared at by the two new men, and glared at by Prince. As far as she was concerned, everything had returned to normal.

She removed Kei's chains while the others talked, sneaking glances at him while she did. She caught him a number of times watching Prince, a thoughtful look on his face.

Eventually curiosity got the best of her. "What are you thinking?"

"What?" He looked back at her and blinked in confusion.

She smirked and jerked her head in Prince's direction.

"Ah. Hmm. Yes."

She raised her eyebrows. "Is that so?"

His face screwed up in frustration. "Sorry. I'm...not used to talking."

She rested a hand on his and squeezed lightly. "It's fine. Just think about what you want to say first. I don't mind." She smiled again to encourage him.

He let out a deep breath of air and sat a moment. "Well, I was surprised he took care of you. I honestly didn't know if he would."

She sighed. "He did. And he did a very good job of it. Truly, he's not so bad. I wish everyone could see that."

"He's..." Kei saw her face and stopped, shaking his head. "I just don't think we'll ever get along. We're too different."

"We need to all work together," she insisted quietly. "Will you try? Just try not to fight at least? You don't have to be friends."

He watched her for a moment before nodding. He motioned to the two new men. "Am I supposed to do the same with them? I don't like them."

She raised her eyebrows and her mouth twisted into a wry smile at his blunt words. "I don't think any of us do. But they haven't done anything. So..."

Kei sighed. "Try to get along."

"Exactly."

By the time she got the last of his chains off it had started to get dark. The men continued with their quiet conversation. What could they possibly be discussing so earnestly? She could have listened in, but it wasn't like she could help. She sat beside Kei off to the side, partly hidden by flickering shadows from their very small fire. She grimaced as she stared at it, they didn't want to risk being seen. At least the cave hid enough they could have a small one. Still, it was going to be cold. Just thinking about it made her shiver.

Kei shifted slightly, moving closer to her. She smiled over at him but didn't say anything.

Avery came over to join them a short while later. "Are you cold, Aro?"

She nodded slightly. "Just a little."

He frowned. "We'll be able to have a bigger fire tomorrow night."

"We're moving then?"

He nodded. "First thing in the morning. We're taking watches tonight, just in case. Tomorrow we'll follow the stream into the woods a goodly way and set up another camp."

"We aren't going to keep moving?"

"We haven't come to any decision on that yet. The sea provides a good amount of food. We won't be so lucky in the woods. Water will be a problem, too. We've nothing to carry extra in. Cain is going to try to make up some water skins from some of the leather we salvaged. We'll see if that works." He smiled at her. "Don't worry. We'll get it all sorted out."

She bit her lip and nodded, wishing silently that they'd stop treating her like a child.

Avery turned to Kei. "You have the last watch. I'll be getting you up."

Kei nodded.

Avery looked back and forth between them a few times, his head cocked slightly to the side as if trying to figure something out. Had he found out that she was actually a girl? He didn't say anything however, just gave a brief smile. "Get some sleep, you two. We've a busy day tomorrow."

As she settled herself next to the fire she noticed Prince watching her and guilt stabbed her heart, forcing her to look away. After everything he had done, she had abandoned him without a second thought when Kei had returned. Yet there he sat, not even with his customary frown, but just simply watching her quietly.

"Gah."

"Aro?"

She looked over at Kei. "I'll be right back." She grinned at him, "Keep my rock warm."

He laughed, shaking his head at her, and settled back down as she got up.

Heading quietly out the back way of the cave, she turned once and looked at Prince. He still watched her. She gave him a slight nod toward the pool and then continued on.

She waited out of sight by the pool, worrying at a fingernail.

"Don't bite your nails. It is unseemly."

She lowered her hand and grinned. "I'm supposed to be a boy."

Prince frowned at her. "That is no excuse."

She rolled her eyes dramatically. "You are such a prince." Her words brought a faint smile to his lips, but it faded quickly and she winced. "I'm sorry."

He shook his head slightly. "You have nothing to be sorry for, child."

She grimaced. "You've done so much for me. And..." She sighed and rubbed at her head in frustration, unsure of how to say what she wanted him to understand. "I just...gah!"

He rested a hand on her shoulder as she struggled with putting into words how much he meant to her, for everything he had done and said. Especially for being there for her. She didn't know what to do, how to be friends with both him and Kei when they didn't get along.

He gave her shoulder a little squeeze. "Stay with Kei. I know you missed him. I will be here if you need me."

She looked up at him and saw he was actually smiling and a small smile came to her on its own. He wasn't mad, so everything would be fine. He had said he would stay, he would be here. His words meant more to her than he could possibly know when everything else seemed to be disappearing around her.

"Come on," Prince said, the smile still amazingly on his face. "Time for bed."

She opened her eyes wide in mock astonishment. "You found me a bed?"

He swatted her lightly upside the head.

She laughed and followed him back.

Kei looked over at her in concern when she settled back down next to him.

"I'm fine." She smiled to herself as she closed her eyes. Everyone was getting along. Everything would be fine.

Morning seemed to come too quickly. She had meant to get up early with Kei and stand watch with him, but he hadn't woken her up. In fact, she ended up being the last to wake. That made her cranky.

She ate the little food they had left for her and proceeded to help pack up. Most of the others had gone out searching for what food they could find. Prince remained in the caves with her, trying to put all their salvaged belongings into portable bundles. She grew frustrated as she found herself reaching for her knives more than once and not finding them there.

Prince remained strangely quiet and she looked up at him. He stood there, fingers resting gently on his chest. She'd seen him do it a number of times before, but hadn't really taken notice. Where his fingers rested though, could have been where a chain or pendant had hung. "Did they take something important from you?"

He nodded slightly and his fingers curled before he dropped his hand. "Important. Yes, you could say so." He looked off into the distance. "I need..." He started, but stopped and looked down at her briefly, before turning suddenly and walking away.

"Uh, strange," she muttered.

Kei walked in from the beach. "What's strange?"

She sighed. "Nothing." She looked over to where Prince had disappeared toward the pool.

Kei followed her gaze and frowned. "Did you fight?"

She shook her head. "No. I don't think so." She worried her lip, trying to figure out what had happened. "I think it's just hard on all of us, losing everything."

Kei nodded. "Harder for him. He had more."

She nodded. "True."

Bo came in, followed by Cain. "You all finished in here?"

She nodded. "I think so. You have any luck?"

He smiled and held up a bulging shirt. "Didn't do too badly if I do say so." He nodded in Cain's direction. "Cain has another. Garic actually speared a few good sized fish. They're cleaning them now."

She made a face, wondering how good a job they could be doing with just sharp chips of rock.

Everyone came in and gathered up their sparse belongings. She only looked back once before following the others up the embankment and into the woods.

Fear pushed and pulled at her, trying to take over, but she tried not to let it show. She was a city girl. Living on the beach had been hard enough. She didn't know what to expect now. She tried not to be afraid. She knew at least some of the others had some experience with it. It helped knowing they would all be looking out for her.

However this wasn't their woods, or their homeland. Childhood stories of wild Fey, magical Elves, and shape changing Were abounding in these woods came back to her. Truly none of them knew what they were walking into. Had the stories been just stories? She knew they all existed, but the tales had often been frightening, not cozy and nice. Even Kei had few memories of his young childhood here. She glanced over at Prince. "Think we'll run into anything we can't handle? Other than slavers I mean."

"I wouldn't think so. Not this close to the beach, or so far north."

She didn't like how his words didn't seem all that certain and again missed her knives. Giving up on that she picked up a big stick as soon as she found one.

They headed into the woods on an easterly course until they came across a stream. Not wanting to give up a source of water, they continued on along its banks. Finally, Bo declared a sizable clearing by the stream the place they would stop.

Personally she considered the spot still too close to the beach, but maybe that was the point. They could still have easy access to the food they could find there.

Her men suddenly sprang into action, seeming to know what needed to be done, gathering rocks for a fire pit, digging a shallow hole for it, and breaking branches off trees with long thin needles for bedding.

She tugged on Bo's shirt. "What do you want me to do?"

He pursed his lips. "Hmm. You can start collecting firewood. Try to find some good dry, dead fall."

She nodded and set about doing as asked, and any other small chores they found for her afterward.

As the afternoon wore on everyone else seemed to be able to constantly have something to do. She found herself sitting next to Cain watching him in amusement as he cursed at the pile of leather before him. "What are you making?"

"Water skins."

"Do you know what you're doing?"

He scratched his head and let out a sigh. "Well. No. It is not helpful we have nothing in the way of tools."

She picked up some leather pants and examined them. "I'd cut off part of a leg. The seams are pretty good. Then you'll just have to sew the bottom."

He raised his eyebrows at her but took the garment and nodded after a moment. He set about sawing at the leather with one of the sharp rocks. She checked out one of the other pieces they had, a leather vest, and began picking apart one of the seams that had been held together with a thin strip of leather. Cain finished cutting and again began staring the piece of leather, turning it over and over in his hand.

With a sigh she took the piece from him. She deftly turned it inside out and decided the cut end would be the best end to sew. She bit her lip. "I'm going to find some rocks."

She came back with a larger flat one and smaller hand sized one. She pulled one of the larger nails she'd scavenged from her pocket and set about pounding a line of holes along the leather.

Cain stared at her in astonishment. "You can sew?"

She paused, holding in a wince. Boys aren't supposed to sew. "I'm a lot younger than my brothers, so I got taken care of by a lot of army wives when they were gone."

He nodded as if her quick lie made perfect sense. Suddenly his face turned solemn. "I'm sorry, about your bro–"

"Don't," she said quietly, ducking her head and concentrating on her work.

He watched her in silence for a while before standing. "I'll leave this to you then. You seem to know what you are doing."

She nodded, concentrating on placing even holes, trying to ignore the ache in her chest. Trying to hide the tears sliding silently down her cheeks.

She had almost finished sewing the bottom together when Prince wandered over. She looked up at him. "I don't know how well these seams are going to hold water."

He raised his eyebrows at her and frowned, looking off into the woods as he thought. "Let me see what I can find that might help."

She continued to work, making a few more makeshift water skins, adding ties to the tops. By the time the sun started to set Prince returned with a shell full of something that looked like tree sap. For all she knew it was. With a small stick he showed her how to smear some between the seams and then weigh it down with rocks. "Do that for the rest, we can test one in the morning, we may need to add more."

Darkness came and everyone returned to camp from whatever they had been doing. She happily greeted Kei. He had been gone most of the day scouting the area. They all ate quickly before curling up in lumps around the fire.

The days continued to pass quickly. The men tried their luck at hunting and continued fishing. She and Prince spent time gathering food and scavenging at the beach. Her water skins seemed to work, so she continued making them. The men occasionally brought her other leather they found. The work made for boring and monotonous days. Boring beat being chased by slavers, so she didn't complain.

Kei and Prince seemed to be almost getting along. They weren't openly hostile at least. She could not say the same for Allen and Garic. She heard them arguing more than once, about what she wasn't certain. They still kept to themselves, but she found them watching her quietly on a number of occasions. It would have unnerved her, but she caught them doing the same to Avery and Kei, too. It made her uncomfortable, but she didn't understand, so she ignored it.

It turned out to not matter very much. One morning they awoke to find the pair gone. Thankfully they didn't take anything they shouldn't have.

# Chapter 14
## Always Trust Your Instincts

Something startled her awake. Staring up at the stars she listened, trying to figure out what it had been. Was it just the wind in the trees, or some unfamiliar animal noise? Whatever the sound had been it didn't repeat and she rolled over, Kei close beside her, listening to the other night sounds around her.

Sleep evaded her and she grimaced, rolling over again and then sitting up. The others all continued to sleep soundly around the fire. She sighed and yawned as she stood and quietly added more wood to it. She poked at it for a while and then looked around at the sleeping bodies again.

She had to pee, but was uneasy at the idea of going off into the woods alone in the dark. The others had warned her often enough not to go off alone. She felt foolish, being afraid of the dark. She wasn't four years old. Still, she grabbed a stick as she picked her way into the woods.

She wouldn't go far, would do what she had to as quickly as she could, and get back before anyone missed her. It seemed the stars had begun fading somewhat, dawn couldn't be very far away.

Trying to quietly make her way back she stopped suddenly, again hearing something that sounded out of place. She turned, trying to figure out what had made the noise, but the sound did not come again. Cursing under her breath she continued on more quickly.

She wasn't certain when she got turned around, but after a short time realized she should have been back to the camp already.

"I hate the woods," she muttered as she stopped.

She looked around, it still wasn't much lighter. She didn't know where she was. Should she call for Kei? Or wait for someone to come and find her? She gripped her stick more tightly.

"Idiot, idiot, idiot." Waiting until morning would have been a better idea. Or keeping the camp in sight, but no, she had been too afraid one of the others would see her and discover she wasn't a boy.

"Gah!" She turned in a circle, but it didn't help.

She continued muttering to herself as her panic grew. Kei would be upset with her. Prince would be furious. She started walking, hoping to come across the stream or the beach, anything to get her bearings. She needed to get back before everyone woke up.

She stopped suddenly as she thought she heard muted voices, people sounds. Yes, off to her left. Relieved she quickly headed for them.

The sound of loudly snapping branches froze her immediately. She peered into the darkness under the trees, glad the sun seemed to finally be rising. She could finally see a little better.

The sight of a giant wolf standing not far from her almost made her scream. A weak whimper escaped her instead as she helplessly raised her stick in front of her.

*Run.*

She blinked and quickly spun, taking off toward the voices she'd heard. Her mind at least seemed to know what to do and not panic.

She ran as quickly as she could, dodging around trees and underbrush, not worrying about being quiet. She slid to halt, stumbling and gasping for breath as she stumbled amidst the men.

They weren't her men.

The voice she had heard in her head telling her to run hadn't been her own thought. Someone had spoken in her mind!

*Stupid girl.*

She spun and ran back the way she had come, toward the wolf. It must have been one of the Were. She hadn't known they could talk in other people's heads. The stories never mentioned such a thing, but it made sense. Actual wolves certainly couldn't speak.

It had tried to warn her. Was it friendly?

She never found out, she barely left the sight of the men she'd discovered before they caught her.

One grabbed her by the back of her shirt and jerked her backward so roughly she fell to the ground, her breath knocked out of her. When she looked up, they had surrounded her.

She scrambled to her feet, trying not to choke on the panic rising within her. The men were talking and laughing. She twirled around, counting. Six. A shuddering breath escaped her.

From their dress and speech she was pretty certain the strangers were slavers, not other escaped slaves. "Rot it!"

One stepped forward. "Where are of the rest of you?"

She shook her head, afraid to speak, and certain she couldn't even if she wanted to. Terror held her frozen. She couldn't even breathe. Every muscle tensed, ready...even though she had no idea what to do.

"We've caught two of you again already, boy," the man said.

She bit her lip. So Allen and Garic hadn't run off, or they had, but been caught.

"They told us more of you are out here. Our fighters, too. We will find them. Tell us where they are and it'll be easier for you."

She shook her head frantically again as the men tightened the circle around her. She didn't know what they were going to do. Would they kill her? Or just put her in chains again? She didn't want the chains. Never, ever again.

She jumped to the side quickly, hoping to surprise them and break away. Her attempt failed and they laughed as they dragged her back. She fought them, kicking and hitting. "Let me go! Stop! Let go!"

She lashed out with her fist and grunted as she caught one slaver square in the face. Without hesitating she swung her elbow back and spun until she felt it connect with the soft tissue of a second one's throat. Fear overwhelmed her as she blocked a punch with her arm, realizing there were too many of them. Her fear became reality as a fist caught her in the shoulder and spun her. She managed to grab his shoulders and deliver a swift knee to the groin as her brothers had drilled into her so many times. She managed a small smile as he doubled over and she brought both of her fists down on his head. She wasn't strong enough to knock him out, but he would be concentrating on his pains rather than her.

Maybe if she would have remained quiet and passive, they wouldn't have started hitting back. They didn't hit lightly. She abandoned the offensive and concentrated on blocking like she'd been taught. Her hands clenched into fists as she reached out, blocking attacks to her face and stomach. It took everything she had just to protect herself. However she'd never fought with so many before, or with grown men who didn't hold back.

More and more blows hit. She wasn't fast enough. She pulled inward, her hands protecting her face, her arms pulling tight to her ribs to protect the vital areas. Ragged gasps were pounded from her as she twisted and turned, still trying to avoid as many blows as possible. Her hands and arms took the worst of the hits and quickly the pain turned to numbness.

They didn't stop until she fell again to the ground, bleeding and bruised. She couldn't say for certain if she had any broken bones or not, but despite her blocks her ribs hurt so much she could hardly breathe.

Gasping for breath and struggling to hold back tears she fought to stand again. The ground was the last place she wanted to be. She didn't want them to be able to start kicking her as well.

"Talk, boy."

She shook her head defiantly, unable to speak beyond the pain that flared through her. She'd never hurt so much in her entire life.

One of them caught her arm, pulling her backward before grabbing her other arm and pinning them both behind her. She struggled against him as the others laughed.

"Well, well," the first man said, walking up to her. He tilted his head to the side, "Not a boy after all are you?"

Startled, she followed his gaze down to her chest. The way the man behind her had pinned her arms, her shirt pulled tight against her, clearly showing breasts. They weren't very large, but they were definitely there. Rot it, when had they grown more?

"Makes things easier. Where are they?"

She sucked in a shuddering breath. Her heart beat so fast she could hardly hear anything else. "No," she managed to say.

The man smiled slightly. It wasn't a nice smile.

She saw his fist coming for her face and turned her head. She wasn't quite prepared for how much it hurt. She closed her eyes after the second, and by the fourth couldn't help but scream Kei's name.

The man paused as she hung limply against the one behind her. She hurt so much she could barely stand. Her ears wouldn't stop ringing. The punches to her stomach made her feel like she had to throw up.

When the man behind her suddenly let go she fell limply to the ground, quickly and instinctively curling into a ball. She couldn't keep the tears away any longer, or the whimpering sobs. The slavers didn't seem to care.

Someone kicked her in the side. They might have been demanding she talk again, but she couldn't hear them and didn't want to. She tried to curl into a tighter ball, but someone grabbed her by a fist full of hair and dragged her backward across the ground. She screamed, loud and shrill. It felt like he was ripping the top of her head off.

He stopped suddenly, having accomplished what he wanted; getting her out of her ball. One of them immediately dropped over her and she fought in a panic as his hand pinned her down by the throat.

Even as they tore her clothing she fought back. She could feel the cold night air raising gooseflesh on parts of her that had no business being exposed. She forced her already swelling eyes closed and steeled herself for what she knew was coming next.

They weren't gentle. More than one set of hands settled across her. Grabbing gave way to pinching, touching became handling. The tears of pain became horrid sobs of utter hopelessness.

Growing up around her brothers, she'd heard stories. She had tried to imagine the horror of such a situation. Her imagination didn't even come close. The screams of the women on the slave ship made so much more sense now.

Her horrid sobs finally stopped as a great wail started somewhere in her soul, echoed through her body, and erupted from her throat to beg the sky for death. She couldn't survive this. She didn't want to.

She wasn't certain when it started, or what exactly happened. One moment everything revolved around pain and darkness, the next she found herself gently wrapped in familiar arms and listening to a familiar voice whispering words of comfort.

She looked up in a daze at Prince, simply amazed to find him suddenly there. She turned her head as a scream cut through his calming words.

She gaped in horror. Bodies lay broken everywhere. Pieces of bodies. Blood and gore covered them, the ground, and the trees. Kei stood a short distance from her, tearing a man to pieces.

But it wasn't really him, just a monster who reminded her of him. He didn't have teeth like a beast, or feral glowing red eyes, or such impossibly long claws. Her sweet Kei wouldn't cause such destruction, wouldn't be covered in so much blood.

"Aro. We have to go. And quietly. Do not call out to him. It isn't safe."

She looked up at Prince, her eyes wide.

"He's gone into the fury. He might hurt us. So quiet. Understand?"

She nodded even as more tears came to her eyes and she looked back at Kei. It was Kei? Her Kei?

The monster turned. His glowing red eyes met hers and a growl rumbled from him as he took a step toward them.

Prince rose swiftly and set her down, pushing her behind him. "Do not come closer."

Kei paused, cocking his head to the side slightly as if struggling to understand.

She peeked around Prince, her hands on the small of his back, afraid to move. Kei looked at her and she saw his sharp canines and the blood on his face. Trembling she whimpered, hiding more behind Prince.

"Go," Prince demanded. "She is safe now."

Kei continued to hesitate, swaying slightly as he watched her.

"You are frightening her. You need to go."

With a mournful howl Kei spun and disappeared into the trees.

Prince sighed and relaxed under her hands before he turned, putting his hands on her shoulders.

She stared after Kei, at the destruction he had caused. She couldn't stop shaking. Prince caught her and lifted her up into his arms as her legs collapsed. "You are safe now, Aro. Everything is fine."

She turned her face into his shirt as she wrapped her arms around his neck and wept. "No, it's not."

# Chapter 15
## Not Fine

Prince silently carried her through the brightening woods. The sun had finally risen, but it still rested below the tree line, creating a muted light beneath the trees. She kept her arms tight around his neck, her face hidden against him, and eyes squeezed closed against the light.

The tears continued to leak out of her eyes, her body still trembled, but she didn't care. Everything hurt too much. She just held on to Prince and tried not to think. She didn't want to remember what had happened. She wanted to forget everything those men had done.

She couldn't do it. Pain wracked her body as a constant reminder and Kei wasn't there. Prince had sent him away. She wanted to be angry at Prince for doing that but she couldn't be. Kei had truly frightened her.

Prince continued to make his way quickly but steadily through the trees. Each step jarred her, even though she could tell he was trying to walk carefully. She clenched her teeth, wishing the pain would go away.

Prince rested his cheek against her head. "Not too much further," he whispered.

She began to nod but stopped abruptly and raised her head, pushing back from him as her stomach suddenly twisted. "Stop! Down! Put me down!"

He hesitated only a moment before doing so. Even so, she only made it a few steps away from him before falling to the ground and throwing up. The action hurt so bad it caused her to do so again and again. The pain wasn't going to kill her, but right then she wished it would. She wanted it over. She wanted the pain to go away.

Prince knelt beside her, his fingers gently pulling her hair back from her face until she finished and collapsed over onto her side.

"I think we should detour to the river," he said, as she curled into a ball with her hands around her pain-wracked stomach and ribs. "You're quite a sight, child."

She couldn't even answer him with a sarcastic remark. All she could do was take small gasping breaths. She didn't want to think about what she looked like. She could see her blood covered hands had started to swell. Her face felt hot and burning, one eye had swollen completely shut. Her lips on the left side of her face were tender and swelling and she could still taste blood even after throwing up.

She glanced over at him, afraid to see if he was angry with her for getting into such a situation. It surprised her to see his face only clouded with worry.

She grimaced and closed her eyes as she slowly sat up. "We need to go."

"We are safe. You can rest," he answered, his voice tired and quiet.

She shook her head, just a little. "No. They were slavers. They said they had Allen and Garic. They told them where we were and who we are. There will be more of them coming for us."

She didn't catch what Prince muttered. She guessed it was a curse. She rose as he did and tried to walk. Her legs didn't want to work. Prince scooped her up quickly without even asking. She didn't complain. The pain of being held in his arms was far less than if she walked on her own.

"Try to rest. We will need to leave camp and you will have to walk then."

She nodded against his shoulder. She knew he wasn't being mean. They would all have to carry everything they could, that wasn't much, but would still weigh them down, and now they didn't have Kei to help either.

The others met them before she and Prince reached the camp. Their loud exclamations hurt her head and she gritted her teeth again. Prince did the talking, explaining what he could about what had happened.

He didn't stop once they entered the camp, but headed directly for the stream, telling the others about the slavers and instructing them to start packing up as he walked. She barely heard most of the conversation, her mind didn't want to work. Too many emotions bounced around in her head. Too many memories. Much of what had happened was a blur. Too much of it wasn't.

He set her down by the edge of the water and she shook her head. "We don't have time."

He frowned at her. "We do. You need to clean your wounds and wash off the blood."

She did as she was told, silently and carefully but as quickly as she could. Prince washed her blood off of his hands and left for a moment, returning with one of his spare pieces of cloth. He used it to wash his face and neck where her bloody hands had left red smears. He wet it again and turned it on her.

He paused after gently dabbing at her face for a while. "Aro. Did..."

She looked up at him through the eye that wasn't swollen shut. "What?"

He looked down and took a deep breath. "Did they rape you?"

She stared at him for a long time before looking away. Yes, he'd fixed her clothes hadn't he, when he'd first taken her into his arms. Her cheeks flushed. She lowered her head. "No," she whispered. "Not...they didn't get that far." They had been close though...so close. Her breath shuddered out of her and she tried to focus on anything else.

His face softened as he let out a relieved breath. He ran the back of his fingers gently down the side of her face that wasn't beaten bloody. "Good. I apologize for not getting there sooner."

She looked away and bowed her head again. She suddenly felt the need to explain. "I went to pee, and got turned around." She let out a deep breath. "I'm sorry you had to come and save me." Her felt her eyes tear up "And Kei...I lost Kei again." The tears started falling again.

He silently wiped them away with the blood.

It didn't take the men long to pack up the camp. They didn't give her anything to carry. For that, she was extremely thankful. She trudged along at the back of the line they made as they picked their way along a narrow animal trail that at least for now ran parallel to the stream. They headed west, the only way they could go really. North would bring them to the slavers cities, east back to the beach where more slavers searched for them. She didn't know if south should be the direction they traveled. Perhaps, but none of them knew what lay in that direction.

She knew they were in serious trouble. Not only were they running from slavers, they had no provisions or weapons, and had no idea even where on the coast they had come ashore. She sighed and winced suddenly as she stumbled and pain shot through her. She wrapped her arms tighter around herself and continued putting one foot carefully in front of the other.

# Broken Aro

As the pain grew worse despite her careful steps, tears again began to trickle down her cheeks. She kept her face lowered, hiding behind her hair and trying not to think about how much she hurt and what the slavers had done. She concentrated on how hungry she was. They had eaten the night before but it hadn't been much. It was never enough. She always wanted more, always felt so hungry. Her brothers would certainly make a joke about her growing right about now.

She wanted to close her eyes against the pain and the hunger. She knew she couldn't. If she even blinked, or let her mind wander in the slightest, the memories came crashing down on her.

"How are you doing, Aro?" Bo's voice came from somewhere ahead of her.

"Fine," she managed through gritted teeth. The sound of his loud voice pierced her throbbing skull like daggers.

"Aro?" He hadn't heard her.

"Fine!" She didn't mean to snap at him, but she really wished he'd just be quiet.

Prince stopped in front of her, forcing her to stop as well. She cursed under her breath. Stopping wasn't good. She didn't know if she could get herself going again.

He turned and bridged the few steps between them to rest a trembling hand on her shoulder. No wait, she was the one trembling. Shaking actually. Yes, stopping had definitely been a bad idea. She squeezed closed the eye that wasn't swollen shut already as the trees started spinning around her. "Wither me."

"You need to rest," Prince said quietly. His soft, quiet voice didn't hurt her head at least.

Shaking it in response to him did, and she knew she was about to throw up again. She managed to turn off the trail and drop painfully to her hands and knees rather than hit his expensive boots.

As before, he knelt beside her, holding back her ragged hair and not making a sound. Wasn't he supposed to make soothing noises or something? She wanted to hit him.

She had very little to throw up other than water and bile and finished more quickly this time. She stayed on her hands and knees, not wanting to lie down even though her body shook so hard she thought she might break apart into a million pieces. She had to get up. She had to keep moving.

She sat back on her heels and covered her face with her hands, trying to regain any kind of control. She heard the shifting of the others close by. Perfect. Now they'd all seen her.

Not that it really mattered. Who were they to her? Allen and Garic had betrayed them. Because of them the slavers had come looking and had found her. She had trusted Kei and he had turned into a monster. She had trusted Prince, but now she knew such an idea to be her dumbest yet. He was a prince. Of course he would always save himself first. And the others? She raised her head to look at them as she lowered her hands. Would they betray her as well? Most likely, if given the chance. Luckily they still did not know her only secret; that she wasn't a boy at all. Because of the slavers, she understood how important keeping up the ruse was.

She pushed herself to her feet, turning away from Prince when he tried to help her stand. "I'm fine. Keep going." They started to argue and she glared at them, "I'm fine!" She stumbled a few steps but they parted silently and followed as she headed down the trail again.

The anger kept her going for a while before her steps slowed noticeably and tears started falling again. Not so much because of the pain, but because exhaustion from everything that had happened was wearing her down. She could hardly keep her eye open.

"Aro, we're stopping for a while," Bo called up to her.

She turned quickly, the anger rising again. "Do not pity me!"

Avery walked up and smiled slightly, nodding his head to indicate something behind her. "The trail is starting to veer away from the stream. We're stopping to decide what we want to do."

She felt like an idiot for getting the wrong idea. It didn't help her sudden anger. Just to make things complicated she was also angry no one seemed to be worried about her. Memories of the Were came to her then. With everything that had happened, the encounter with one of the creatures she'd only heard stories about had completely slipped her mind. He had called her stupid. Right then, she agreed.

She crossed her arms and followed him back a few steps. She didn't sit with the others, but found a tree to lean against and crossed her arms, trying to hold the pain and the anger in.

Too many emotions pounded through her, screaming and wrenching, fighting for dominance. She couldn't control them or even make sense of them all. She shuddered, pain lancing through every part of her. Images and snips of voices flashed through her head. Terrifying images, horrible words. Fear held her frozen. Couldn't escape them.

Her thoughts shifted, twisted, balanced on the edge, ready to break. Something snapped inside of her...all of her feelings tumbled and broke and...warped into one solid thing.

Anger.

It filled her, every part of her. Her shallow breathing sped up. She hated the Gelanians for attacking her country. She hated the Frans for taking her as a slave. They'd destroyed her life. They'd helped destroy her home. They'd taken or killed her family. They made her a *slave*. Then they'd attacked her, they'd beaten her, and tried to do even more. *Filthy, horrible men.*

Her thoughts shifted again. It was their fault. The men, always fighting, always wanting more. Always taking.

Everyone but Prince talked for a while, trying to decide whether to stay on the easier trail, or go through the brush and keep to the stream. She watched Prince for a while. He didn't add to the discussion, he didn't do anything. So like the nobility.

Something tickled at her brain, for a moment pushing away the anger. Little things she'd hardly noticed edged forward, how he'd known so much about the slavers and what would happen when they reached port. She stood up a little straighter. He'd known how to survive here, what to eat. She'd trusted him blindly on what was safe from the sea, even though much of what he'd fed her hadn't been familiar. He'd made that strange healing paste from plants in the forest. They were on a different continent, how could he know these things? The answer was obvious and brought forth her anger once more. He'd been using them, for what she didn't know.

The other men continued their debate, growing frustrated as it became clearer they had no idea what to do.

"Just ask Prince," she finally snapped. She wanted to get moving whatever they choose to do. Sleep had begun pulling at her, and the last thing she wanted to do was close her eyes and dream.

Every one of them looked up at her in surprise.

Bo looked over at Prince and then back to her. "What do you mean?"

She grimaced and looked away, specifically avoiding Prince's eyes. What if she was wrong? "I think he's from here, these lands. He should know something at least."

Her words caused more of a ruckus than she'd thought they would. She grimaced at all the noise, moved her hands to her head, and tried to hold her brains inside.

"Is this true?"

Prince pressed his lips together angrily, but nodded.

Everyone started yelling at once.

"Very well," Prince eventually snarled. "If you will all be quiet I'll tell you what I know." Everyone thankfully grew quiet immediately.

He picked up a stick and leaned forward, flashing an angry glare at her before looking down at the bare trail before him. He started drawing lines in the dirt with quick, efficient strokes. "The shoreline. Running from north to south here, mountains." He paused and looked up at the others. "Don't think of crossing them, they aren't passable. They are to be avoided. If you think the forests are full of nasty creatures, the mountains are much worse."

He drew few more lines. "The north is held by the Frans. Their border extends to here." He drew another line. "The southernmost part of their lands is forest that extends to the sea. The border is marked by the tree-line." He pointed further down, and drew another line cutting the land between the mountains and the shoreline in uneven halves. He tapped the larger space next to the mountains. "The forests. They are inhabited by the Were, the Fey, and creatures that come down from the mountains. Humans are not permitted in them. Stone markers show the borders, as some forest had been granted to them when they first settled here. Mostly everything has been cut and cleared. A few were smart enough to leave some for hunting and foraging. Some even replanted."

Avery pointed to the other area. "So this is where the people are. Are they split into countries?"

Prince shook his head. "Not as such. The whole area is divided into many small city states. Each has a small walled city and its ruling prince. Few live beyond the walls, the odd farmstead. It is mostly crops and pasture-land."

"Why the walls?" Bo asked.

"To keep the monsters out," Prince answered with a faint smile. "Mostly they are all fighting each other over land." He drew a line down the center of the humans land. "There is one main road that connects them all. It even runs up into Franua. We should be coming across it soon."

Bo and Cain regarded each other quietly for a moment.

"We should find that road," Cain decided and Bo nodded his agreement.

Avery turned to Prince. "Do you think we are still in Franua?"

Prince nodded. "The forest still runs to the shoreline, so yes. How far in, I don't know."

"How bad are the winters here?"

"This far north, bad," Prince replied with a frown. "Lots of ice, lots of snow."

The men all grimaced. "We need to get to one of these cities before the bad weather hits," Bo declared.

The men started talking quietly, making plans, and she closed her eyes and leaned her head back against the tree. At least they had a plan now.

Dark images suddenly appeared in her mind, trying to swallow and drown her. Her eyes snapped open. Fear overwhelmed her hatred for a moment. She sucked in a deep breath, trying to push the clawing hysteria away. Somehow she managed, concentrating on the hate until the shadows in her mind mostly drifted away. She glanced at the others quickly, hoping they hadn't noticed her distress.

Prince looked solemnly at her. "You told my secret."

She shifted uncomfortably against the tree. "It wasn't a secret. You never told me, I just guessed."

"There was a reason I didn't say anything."

"And what would that be?"

He paused and glanced around at the others before looking back at her. "I can't expect any of you to understand what it means to be a prince in these lands. It is much different here, much more dangerous."

She rolled her eyes. "That is the stupidest thing I've ever heard! Why don't you just say you don't trust us?"

He inclined his head slightly. "There is a bit of that as well."

His answer wasn't really a surprise, but for some reason his admitting it hurt. "You can trust us."

"You wish to talk about trust?" His face looked far too innocent as he raised his eyebrows. "So should I tell your secret? The one you never told me, but I guessed?"

Dumb, arrogant, blighting idiot prince. She tried to keep the anger from her voice, but it didn't really work. "You should have just told us! What you know can help us here! Mine isn't good for anything."

Prince smiled slightly and tilted his head to the side, still all fake innocence but real anger. Yes, he was rather furious with her. She didn't really care.

The others watched them both in morbid fascination.

"It would be good for you," he finally said.

She grimaced. "Good way to get me killed."

Avery interrupted them. "Aro, what are you hiding?"

She clenched her teeth and continued to glare at Prince. "You'll tell them if I don't. Won't you?"

"Yes, I will." His faint smile wasn't friendly. "It's your choice."

"That isn't any kind of a choice." How exactly was she supposed to tell them? "I don't want to tell them at all," she muttered. She closed her eyes, thinking quickly through her anger. It didn't matter really. Her pretending to be a boy hadn't saved her. They hadn't either. "Fine, then."

Everyone waited for her to reveal her secret. She stalled, leveling her gaze on Prince. "You were right. About depending on others. If I want to live, I need to start taking care of myself."

"Aro, that is not–"

An idea came to her. Raising, a hand she cut him off and looked over at the men, her face grim. "I saw a Were." When they all started to speak at once she raised a hand to silence them. "Let me tell you the whole story. Before I ran into the slavers, I saw a giant wolf." She pointed to her head. "It spoke in my head, telling me to run. I thought it was me thinking it, so I did...straight into the slavers. I didn't know Were could talk in your head like that."

Prince raised his eyebrows and shook his head slightly. He wasn't going to let her get away with not telling everyone she was a girl. For a moment she rather hoped he would pity her and leave her alone. She didn't want to deal with this right now, even if it was a distraction from her memories.

She paused, trying to think of how to say the words. "The Were had one last comment before he disappeared." She glanced at Prince. He watched her intently. No more stalling. "He called me a stupid girl and ran off."

She looked back at the men. They all stared at her in shock.

Avery leaned in toward Bo. "Was the secret that she saw a Were or that she's a girl?"

"Rot it," Bo snapped. He rubbed his forehead, clearly at a loss. "This is…this is…"

Avery remained innocent. "You didn't know?"

Both Bo and Cain glared at him. "And you did?"

Avery grinned and winked at her. "She's a tough girl, but definitely is one. Too curvy and pretty for a boy. And seriously, did you think both Kei and Prince prefer boys? You've seen how they've been acting with her." He made a tsking sound. "You two need to pay more attention."

She watched Bo and Cain try to hide the fact that they had thought Prince and Kei liked boys. Normally she knew she would have burst out laughing and made some sarcastic comment at them...but she didn't. She couldn't. Not even a small smile would form on her lips. She worried at her swollen lip as she tried to figure out what was going on inside her head.

"Well," Bo said finally.

Cain shook his head but smiled up at her. "I understand why you didn't tell us."

They both looked more shocked than anything else. Avery was clearly amused. She let out a deep breath. That hadn't gone so badly. "We don't have any problems then?"

"Don't worry, pup," Bo said. "Nothing has changed."

She doubted that, but nodded. Pain shot through her head.

"Well enough of all that," Avery said quickly. "What are we doing now?"

"You three jump into the stream and head east as far as you can." Bo's eyes flickered over to her, and she knew he meant as far as she could make it before collapsing. "Cain and I will make a false trail for a while and then come and join you."

She didn't comment on how quickly Bo had changed the topic. She didn't protest when Bo lifted her over the low brush between the stream and the trail and gently set her in the water. She did flinch, even though she didn't really know why. Prince and Avery both jumped over on their own.

She let out a little gasp as cold water quickly started to fill her boots. The stream wasn't very deep, not even up to her knees, but she didn't remember it being so cold.

As they started walking carefully upstream, Avery touched her arm, making her jump. "You don't have to worry," he said quietly. "We aren't going to hurt you or anything."

She glared over at him in response. She didn't want to be reminded.

He shrugged. "Bo and Cain like their women, uh… more mature."

She grimaced. "Fine. I'm not done growing. No need to rub it in."

"Oh… I didn't mean to imply…" A shy grin spread across his face. "Of course, you're my kind of girl."

"I don't want to talk about this," she said flatly

Prince turned on them both. "You touch her and I will kill you," he snarled before spinning around and moving angrily ahead of them.

She raised her eyebrows in surprise. She certainly hadn't expected that response, not with the way he'd been acting and being angry with her for telling his secret.

Avery only laughed. "You were right about him. He definitely has taken the role of overprotective brother."

She clenched her teeth together, suddenly angry again. Of course. Prince was just like a brother. She didn't want to think about her brothers right now. Missing them. She couldn't...

She pushed the heels of her hands against her temples at the sudden pain in her head.

"Aro? How are you doing?"

She turned her head away. "Just stop talking."

He flushed and looked down at the water. "Sorry. I know things are hard right now."

"Hard? Blighting idiot," she muttered as she lowered her hands and started walking faster before Prince pulled too far ahead of them.

# Chapter 16
## Anger and Forgiveness

The cold water certainly took her mind off of almost everything else.

She stumbled along, trying not to twist her ankle on rocks or submerged debris. She kept her arms wrapped around herself, more from her shivering than pain. Prince had moved far ahead of them. Sometimes she lost sight of him altogether as the stream gently curved and overhanging scrub and branches blocked her view.

She didn't worry about it. They both could certainly use time to cool their anger. Besides, she wasn't alone. Avery kept pace with her, and a close eye on her. She kept her mouth clamped shut to keep from yelling at him. Would everything change now that they all knew she was a girl?

She paused suddenly as she caught sight of Prince sitting up on the far bank. Maybe he'd calmed down already? It could be possible, they'd been walking for quite a while, long enough she couldn't feel her feet.

As they approached he nodded his head upstream. "I found the road. We can wait here for the others."

She looked upstream and could barely make out what looked to be a crude wooden bridge in the distance. Looking up at the sky she frowned. It wasn't even noon yet. She had hoped they would be traveling most of the day. Yes, she was tired already, but not tired enough to pass out and avoid the dreams she knew would torture her.

"There is a well sheltered clearing just behind me," Prince continued quietly. "The others should find us easily enough, but there is enough cover we can have a fire."

A fire sounded like a fine idea. She knew his words should have at least made her smile, but inside she felt...nothing.

Prince stood and pushed his way through the brush. Avery jumped up onto the bank and turned, holding his hand out to her.

She froze and stared at the hand for a moment and then glared up at him. "I'm not some useless girl!"

He let out a weary sigh. "I know you aren't. Now be quiet and get up here. I'd rather be sitting in front of a fire warming my feet than fighting with you."

She clenched her jaw to keep from saying anything else and held out a swollen, darkening hand. He stared at it for a moment before grabbing her by the wrist and hauling her up the muddy, crumbling bank.

She tucked her hands back under her arms and started pushing her way through the bushes.

Avery followed behind her. "Rot it, Aro. How hurt are you?"

She didn't answer him.

Walking with almost no feeling in her feet was painful. The bushes that surrounded the clearing grew thick and thorny. She had some new scratches on her face and was certain she'd lost some hair as well. By the time she stumbled into the clearing Prince had collected a number of rocks and had started placing them in a ring for their fire.

Prince continued working on the pit, only briefly glancing up at her once. *Gah.* He was still upset with her then. Fine. She wasn't any happier with him.

Avery walked around her and started putting his things in a pile Prince had started. He silently began gathering up twigs and small branches that littered the clearing. She started to help.

"Sit down."

Her head jerked up at the sharpness of Prince's voice. "I can help."

"Just be quiet and sit down," he snapped at her.

She gritted her teeth as tears sprang to her eyes. He didn't even look at her, just kept working on the fire.

She sat and wrapped her arms around herself tightly. She wasn't going to cry.

He and Avery got the fire going and worked silently for a while, gathering a large pile of branches. When they finished both sat and took off boots and socks, setting them by the fire to dry.

She grimaced, she should have thought of that. Pulling up a pant leg, she began fumbling with her boot laces. She cursed. Her swollen hands were useless on the tight wet knots. She gently rubbed at her knuckles. Bruises were forming but at least the torn flesh from where she'd punched some of the slavers in the teeth had stopped bleeding.

She didn't even hear Prince come and kneel beside her. She jumped as suddenly she found him on his knees in front of her, undoing her laces. She looked up at him, startled, but didn't say anything.

"Her hands are really bad," Avery commented.

"Yes, they are," Prince said quietly, keeping his head bowed as he worked. "What did they do?"

She frowned. "Nothing. It's from blocking their hits and fighting back."

He raised his head to look at her in surprise as Avery unexpectedly chuckled.

"I'm not some useless lady," she snapped.

"Apparently not," he murmured. He got her boots and socks off and rubbed her feet down with one of the shirts from his collection before wrapping them snuggly in it. "Let me see your hands," he demanded.

She held them out and ignored his sigh. She looked passed him, staring at nothing as he gently moved his fingers along her hands and forearms. "I don't think anything's broken," she told him.

"Agreed," he said finally. "However, you may have some fractures, and you've ripped open some of your old cuts." He went to his things and came back with a small leaf wrapped bundle. She wasn't surprised to see it was a small shell full of the purple paste. She let him apply it to her hands and to the new cuts on her face. When finished he wiped his fingers and looked at her sternly. "Lift up your shirt."

She gaped at him for a moment before snapping her mouth closed and vehemently shaking her head.

He frowned at her. "Keep yourself covered." He gestured to her chest. "But you've been holding your side all day. Let me see it."

Lips pursed tightly together, she did as he asked, lifting her shirt up exposing her stomach and ribs. She looked away in embarrassment until he gasped.

"Wither me, what did they do?" She looked past Prince to see Avery had come closer.

She hated them looking at her. Her face burned. "Enjoying yourself?"

Her body jerked as Prince gently moved his fingers along her ribs. He frowned up at her when she tried to pull away. She looked down and had to admit she looked almost as bad as she felt. Her stomach and side had turned into a shocking array of black and purple bruises intermixed with the odd swollen welt. Her breath quickened in rising panic as he continued to gently feel along her ribs. "Are they b-broken?"

Prince shook his head. "Amazingly, not that I can feel." He glanced up at her. "You're a tough child."

"Stop calling me a child!"

Avery just shook his head and kept cursing under his breath.

Prince gestured she could lower her shirt and she did so quickly. Relief at being covered, and that he'd stopped touching her, nearly overwhelmed her.

He stood in one fluid motion. "I will collect us some water."

"And food," she said quickly. "I'm starving."

He looked back at her as he grabbed a number of water skins. "Food is not going to be easy to find."

"Then why are we out here?" Too many emotions thrashed around in her head. Her voice rose, "Dying under a slaver's blade would be preferable to starving to death!"

His lips became a fine line of anger. "I'll find you something. You need to rest and calm down." He stalked off back toward the stream.

She muttered curses under her breath.

"He's only trying to help you," Avery said in exasperation.

She turned on him. "I don't want to hear it!"

His cheeks flushed at the harshness of her voice. "Why are you so angry at us?"

She stared at him, taken aback by his words. Why was she? "Because…because everything hurts...and I'm afraid," she answered in a rush. "All I can see are the men who hurt me. With you all, I keep expecting the fists and hands to start falling. To hurt me. I can't help it. It won't go away. I hate it. And them. I can't stop it. I just want it to stop."

He opened his mouth and then closed it quickly before turning to look solemnly into the fire.

At least he'd stopped talking.

Staring at the fire, she forced herself not to sleep. Avery kept away from her and didn't try talking to her again, but he did occasionally look at her with sad, wounded eyes. She ignored him as the day dragged on and he collected more wood and puttered around their new camp.

She tried not to think about Kei. It was hard to do. She missed him and wanted him with her, but at the same time memories of his transformation and what he'd done to the slavers overwhelmed every other thought of him.

Bo and Cain found them before Prince returned. They greeted her warily as they sat down with weary thuds and pulled off their soaked boots and socks.

She sat wrapped in her fear and pain and stared at the fire. She could hear Avery talking quietly to them, probably about her. She didn't care. Maybe they'd leave her alone.

Prince returned before dark, dirty, scratched, and looking ready to collapse. She stared at him in shock as he stumbled in and dropped down beside her, tossing a knotted shirt in front of her. "Food. Eat it."

She pounced on the bag, her swollen fingers fumbling at the knots. Luckily the thick cloth wasn't tied tightly and she managed to get into the body of the stuffed shirt, finding it full of berries. She started jamming them into her mouth before looking guiltily at the others.

"You eat it," Bo said with a faint smile. "You're skin and bone."

"And you need food to get better," Cain added. "We can't have you slowing us down after all." Even though the words themselves were harsh, it was something she understood.

She glanced down at Prince. "Just eat the food," he snapped.

So she did. She found the arms of the shirt had been filled with various kinds of some sort of root, already scrubbed clean. She ate until she worried she would get sick. "I'm full." She told the men, pushing what remained toward the others. They didn't fight over what remained, but they finished it off quickly enough.

She looked down at Prince. She'd never seen him so exhausted. Or so dirty and disheveled. It caused a different kind of pain in her chest. He'd taken care of her. Again. She wanted, she needed to take care of herself now, but...She looked down at her bruised and swollen hands. Sometimes a person just couldn't, could they? Maybe sometimes, you did need someone. Still, it was hard to speak, hard to keep the anger and fear inside of her out of her voice. "Did you...Did you have some?"

He sat up and regarded her carefully for a moment before he nodded. "I did." He leaned forward and cupped her uninjured cheek in one hand, wiping his thumb gently across her lips and over the corners of her bruised mouth. "You are the messiest eater I have ever seen."

She looked down at her dirty hands. "I'm sorry," she whispered.

He sighed and removed his hand. "As am I." He tucked some hair behind her ear. "You need to sleep now."

She shook her head frantically and glanced over at him. "I don't want to close my eyes," she admitted. "I see...bad things. When I close them."

He put his arm around her. "I'll be here."

She tensed at first, but then took a deep breath and relaxed. This was Prince. He had never hurt her, and honestly, she didn't think he ever would. She forced herself to relax and curled up next to him. At least now she didn't have to worry about what the men thought. She closed her eyes tightly and allowed herself to consider sleep. The dark images came, but she fought them back thinking of Prince on his black horse keeping them away.

She awoke with a start sometime in the night. She sat up carefully, looking around. All the men were sleeping. She frowned. Had someone called her name? She looked around again and gasped.

A pair of glowing red eyes stared at her from within the bushes.

"Kei?"

The eyes blinked and she heard a rustle of branches before they suddenly disappeared. She sat up for a while more but they didn't return.

The next day they pushed on, now paralleling the road. They traveled slowly, spreading out and foraging as they went. Prince moved amongst them, showing them plants they could eat, teaching them what was poisonous. They stopped early to camp near another small stream.

As it grew dark, she searched the shadows for any sign of Kei but didn't see anything. Staying close to Prince as she slept seemed to keep the nightmares from being too bad, though they still came. She woke again in the night and same as before saw the red eyes watching her, but they again left quickly when she called out Kei's name.

The next morning the men were surprised to find a pile of weapons next to her.

The men went over the weapons, perplexed, and she scowled at their stupidity. "It's Kei." She started digging through the pile. "These were the slaver's weapons. He brought them to us."

They sorted out the weapons, mostly various knives, daggers, and two swords. Cain took one, Prince the other. She felt so much safer having knives again. It bothered her she couldn't smile about that.

The days blurred together. They walked, foraged, and camped by water when they could. There at least seemed to be an abundance of it in the forest. That was one less worry for them. Food remained hard to find, so they all remained hungry.

She watched for Kei. During the day she never saw any sign of him. Any time in the night she awoke she would see his eyes though. He was following them. It made her feel a little better, and disturbed her, too. His eyes had remained red, and she knew they shouldn't have. Avery had said the few times Kei had gone into the fury in the army, he'd always returned back to normal in a few days at the most.

As she curled up beside Prince she whispered a good night to the others. She didn't talk to them much anymore or them to her. She couldn't stand it when they touched her. Her anger and fear wouldn't go away, and any time anyone tried to talk to her she always ended up being mean or snapping at them. Prince seemed to be made of unending patience, or he knew she didn't really mean the things she said. With him she was better. She didn't flinch from his touch at all anymore. He'd saved her, he always did. She had no trouble drifting off to sleep in his arms, her head tucked under his chin.

She awoke and saw the sun hadn't yet risen. As usual she wasn't certain what had caused her to awaken, but she immediately sat up and looked around for Kei. When she saw his glowing red eyes she carefully shifted away from Prince and stood. The eyes winked out, but she hurried in the direction she'd seen them.

Their campsite wasn't surrounded by thick and thorny brush, but she still struggled her way through the undergrowth and around trees trying to find Kei.

It quickly became apparent he hadn't waited for her. "Kei," she whispered loudly. "I want to see you!" She pushed forward and almost stumbled into a small clearing.

# Broken Aro

She stopped suddenly as the moon broke from the clouds and lit the clearing before her.

Kei stood there facing her, his body tense as if to flee, or attack. The moon shone off his hair and glinted off of the long claws that moved slowly at his sides, quietly clicking together. Once she saw them she couldn't take her eyes of the impossible length of them. They looked so deadly, so sharp.

He looked up at her and blazing red eyes burned from behind the locks of hair that always fell over his face. Even after days he was still angry, still wild.

"Kei..." she whispered, her voice cracking as her heart lodged in her throat.

She took a step forward and one of the clawed hands rose. "Stay there."

She stopped suddenly at the strange sound of his voice; rough, ragged, full of anger and pain.

She clenched her teeth then. Why was he angry? What pain did he have? She was the one feeling those emotions, not him. It hadn't happened to him, it had happened to her.

"Are you doing well?"

The absurdity of his question made her angrier. "No," she snapped and took another step forward. "No. I'm not."

She watched his eyes flicker over her. She knew what he saw the green and yellow of bruises still on her face, and a darker spot of purple on her cheekbone. Her hands had become mottled as well, though the swelling had at least receded. They continued to be stiff, but she could at least use them again. She was glad for her shirt as it hid the worst bruises that still ran down her forearms and side.

His head lowered and hands clenched, the claws clacking together again. "I'm sorry. I didn't get there in time."

Her anger, her hatred, had never been directed at Kei. It was starting to now though. "I guess it's your fault then." His head shot up at her harsh words. "Since it certainly couldn't be their fault they did that to me. It's certainly not my fault, for not listening and going off on my own."

"Aro…" He shook his head and turned away. "I'm sorry."

She gritted her teeth again and started walking toward him, but he twisted abruptly and quickly backed away, both hands out. "No! Stay away from me!"

She stopped and watched him for a moment. She saw those red eyes had started burning brightly, noted the sharp, quick breaths he was taking. He reminded her so much of herself.

"I need to go," he said.

"No."

He growled at her, showing teeth, showing canines that were long and pointed. She ignored his warning and glared at him while she strode forward. He jumped back, trying to keep his distance and she stopped. "You will stop that right now!"

He shook his head violently. "You don't understand…"

"No!" As her voice rose her hands clenched tighter at her sides. "You aren't leaving! You aren't leaving me again! You promised you wouldn't and then you did and I've needed you, I've…" She could barely speak because the tears had started again. "They always left, but they came back. But now they aren't. My brothers. You're the last one I have. You can't…you can't leave me, too."

"Aro," he whispered, his voice full of sadness. "I'm sorry. I'm dangerous. I could hurt you." He growled again. "I can't calm down. I can't make it go away." His teeth flashed again. "When I saw what they were doing to you...I've never been so furious in my life. I've never lost control so quickly, so much."

She choked on a sob and rubbed at her eyes. "You won't hurt me," she insisted.

"I will. It's what I am."

Troublesome Fey. He just didn't understand. He was family. He was all she had left, all she would ever have. She knew she'd never see her brothers again. She was all he had, too. They needed each other. Why couldn't he understand that? She sniffled and wiped her nose on her sleeve before taking a deep breath and looking up at him. She stood closer to him now. Only a few steps away. She could see he didn't like that by the way his body had become so very tense, as if it would shatter at any moment.

"Liar," she finally said loudly, making him start.

His brows drew together and his body shifted to spring away as she started closing the distance between them. She jabbed a finger at him before he could move. "Don't you dare move! You will stay right there!" He swayed again and her words snapped out like a whip, "Stay. There."

He froze in place, not moving a muscle until she stood right before him, and then the trembling started.

"I don't want to hurt you." His words came out quiet, choked, afraid.

She reached out slowly, ignoring his flinch, and put a hand on his shoulder. She stared at his face but he wouldn't look at her, keeping his head bowed.

She moved her hand slowly across his shoulder and up to curl about the back of his stiff neck. "You won't hurt me," she told him quietly. "You won't ever hurt me, Kei."

She pulled him gently to her as she slowly moved even closer, drawing his head to her shoulder. "You protect me. You take care of me. You won't ever hurt me." She kept up the quiet litany as she brought her other arm up and held him as she leaned her head against his. "You are my Fey. My Kei. You won't ever hurt me."

His rapid breathing slowed and the trembling subsided as she gently stroked his hair. He still remained rigid in her arms. He did not embrace her back, but kept his arms stiff to his sides.

He turned his face slightly, took a deep breath. "Aro...I can't..."

She kept her voice firm, "You can. You will." She gently pushed him back a little, moving her hands to cup his face, fingers forcing his chin up so he had to look at her. She stared into his eyes, noting they were still red, but not burning as wildly as before. "You are mine, Kei. And I am yours. You will never hurt me. Do you understand? Never."

"Aro..."

"Never," she said determinedly

He sighed and closed his eyes for a moment, and then opened them and nodded.

A faint smile crossed her lips and part of her rejoiced at that. He was hard to get through to, but she could see now he'd given up fighting her. Good. She wasn't done yet. Her hands tightened slightly on his face. "You will never leave me again."

His jaw clenched under her hands, the red eyes brightened.

"I said you will never leave me again. Ever. Do you understand?" She had to make him understand, because she didn't think she could survive being alone without him again. "Even when you are wild, you will not leave me. Because you will not hurt me, you will protect me. You will not leave me," she said again.

He stared at her, fighting something within himself. His body began to tense again.

"Kei," she said warningly. "Don't start this nonsense again. You will stay with me. I can't be alone again. I can't stand it."

His face crumbled at her words and his head bowed again. She moved her hands up his face, pushing back his wild hair as he nodded.

"I understand." He looked up suddenly and she dropped her hands to his chest. "We will stay together. I will stay with you. You will stay with me."

She nodded solemnly. "Yes. Together."

"Forever."

She nodded again as he let out a deep sigh. He surprised her by gently wrapping his arms around her and pulling her close. She could feel his claws rest carefully across her back. She wasn't afraid. She believed her own words. She relaxed against him and let him hold her.

This was right. She was safe now. Protected. She closed her eyes and tried to let the fears inside of her go. Only normal darkness greeted her. She smiled against him in relief. Kei had been what she needed. He had brought her back to herself.

"We should go back to the camp," she whispered into his chest.

He stiffened slightly and pulled back just enough so he could look down at her. He shook his head. "I can't. I may be safe with you. But not with the others."

She grimaced. He was probably right. She sighed. An idea came to her and she raised her hands to his face again, holding him steady and looking into his red eyes. "Then we'll make you safe. Understand?"

"I don't–"

"Give it to me," she said firmly, not taking her eyes from him. "Give it to me, the anger, the hate, the rage."

He didn't look away from her, perhaps he couldn't, but he frowned. "I–"

This was right. She could feel it. More than anything, she needed him and would do anything to keep him by her side. "Please, give it to me. I'll take it from you."

His eyes bored into hers, searching for something, and then he nodded. "How do—"

"Just let it go…" she whispered.

Her words had hardly left her lips before she felt him do it. A prickly, buzzing sensation came over her, into her. Anger and rage and fear and hate suddenly poured into her, burning through her and she gasped at the shock of it. Not at the feelings, those she had been living with, but that they were so strong, and came from Kei.

Kei's arms tightened around her, but she didn't mind. His embrace helped, supported her as his wild Fey power flowed into her. It didn't hurt. Much. Once she knew not to fight it, to let just let it flow and wrap itself around everything inside of her. It filled the empty parts before the rest slid away, dissipating inside of her. Strange.

She could see it was working. It wasn't just coming into her, but draining from him. She watched in amazement as she saw his eyes start to change. The red faded into orange, then into yellow, and finally the light itself faded away until only his golden eyes remained.

She gasped. "See?" She still felt dizzy and buzzing from the Fey power that had coursed through her. *Was it still inside of her?* She had no idea and didn't really care.

He frowned down at her, his teeth worrying his lip. She saw his teeth had returned to normal. She noticed she could no longer feel claws around her either, only his hands. "How are you?" He sounded worried.

She nodded and lowered her head. She was getting a crick in her neck from staring up at him. "Fine."

His hand moved under her chin and forced her face back up and she got worried as his eyes searched hers. She panicked. "What? What is it?"

He let out a breath suddenly and smiled slightly. "Your eyes turned red. But it's starting to fade now."

Her eyebrows visited her hairline. "My eyes?"

"Mm hmm," he said and his smile grew and he hugged her close again. "You're the strangest girl I ever met."

She punched his chest lightly. "Troublesome Fey."

He chuckled and pushed her back, putting his hands on her shoulders and bending a bit to look at her eyes. "Just about back to normal."

"Normal? Who's normal?"

He grinned again. "Certainly not either of us," he agreed.

"Let's go back." She sniffed. "You stink."

He glared over at her and scrunched up his nose. "I'll walk you back, then go and clean up."

They walked hand in hand through the clearing and her mind wandered, peaceful and quiet for once. Kei had come back to her.

"Aro."

She nearly jumped out of her skin. She stopped abruptly to stare at Prince who had appeared suddenly at the edge of the clearing. He looked from her, to Kei, and back again, a slight frown on his face. "Are you coming back to camp?"

She nodded quickly, hopefully she wasn't about to get yelled at for leaving the camp on her own.

Prince looked over at Kei. "Are you safe now?"

Kei nodded stiffly and looked down at her. "Return with Prince. I'll go and get cleaned up."

Before she could answer he was gone.

Jen Wylie

# Chapter 17
## To Have a Purpose

She did *not* like watching him leave again, even though she knew he'd be back. Well, she was pretty sure he would be. If not, she'd hunt the Fey down and drag him back by his little pointed ears.

Nervously worrying her lower lip with her teeth, she walked toward Prince. How much he had seen? She stopped in front of him and winced. The moonlight reflected off his pale drawn face. He wasn't happy.

"Don't do that again," Prince said. Though he kept his voice down, his words came out slow and stiff.

She sucked in a sharp breath. Had he seen what she had done with Kei?

"When I woke up and found you gone again..." He looked away, his lips tightening into an angry line.

*Gah!* She hadn't even thought of that! Impulsively she stepped forward and wrapped her arms around his waist, laying her cheek on his chest. "I'm sorry."

He stiffened in surprise at her action, but after a moment he relaxed and put his arms around her, too. He let out a heavy sigh. "You are such a troublesome child."

She smiled slightly against his chest. "I don't know why you put up with me."

He chuckled and reached a hand up to ruffle her hair. "Sometimes I wonder myself."

She looked up at him. "I still need you. If you...I mean...even with Kei back." Her cheeks flushed as she fumbled to say what she felt inside. Prince and Kei were completely different, however both of them had grown to mean so much to her. They truly had become the family she had lost.

"I told you before, I am here if you need me."

Looking down at her, a small smile formed on his lips. She hoped his smile meant he was glad she still needed him. Whatever the reason, it certainly looked better than his customary frown. She reluctantly pulled out of his arms. "We should get back."

They picked their way carefully through the trees and she found her mind wandering in circles. "Prince," she said as she followed him. "I won't be able to stay with you forever will I?" She winced at her choice of words and stopped as he turned to face her. "I mean, when you get home. We won't be able to stay together will we?"

He sighed and gave a slight nod. "I'm sorry."

She bit her lip. "Is that the reason why you haven't said anything? About us all taking you home?"

He raised his eyebrows slightly. "I didn't–"

"Because we should," she interrupted. "That's what we should do. We're lost here. Taking you home would be a good thing for us."

"It is very far away," he said evasively.

She shrugged. "It's not like we've any pressing business to attend to. How far is your city?"

"Very."

She frowned at his short response. "Good. I mean, that means at least you aren't from Franua."

His eyebrows went up again and he looked shocked. "I am not."

She started walking again. "Well, I'm glad that's settled."

He muttered something under his breath.

She managed not to smile, but was happy as she was pretty sure she could have if she wanted to.

When they reached the camp they quietly found their spots by the fire and waited up for Kei. He returned not too long after them, damp and shining in the moonlight. When he hesitated at the camp's edge she held her hand out to him. With a blush he hurried over and took her hand as he sat beside her. "Welcome back, Kei," she whispered.

A faint smile crossed her lips as she sat between them. Kei had returned, certainly she could get better now. The memories and nightmares wouldn't dare to haunt her with both a prince and a Fey watching over her.

Prince rested a hand on her shoulder. "Time for sleep."

She nodded and lied down, facing Kei. He still held her hand and didn't let go as he gracefully slipped next to her. She smiled at him a little. The smile grew when he grimaced over her shoulder as Prince settled in behind her. He was not quite touching but very close, his arm sliding over her waist. Kei clearly wasn't happy with the situation.

"Silly Fey," she murmured. She wondered if it was jealousy, or if it was just his dislike for Prince making him unhappy. She squeezed his hand. "I need you both," she whispered very quietly. "Keep the nightmares away?"

His grimace faded quickly and he glanced down shamefully as he nodded. He looked back up at her. "Am I part of those nightmares?"

She closed her eyes and squeezed his hand, faking a very faint smile. "No," she lied. The hand at her waist tightened slightly and she held in a sigh. Did Prince know she was lying? Probably. Sometimes she thought he knew more about her than she did. He thankfully didn't say anything and she quickly drifted off to sleep.

"Kei! You're back!"

Aro sat up, rubbing the sleep from her eyes as she yawned. She saw everyone, surprisingly Prince also, standing together by the fire. She guessed they talked about Kei coming back. Since she knew the story she stumbled a few steps into the trees to relieve herself.

She wasn't gone long, however by the time she returned the men had already begun arguing about something. She grimaced as she walked up to them. Starting the day off fighting wasn't her idea of fun.

"It's not appropriate," Bo said angrily.

Her brows drew together as she joined them. "What's not?"

They all looked at her as if surprised to find her standing there.

"Never mind," Bo snapped, pursing his lips together over further words.

"Our sleeping arrangements." Prince answered at the same time.

She blinked in confusion, trying to get her sleepy mind to understand what was going on. A flush crept over her cheeks as she suddenly understood. The others must have woken up before they all did. She bit her lip and looked at Prince. He didn't look angry, just annoyed. Her blush didn't go away, if anything it got worse as her mind put together the picture of what the others must have seen. A young girl curled up between two older men. Yes, such a thing would certainly not be considered appropriate. "I'm sorry," she murmured, looking at the ground as she clenched her fists.

"It's not your fault." Cain said gently.

She nodded, somehow managing to keep tears of embarrassment away. Anger rose up within her, but she managed to squash it down and not yell at anyone.

"We should get moving," Bo said suddenly, changing the topic.

Relieved, she agreed with the others. As she helped to pack up their small camp she couldn't ignore the hollowness in the pit of her stomach. Yes, she was hungry, but certainly it was caused by the knowledge she wouldn't have her dreams protected by Kei and Prince again.

When they stopped to rest later that day she sat and watched all the men, trying to decide how to broach the subject of them all taking Prince home. She munched on mushrooms someone had found, watching the others share and slowly eat the little food they had been able to forage during their morning travels.

"I was thinking," she said suddenly, and forced herself to continue as everyone looked over at her. "If we didn't have anything else planned, we could take Prince home."

She looked down at her hands as silence answered her proposal. "Or not."

"No," Bo said. "It's a valid idea."

She looked up in relief. Kei and Prince were staring at each other. As usual the look wasn't a nice. She couldn't understand why the two didn't seem to be able to get along at all. At least the others were better with Prince now, which was why she'd been confident in broaching the subject.

"How far is your city?" Bo asked Prince.

Prince turned his attention to Bo and frowned. Aro was unsure if the frown came from the topic or the question. "Far."

Bo raised his eyebrows. "That's all the answer we're going to get? Are you going to continue keeping your secrets then, *Prince*?" He stressed the last word, effectively pointing out none of them actually knew Prince's real name.

"I think we've had enough secrets between us all," Cain added quietly.

Prince's jaw tightened as he regarded them. "I told you, the cities fight amongst themselves. Knowing who I am and where I am from would not be a good idea."

"You don't trust us." Cain commented.

Prince actually chuckled as he shook his head. "It is more that I don't trust one of my enemies not to try to torture the information out of you." He glanced over at her. "And accidents do happen. A slip of the tongue, or someone overhearing something they should not. I cannot risk it."

"It's not easy, being a prince," she said quietly.

"No," Prince agreed. "Not in these lands." He stared at her and she tried to force a smile. He sighed and looked back at the men. "Should you agree, you would of course be compensated. Rewarded. I would ensure you each received enough to be able to start a new life here, should you wish to."

She raised her eyebrows. She hadn't expected him to make such a generous offer. Or any offer at all actually. The men seemed surprised as well, and began exchanging looks that involved some shrugs and small smiles.

"Very well," Bo finally answered after the men all came to a silent agreement. "We'll get you home." He paused a moment. "On the condition you tell us as much as you can about these lands, the people, customs, laws, and dangers. Anything we might need to know."

Prince nodded. "That is acceptable." The men started talking to each other all at once. He looked over at her. "Happy?"

She smiled and nodded. Yes, she was, and relieved as well. She didn't even want to think of having to part ways with Prince. She wasn't an idiot, she knew they would eventually. However, he had become part of her family and she didn't want to think of losing him anytime soon. She rather liked the idea that he lived far away.

He smiled faintly. "I suggest you see to your Fey before he falls into a fury again."

She turned quickly to see Kei, white as a sheet and eyes faintly glowing. Not good. She scrambled to her feet.

He grabbed her arm and immediately started dragging her into the trees for some privacy. "We need to talk."

She bit her lip as he pulled her along. She hadn't considered how Kei would react to the idea of them helping Prince. She should have known he wouldn't be happy.

He turned on her when he finally stopped, "Are you insane?"

She scowled. "No."

"What were you thinking?" He shook his head in disbelief as she cringed. "You don't know who he is!"

"Kei..." she began, wanting to try to explain.

"No!" He growled and began to pace in front of her. He stopped suddenly and turned to her, his face pained. "Is this a test? Are you testing my loyalty?"

"Huh?" She had no idea what he was talking about.

He grimaced and closed his eyes tightly, running his fingers angrily through his spikey hair. A growl rumbled out of him.

"Kei?" She began to get worried over his obvious distress. She understood his anger, just not the degree of it.

He took a deep breath and lowered his hands, searching her face. She had no idea what he had been searching for but the anger seemed to suddenly fade away. The light in his eyes died.

His face broke into a sudden unexpected grin. "Never mind."

She gaped at him, totally confused. "I think you're the one who's insane," she muttered.

Kei laughed and wrapped his arms around her, lifting her up.

She gasped in pain as his arms tightened around her bruised ribs.

He set her down quickly. "What's wrong? Did I hurt you?"

She sucked in a deep breath and faked a smile. "I'm fine. I'm just still a little sore from..." her voice trailed off and she looked away.

"Show me," he demanded.

She grimaced and lifted her shirt a little, showing the lovely mass of yellow and green and purple.

"No," he whispered, his voice cracking in pain. His fingers reached out, gently brushing her skin and making her shiver. He drew them back quickly. "I'm sorry!"

"It's fine." She glanced up and saw his stricken face, his eyes lightly glowing again. "Really. It's much better now."

His hand moved toward her again and stopped. "You need to eat more. I can see your ribs."

She jerked her shirt back down, suddenly both angry and embarrassed. She took a deep breath, trying to calm down. She wouldn't let the anger take over again, not with Kei. "We're all hungry," she said, managing to keep her voice level.

"Aro! Kei!"

She turned her head toward where they had left the others. "Time to head out again."

Kei nodded and followed her back in brooding silence.

# Chapter 18
## Could You Repeat That

Before the sun set, they came across a freshwater spring and decided to camp by its side for the night. After the gathering of wood and eating the little food they'd found, she moved off to the side, alone. She practiced with her knives, throwing them over and over again into a nearby tree.

Kei had climbed an old giant tree earlier in the afternoon and reported he could see the end of the forest. They would leave its shelter within a day or two at the most.

The others had mostly settled down around the fire for the night, but she kept throwing. The fear of sleep made her restless and angry. It wasn't a question on whether or not she would have nightmares, she did every night. What worried her was tonight there would be no Kei or Prince next to her to keep them from overwhelming her. The fear wouldn't go away.

She walked to the tree and jerked a blade from it.

"Aro, time to get to some sleep."

She jumped and turned, startled to see Bo so close to her. She looked down and then turned and pulled her other knife free. "Sure," she said quietly, tucking the knives into the crude makeshift sheaths she'd made for them.

She followed him reluctantly back to the fire, sitting down when he stopped and turned to look at her. "Good night," he said.

"Night," she replied, forcing herself to lie down. She closed her eyes over the others quiet comments as well.

She woke kicking and screaming, pushing at the hands that held her down. Terror held her trapped in its grasp so tightly it took her a while to realize she was awake, that she had just been dreaming. Angrily she slapped away the hands trying to calm her, or perhaps they had been trying to wake her up. She sat up, putting her face in her hands as she gasped for breath. She didn't even bother trying to control the shaking when it started.

Bo leaned forward. "What's wrong?"

Avery spoke at the same time, "Did you have a nightmare?"

She lowered her hands and glared up at them. It surprised her to see everyone kneeling around her, worried looks on their faces. It brought forth her anger again. She scrambled to her feet and stumbled to the pool, ignoring their further questions. They didn't understand at all. Of course something was wrong. Of course it had been a nightmare.

Dropping to her knees, she quickly splashed freezing cold water on her face. She ran wet fingers back through her tangled hair. She continued to shake as she wrapped her arms tightly around herself and stared at the reflection of the moon on the water. Memories of pain stung her. "It wasn't real," she whispered to herself.

She heard someone walk up behind her and when they rested a hand on her shoulder she shuddered at their touch. "Don't touch me."

Avery removed his hand. "Are you going to be able to sleep now?"

She bowed her head and cursed the tears that threatened to fall. She didn't want them to start. They had a tendency to never want to stop. "Leave me alone," she snapped.

Someone said something far behind her. Avery answered, "I don't know."

She turned and glared up at him. "Just go away!"

He sat down beside her instead. She tensed as he put an arm around her shoulder and pulled her close to him. Clenching her teeth, she fought the fear that tried to wrap itself around her. Avery wouldn't hurt her, not ever. He was her friend, her brother. She struggled to push the fear away, to hold in the simmering anger that didn't make any sense.

He started gently stroking her hair. "There," he said. "It's not so hard." He looked down at her. "You don't have to push me, I mean us, away you know."

He was right. She knew it, but the knowledge didn't make it any easier to do. She sighed and forced herself to relax. "Gah! I hate this!"

"It'll get better," he said gently.

She hoped so.


She fell asleep with his arm around her. She awoke alone, hoping it had all been a strange dream, but it hadn't. She sat up, shaking her head.

"Aro, come here," Avery called to her.

She drank quickly from the pool and washed her face before going to him. She bit her lip as she approached. Would he say something strange about the night before?

He didn't waste any time getting to the point. "We've all been talking and decided you need to work off some of that anger. We're going to give you further lessons in fighting."

She raised her eyebrows. "Um..."

Avery flashed his charming grin. "You'll be practicing your knives with me. Bo will help you with hand-to-hand. Cain and Prince will teach you sword-work, and Kei, scouting."

A grin spread across her face at his words. They were going to teach her to fight? She could certainly deal with that. She nodded quickly. "Yes!"

He drew one of his knives. "Ready?"

"Right now?"

He nodded and she grinned again.

They fought until the others called to them it was time to head out. She drank from the pool until she sloshed and then moved out to scout with Kei. The others would continue their slow travel near the road as they foraged for food. She and Kei would roam further, keeping an eye out for humans on the road, and Were and Fey within the forest.

She enjoyed traveling with Kei. He made her feel safe, and even loved. He acted like one of her brothers, grinning and teasing her as they ran through the trees. He began teaching her how to move quietly, how to climb trees, and how to hide. He pointed out animal tracks and spore and taught her how to identify not only what animal had made it, but how long ago as well.

Everything became a game and she found herself relaxing and enjoying herself more and more. She almost wished their stay in the forest wasn't coming to an end so quickly.

"Aro, come look," Kei called.

She quietly ran to his side and dropped to a knee next to him.

He put a hand down to the ground, fingers spread. Her eyes grew wide at the size of the print next to it. "Wither me! What made that?"

Kei grinned over at her. "Were."

Her eyes opened wider.

"Look," he said. "See how large and deep? There are normal wolves here, but their prints are smaller. The heavier the animal, the deeper the print. Large cats usually don't have claw marks."

She nodded along, paying close attention.

He pointed to the degrading edges of the tracks. "Made sometime yesterday."

Relief washed over her at that. She'd met a Were once, and didn't really want to do it again anytime soon.

They set out again moving more slowly as they came to an area that suddenly blossomed with larger and larger age-worn rock outcrops.

Kei stopped and rested his hand against moss covered stone. She looked up around them, some of the stones rose twice as large as her, and not far away she saw once that jutted up high into the trees.

"What's good, and what's bad?" Kei watched her closely, waiting for an answer.

She looked at the rocks around them. This was easy. "Good, we could hide in them. If we were attacked we'd have something at our backs. Bad, we could be ambushed." She bit her lip, thinking. "We could use them as shelter, too. There might be caves, or we could make something." She paused, trying to think what else Kei might expect her to say.

"And food," Kei said finally. "Small animals, snakes. Different plants grow here." He frowned. "We'll have to ask Prince."

He didn't sound like he relished the idea and she chuckled.

He made a face and mock growled at her. "Let's explore. Stay close."

She nodded and followed carefully after him. Eventually they came across another of the many small streams flowing through the forest and they paused to drink. "Should we camp here tonight?"

Kei stood and looked around. It was getting late in the day so she wasn't surprised when he nodded. He turned, sniffing the air. "They aren't far." He looked back at her. "I can get to them quicker on my own. You wait here."

"Sure," she said a little dubiously. She didn't like the idea of being alone.

He rested a hand on her shoulder. "I won't be long at all."

He paused again so she forced a smile and pushed his hand away. "I'll be fine. Hurry, before it gets dark."

He frowned and let out a little growl of frustration before dashing off.

She watched him run, moving swiftly and silently around rocks and trees. She envied how graceful he was, and fast. But then again, he wasn't human either. Strangely, she often forgot that fact.

She knelt and washed up in the stream, rolling up her sleeves and running wet hands over and over through her hair. She would love to have been able to bathe, but the chill weather wasn't agreeable to that.

She waited by the stream for a while before eventually turning and looking up at the largest rock. It wasn't far so she made her way carefully over to its base. She stared up at the top. It couldn't be that hard to climb it. It would be interesting to discover what she could see from such a height. Maybe she could check to see if anyone was following them.

She started climbing, easily finding foot and hand holds. The rock wasn't at all crumbly, so she didn't need to worry about losing her hold. She found climbing to be not at all as hard as she thought it would be. The exertion felt good. She had almost reached the top when she heard Kei down below.

"Aro! I said stop!"

She turned a little and grimaced down him. Silly Fey. Did he think she would fall? She waved at him and continued up.

She wiped sweat off her forehead after she hefted herself up onto the top. It was worn smooth and almost flat with bumps of greenish-brown moss scattered across it. She wiped her hands on her pants as she turned around admiring the view. She could see over the tops of most of the trees. To the south she could see the hatched colors of the fields and pastures Prince had mentioned. Kei had been right about how close they had come to leaving the forest.

Turning her attention back to the forest she let out a sigh. Unfortunately she couldn't see very well through all the branches. If anyone else was out there, they remained hidden.

She took a deep breath of the fresh air before preparing to head back down.

"Good afternoon."

She choked on a gasp as she froze, fear skittering up her spine at the sound of the unexpected voice behind her. Her hand moved slowly to a knife on her belt.

"No need for weapons. I intend you no harm," the voice said quietly. It was definitely a man. Not young, but not old either.

"Rot it." She squeezed her eyes closed tightly. Fear enveloped her. She could hardly breathe. Had the slavers found her again? Keeping her hand on her knife despite his words, she turned slowly to face him. How had he gotten up on the rock? There had definitely been no one else on the top when she'd climbed up.

She let out a little sigh of relief to find him near the other side of the rock sitting on piece that jutted up like stool near the edge. She regarded him carefully and bit her lip at what she saw. His black hair had been cut short and showed slightly pointed ears. The points strangely curved backward though, rather than pointing up like Kei's did. She stared at the bizarre beauty of his eyes. They had no whites and thin vertical slits. She didn't even know how to try to describe their iridescent color. They shone in a wash of blues and greens dipped with hints of gold and red. He definitely wasn't human.

*Gah.* She had no luck at all. Well, at least he wasn't a slaver. "What are you?"

He grinned and spread his hands. "What do you think I am?"

Did he think this was some sort of game? "Elf or Were?"

He chuckled. "No. Guess again."

She frowned. "Well you're not a Fey. Your ears and eyes are different."

He shook his head with another laugh. "That is true."

His game began to irritate her. "Then what are you?"

He winked. "Something else."

She took a step backward as she remembered Prince speaking of horrible things coming down out of the mountains. Could this creature be one of them? "What do you want?"

"Just waiting for someone," he said with another unnerving smile.

She squeaked as a rock clattered behind her and turned to see Kei pulling himself up. Before she could speak he darted to her side, grabbing her hand and pulling her close to him. "Aro?"

His closeness helped push the fear away. "What is he?"

Kei shook his head slightly. "I don't know."

The man looked hurt. "Come now, Kei. You don't remember me?"

Kei sucked in a sharp breath. "You were on the beach. When I finally made it to shore." His brows drew together. "But..."

Aro looked up at him in surprise. He hadn't told her that! She tightened her hand in his. Things were suddenly getting too strange.

"No, Kei. Think back further. It's been a while," the man continued. He imitated rocking a baby. "I suppose it's possible you don't remember." When Kei didn't answer he continued, "How are your parents?"

"Dead," Kei replied flatly.

"Ahh, I knew them. A long time ago," the man said sadly. "Are you carrying on their quest?"

Kei blinked rapidly in surprise, glanced at her, and then looked back at the strange man. "No."

The stranger frowned. "Do you know why your parents went west?"

Kei nodded sharply, relaxing his arms around her a little. "They had been searching for an artifact that would heal the Fey." He frowned slightly. "There was a prophecy saying the artifact would come from the west."

The man nodded. "Yes." He looked back at her and she felt like someone suddenly started pushing down on the inside of her head. "You've never heard of the prophecy."

"How did..." She bit her tongue.

He winked. "I read minds. You should learn to guard yours. Elves and Were both mind-speak as well." His glance shifted to Kei. "Though the Fey do not." The pushing sensation came again. "You've experienced this with the Were already. You have not, however, seen the artifact his parents searched for."

He looked back to Kei and she cried out as the Fey winced and raised a hand to his head. "Get out!"

"What are you doing?" The anger rose within her again, rising above the fear this stranger caused. She took a step toward him but Kei squeezed her hand and pulled her back to his side.

The man looked back at her after a moment. "It would be best if you stayed out of this, little one."

Opening her mouth, she snapped it closed again at the dark look he gave her. No, she didn't want to anger this man, or whatever he was.

He laughed suddenly, the loudness of it startling her it was so unexpected. Kei put his arm around her, pulling her closer.

"I waited long for your parents return, Kei. Though they did not, your presence is most interesting. Do you know why? Did they tell you?"

Kei shook his head. "No, I was...stop it!"

She looked up at him; his eyes were squeezed tightly closed, pain and anger harsh on his features.

"You were young, when they died," the man finished for him. He frowned. "And you do not know what happened to the book. That is...a great loss."

"What is he talking about?"

Kei grimaced and finally opened his eyes. They were orange, but very close to red.

"Kei is very important, according to the Fey seer. He will have strong connections to the queen. Unfortunately, I do not have the book. So I don't know if there were further words on his future."

Startled at the man's words she looked up at Kei. His eyes hadn't changed. At least they weren't redder.

The man turned his attention back to her. She decided she preferred being ignored.

"I sensed magic over the sea. Fey magic. That recently is something very rare. Most of the Fey are too wild to use it. Yet there is was, and it led me to Kei." He smiled faintly. "You are human and yet I sense, very faintly mind you, Fey. That is unexpected."

She gasped suddenly as the heaviness returned to her head, and with it pain. Images, no memories, began flipping past her eyes. "Stop it." She whimpered, sliding to her knees. He didn't stop. Scenes of the slave ship, the wreck, the beach, the slavers, continued to flash by before suddenly the scene of her taking Kei's fury hovered and then everything disappeared as he withdrew from her mind.

She choked on sobs and leaned against Kei as he knelt beside her, his arms tight around her.

"I see," the man said.

She flinched suddenly as a body loomed over her. Glancing up, she was beyond surprised to find Prince now standing between her and the stranger.

Prince drew his sword. "Who are you?"

"I am Damon." Peeking around Prince she could see the man smiling slightly. "Thank you for asking."

"Leave Aro alone," Prince said stonily. "Have you grown so weak you must torture children?"

Damon scowled. "You do not want to play such games with me." He glanced over at her. "She is not so much a child any longer."

Prince stiffened, his fingers tightening around the hilt of the sword.

Damon grinned. "I will take my leave now." He nodded slowly. "Be well, Prince." He turned to her and gave a short bow. "Grow strong, little one, and learn to guard your mind." He smiled at Kei. "It was good to see you again, Kei. I will be watching." With a wink of an iridescent eye he turned and stepped off the rock edge leaving them all staring after him open mouthed.

She shivered against Kei as Prince turned, sheathed his sword, and crouched down in front of her. "Did he hurt you?"

She shook her head a little. "He..." She took a shuddering breath. "He went in my head. He made me remember things."

Prince grimaced slightly and gently brushed hair from her face before looking at Kei. "You knew him?"

Kei shook his head. "He knew me. My parents. From before we crossed the sea. I don't remember him. I must have been too small."

Prince nodded, accepting Kei's words.

"What was he?" She still couldn't quite figure out, or believe, what had happened.

Kei shook his head, but Prince answered, "A Dragos."

She looked up quickly as Kei sucked in a sharp breath. "What are they? I've never heard of them."

Prince stood. She took his hand when he offered and let him pull her and Kei up. "The oldest and rarest of creatures. Dragons that can take human form. They are more powerful than anything else that walks these lands."

She bit her lip. "Are they evil?"

Prince sighed. "They are neither good or evil. They do what they want." His dark brows drew together. "I dislike that he has taken an interest in you."

She snorted. "Me, too." She glanced over at Kei. "I think I'm not the one he's interested in though."

He regarded her and Kei quietly for a moment. "Tell me everything he said."

She opened her mouth to protest and then changed her mind. With a small sigh she repeated everything they had all said as much as she could remember.

"What do you think?"

Prince shook his head. "I'm not sure what to make of it all. He really didn't say much. Though he mentions Kei having a connection to the Fey queen." He paused a moment and shook his head again. "Fey are immortal. The prophecy could be speaking about any time in the future. What is more worrisome is having the attention of a Dragos. That is..." He grimaced, clearly worried.

"Really, really bad," she offered.

He smiled slightly. "Yes."

"How about we head down to the others." He paused. "Do you want them to know about this?"

She shrugged. "Sure. I don't want to keep secrets anymore." She paused. "What's a seer?"

Prince looked surprised, not at the question, but that *she'd* asked it. "Someone who can see the future," he said finally.

She thought that over. "He said Fey seer. Are there more?"

This time his eyebrows went up. "Yes."

He didn't elaborate and she frowned. "I'm not stupid."

"I know."

"I had tutors," she added defensively.

A smile quirked at his lips. For some reason she found it distracting. "We should get back to the others."

They didn't seem to know what to make of the whole encounter. She didn't know if they thought there was some truth to what the crazy Dragos had said. She just was pretty certain he'd gotten so old he'd gone and lost his mind.

Kei did not leave her side the entire night, that for some reason made her feel deliriously happy and relieved. When Bo looked disapprovingly at him as everyone settled down to sleep the Fey merely growled and pulled her down next to him. He took her hands in his as they lay curled up facing each other.

She smiled suddenly as he looked over her shoulder and growled quietly. A moment later Prince's hand slid over her waist. "Good night, boys," she whispered as she closed her eyes.

# Chapter 19
## After the Long Cold Winter

"I hate winter," she muttered.

Prince glanced up at her. "It's almost spring."

She supposed he should know. He came from these lands, but scowled at him regardless.

After they had finally left the forest they'd traveled the nearly deserted road to the first of the human cities. They hadn't stayed long. It had been too small and too close to the border of Franua for their taste. The second city wasn't much better, however the third suited well enough, it even had a seaport.

It ended up they could have travelled further, the snows started weeks later than expected. The added time gave them a chance to find work and earn the money needed for a place to live. It had not been an easy time, yet they had done it together and eventually everything had worked out.

Their new home consisted of a small room on the second floor of an ancient, decrepit building close to the docks. They couldn't afford much better, but at least it had a large stove for heat and cooking. There wasn't anything else she could say nice about it. It was drafty, there were bugs and rats, it smelled funny, and the neighbors left much to be desired. Cramming six people into one room should have been nearly impossible.

The only thing that made it bearable turned out to be the men's work schedules. Bo and Prince both worked nights at taverns. Avery and Cain worked days at the docks. Kei they couldn't risk letting work at all. A knit wool hat hid his pointed ears, but close inspection would show his eyes were not normal either. He risked hunting and gathering wood in the far forests. She got to cook and clean.

She was rather irritated they didn't want her to work. She certainly could have found something as a servant or barmaid. At the same time she understood. They had become her family, and in doing so had also become overprotective. Part of the problem was her uneasiness in crowds and around other men. Over the months things had gotten a lot better. Her anger and fear had mostly faded away and her nightmares weren't nearly as frequent. Still, she was uncomfortable going out into the city alone and avoided doing so.

The men continued to teach her to improve her fighting skills when they had the time. It became the only thing that kept her from screaming and going insane. They did not have much else to occupy their free time. Sometimes John would bring home a small, tattered book and read to them. Most often they just talked and told stories of their past and people they had known.

Though she had never before been one to gossip, she found boredom got the better of her and she actually paid attention to the local goings on the men would report when they returned from their jobs.

Some of the news and stories were interesting. Tales of Were, Fey, and Elves were more common here. Interestingly, they still took on the form of stories for the most part. There were very few actual events ever spoken of. From the little she learned about them that made sense, they all lived in the forests and didn't interact with humans very often. Apparently humans were lesser creatures, at least to the Elves and Were. The Fey were just all insane. She worried about Kei sometimes, wondering how he felt about all these stories. He never said anything though, and missed many of them while on his trips to the forests.

Winter dragged on forever. The cold and snow had kept them in the city for almost half a year. At least they didn't freeze, and though the food wasn't of the greatest quality, they were able to afford enough they never went hungry. They slowly bought supplies when they had the money to do so; a pot, utensils, an ax, and packs to carry it all in.

She became adept at making soups and stews. They being one of the easier meals to cook and because it seemed someone was always sick with a running nose or cough.

She glanced over at Prince. He hadn't been looking well for a while, though he didn't have any visible signs of a cold. He just looked pale with dark rings always under his eyes. She constantly worried about him, though she tried to hide it because it just made him angry. She could only hope the reason he looked so awful was just because he didn't sleep well with working nights.

Everyone else was sick again, including her. She wiped her nose on her shirt sleeve and grimaced as she got boogers on her arm instead. She'd been growing like crazy and nothing fit anymore.

"Arowyn, you truly do try my patience," Prince muttered.

She winced and pulled a square of old cloth from her pocket and wiped her arm off before blowing her nose. "Sorry."

He only sighed.

She bit her lip and went back to cooking. Avery and Cain had already left for work at the docks. Bo was due back in a little while. Kei would return from hunting in the forest sometime the next day.

"You should get some sleep," she told Prince.

"Come lie down with me then," he said quietly.

At least that's what she thought he said and she turned to look at him quickly. "What?"

He smiled faintly. "Nothing."

She stared at him, sitting on a pile of ratty blankets leaning against a rotting wall. Her prince dressed in torn and stained clothing and living in a dump. It broke her heart. She set her spoon aside and went and sat down next to him. Taking his hand she sighed as she leaned her head on his shoulder. "Spring is coming soon you said?"

He surprised her by leaning his head against hers. "Yes."

"So we can leave soon."

"Yes."

She forced a smile. "Well that's a relief. I'm quite sick of this place." She turned her head and he lifted his as she did. Pulling her hand from his she gestured to the blankets. "Lie down. You need some sleep." He frowned and she grinned. "I'll tuck you in."

He chuckled and did as she told. She pulled a blanket over him. He slept during the day now, since he worked at night. Their old routine had been interrupted by necessity. Maybe that was what he'd meant. He missed the past, too.

Impulsively, she scooted herself in under the blanket as well, curling up in front of him like she used to. Like so many times before, his arm moved to its spot around her waist and she smiled at the memories. He pulled her a little closer and his cheek rested against her hair. That was different, but she didn't mind. She'd missed him and safe and calm feelings he'd always brought her while she slept. "Sweet dreams, my prince," she murmured.

She closed her eyes, just for a moment, before waking at the sound of her name.

Carefully sitting up, she turned to see Avery standing by the door, a stricken look on his face.

"What's wrong?" She spoke quietly to avoid waking Prince, quickly but gently moving away from him and getting up. "Why are you back so early?"

Avery grimaced and pulled off his wool hat and mitts, tossing them to the side. "Everyone is sick. Most of the crew didn't show up today so the foreman sent the rest of us home."

She frowned. Worry knotted her stomach, not just because it seemed a sickness was going around, but the fact Avery had been sent home. They couldn't afford him not working.

Before she could comment he glanced over her shoulder at Prince. "You need to be more careful."

She stared at him blankly. "What?"

He grimaced again. "You're not a child anymore. You've," He made wavy lines in the air in front of her, "grown up. And out," he added with a flushing of his cheeks.

Her own cheeks flamed as she glanced down at her breasts. Yes, they had grown along with the rest of her this winter. She hadn't paid them much attention, except to silently complain when they got in the way. She needed to get something to keep them from bouncing around, but they didn't have money for clothes.

"Just be more careful," Avery said again. He looked away and added quietly, "You're beautiful, you know. I don't want to see you hurt."

She gaped at him even as her face burned hotter. She was beautiful? She snapped her mouth closed. "I'll be fine," she answered. She eyed the growing hole in his black wool sweater. "Give me your sweater. I'll fix it before the entire thing unravels."

He pulled it off over his head and turned his head away from her as a fit of coughing started.

She bit her lip and rested a hand on his shoulder, "Come and sit down."

She went back to the stove to stir her current batch of soup. When she looked back at him he sat on another of the makeshift beds, staring at Prince with a sour look on his face.

He caught her watching him and his gaze dropped. He absently rubbed his chapped, calloused hands together. "Do you love him?"

His whispered question shocked her speechless. She turned quickly back to the soup. "Of course not," she finally managed to choke out. "I'm not an idiot."

He snorted and she turned around again to glare at him. He started coughing again and that was the only thing that saved them from an argument. By the time he stopped Bo was walking in the door.

"Hey, Bo," she greeted him.

"Hey there, pup." He glanced over at Avery and frowned.

"So what's the word?"

He coughed, shook his head and cleared his throat. Avery started coughing again and he grimaced. "Sickness going around it seems."

"Really?" She sighed to cover her snippy remark. "Any deaths?"

He nodded. "A few elderly I heard." He pulled off his hat and added it to the pile by the door. "We'll just have to wait and see I guess."

She nodded. Elderly and young children dying from winter illness certainly wasn't uncommon. When healthy young people started to succumb then it became time to worry. "At least spring is almost here."

Bo and Avery both went to sleep leaving her alone with her thoughts and worries. She puttered about the room, tidying and doing little chores.

Eventually she sat herself in the corner trying to keep quiet as she did mending, occasionally peeking at the boys. Bo and Avery huddled under their blankets snoring away. Prince rested quietly and she found herself watching his face as he slept. "Wither me," she muttered.

With a grimace she went back to mending the hole in Avery's sweater.

Her brothers had talked to her about love. They'd awkwardly explained the difference between love and lust. They had discussed how love came in many different forms and how loving someone, and being in love with them, could be two different things. She'd never much thought about it. She had certainly never been in love with anyone. There had been local boys she found sweet or handsome, but she had never followed them around all doe-eyed and stupid.

She smiled slightly to herself. She was fine then, because she wasn't doing anything like that now either. Sure, she loved all her men. They were her family now. She leaned forward and peeked over at Prince again. He was just a little special because she felt...

"Gah." She raised her hands to her face. "I am an idiot."

She took a deep breath, trying to sort through her emotions. No, it wasn't love, not the type Avery thought. Her feelings for Prince were special, different, but more like a favorite brother. Kei was special, too, so certainly this was normal. Though of all the men, it would be like her to fall in love with the one she couldn't have. The one who would never love her back. He was a prince. She was...nothing.

If she tucked her feelings away in her mind, perhaps she wouldn't show them as much. She could do that. She had been practicing after all.

Since they had met the strange man named Damon in the woods, she had worked on building a wall within her mind. He was insane about all of the talk of prophecies. However she did agree she should learn to keep her thoughts from being invaded by others. She didn't want people like him in her head. Over the long winter months she had built what she hoped was a sturdy fortress in the back of her mind. Damon had told her to build walls, and she'd taken his words literally. She didn't know what else to do. Constant practice at envisioning her fortress seemed to do something though. Luckily she'd grown up learning to concentrate while practicing with her bow. Of course, she had no way to tell if her fortress actually existed or if it was any good or not. She certainly didn't want to seek out Damon to find out and humans and Fey didn't read minds.

By the time Avery awoke later in the afternoon she had almost returned to a good mood. He came with her to collect water from the well and later they practiced sword work in an empty alley tucked behind their building. They weren't at it long before she called a stop and dragged him back up their room and put him back in bed. He didn't argue and fell back asleep quickly.

She waited impatiently for Bo and Prince to wake up, and for Cain to return home.

When everyone finally woke up she started silently dishing out soup into crude wooden bowls. She caught Avery still glaring at Prince. "Avery, pay attention or you're going to spill."

He looked at her sourly before returning his gaze to his food and keeping it there.

When Cain came in she went to meet him at the door. "What's going on out there?" She turned back to look at the men as Avery started coughing again. "Bo said it's getting worse."

Cain shook his head. "Still is. The baker's daughter died this morning," he paused before adding, "and it's snowing again."

She grimaced. Children had started dying now, too. That was a bad sign. "Anyone talking about the symptoms?"

He nodded as he made his way into the room and she fetched him a bowl of soup. "Starts out like a normal cold. With some people it stays one. No worries. Others it gets worse, the cough gets worse. Then the cough goes but a fever comes. If the fever doesn't kill you then the buildup in the lungs does. Person can't breathe."

She glanced over at Avery and Bo, both of them had been coughing. As far as she knew, she and Cain only had running noses, and Prince merely looked like he was going to keel over.

"Seems to happen fast," Cain continued. "Don't know if that's a good thing or not."

The topics turned to other things and she chatted along with them as Prince and Bo got ready to leave.

Prince's shift started earlier so she followed him to the door while the boys kept talking. She waited uneasily as he dressed for the cold. She tried not to fidget when for some reason she found herself not wanting to start the ritual she had begun with each of them before they left for work. Her mind wandered and then suddenly he stood waiting by the door staring at her.

"What's wrong?" He kept his voice low, his typical frown crossing his face.

"Nothing." She forced a smile before holding out her arms. "Hug." She tried not to hold him too tightly, or for too long, uncomfortably aware of Avery watching her. "Be safe."

"You, too," he answered. He broke the ritual with another frown as he stepped away. "Are you sure nothing's wrong?"

*No, she was worried someone would get sick and die. Worried she would lose him.* She couldn't tell him such things though, so merely forced another smile. "Just tired. See you in the morning."

He nodded, though the frown didn't leave his face. "Don't forget to bolt the door."

"I won't."

She almost sighed with relief when he finally left. She went back to the others and sat quietly as they continued to talk and Bo went and shaved with the small, straight razor they'd bought. He nearly slit his own throat when he suddenly started coughing and she jumped up. "Let me."

He grimaced, but handed over the razor. "Be careful with that, pup."

She chuckled. She'd shaved her brothers often enough in the past, she wasn't worried. "Be careful tonight." She carefully slid the blade along his skin around his scar. "If you're not feeling well come home."

A faint smile curved his lip as he struggled not to move. "Yes, mother."

She grimaced down at him. "I'm serious."

"I know. You don't need to worry about me."

She stuck out her tongue. "I worry about all of you, idiot. You're my family."

He smiled and closed his eyes for a moment. "I know what you mean. I'll be careful."

"Good boy," she said with a smirk.

He chuckled.

He left not long afterward and after demanding her hug and reminding him to be careful she did her evening chores before curling up in her pile of blankets. She tried not to think of Prince, or of anyone, getting sick. The last was harder since Avery coughed all through the night.

# Chapter 20
## Break a Little More

When Prince returned early the next morning she ran to the door, nearly knocking him over. She didn't even let him take off his snow covered winter clothes before dragging him to Avery's side.

"Feel his forehead. He's hot isn't he?"

Prince pulled off his mitts and handed them to her as he crouched down next to the sleeping form of their friend. "Yes."

She raised a hand to her forehead and started to pace.

Prince moved his hand over Avery's face. "He hasn't woken up?"

She shook her head, trying to keep from panicking. "And he's not been coughing, not since I woke up. Rot it! I don't know what to do!"

He stood and put his hands on her shoulders, keeping her in place. "Where is Cain?"

"He went out to see what's going on. If anyone has anything for the fever."

He nodded his approval. "Good. Calm down."

She closed her eyes and took a deep breath. Prince was right. She couldn't afford to panic. She had to take care of Avery. She couldn't let him die. "Sorry," she whispered.

He pulled her into an unexpected embrace. "He will be fine. Try not to worry."

She wrapped her arms around him and held him tightly for a moment, holding back tears. With a

206

shuddering breath she pushed away. "You're right. You have something to eat, and get some rest. I'll see if I can get him to at least have some water."

She couldn't wake Avery to drink and cursed in frustration. She placed her hand on his forehead again, grimacing at how hot it felt. Jumping up, she got a wet cloth and wiped his face gently with it before placing it over his forehead.

Kneeling beside him, she tried to figure out what else she could do. Maybe colder water would be better. She sprang up again and grabbed a clean bowl. "I'll be right back," she told a startled Prince. "I'm getting some snow."

"Good idea," he replied. When she hesitated he nodded at Avery. "I will watch him."

She ran down the stairs and outside and filled the bowl quickly with new snow before running back up. She dumped the snow into one of their water buckets and watched it quickly melt. She tested the water with a finger and then ran and got more snow. Satisfied the water would be cold enough, she wet the cloth and again and wiped down Avery's face and neck.

"Should I take the blankets off?"

Prince frowned. "I don't know."

"Gah!" Panic rose within her. She didn't know what to do. "Where's Bo? Shouldn't he be back by now?"

"Calm down," Prince answered wearily. "He's not late yet."

Bo had been coughing, too. What if he was lying passed out from fevers in an alley somewhere? She wished Cain would hurry back. She took a deep breath in an attempt to calm down.

"Should I open the window? Let some fresh air in. It's stuffy in here." She was babbling, and knew it, but couldn't seem to stop herself.

Prince got up. "I will do it. A little fresh air is a good idea."

He pulled rags out from around the shutters of their one window. Cool air slowly filled the room as he pulled the shutters open and she jumped up and started fanning the air with her hands, trying to get it moving around more quickly.

"Aro."

He walked up and pinned her arms to her sides. She looked down, trying to keep her lips from trembling.

He pulled her against him, holding her tightly and stroking the back of her hair. The tears started and she gripped him tightly, wishing they would stop. "I can't do this. I can't lose someone else."

He rested his cheek on the top of her head. "Falling apart is not going to help him."

"I know." She closed her eyes and took a number of deep, shuddering breaths until at least a semblance of control returned. She pulled away reluctantly. "Thanks."

He smiled. "I'm always here."

She smiled a little in return and turned away before he could see the blush rising to her cheeks.

She looked at Avery and saw his eyes were open. With a happy cry she jumped forward and dropped to her knees beside him. Pulling the cloth away she tested his forehead again. "How are you feeling?"

He stared at her for a moment before closing his eyes. "Horrid," he whispered.

She leaned forward; his voice had been so quiet she had barely been able to hear him. "Cain is out looking for something to help with your fever."

He nodded a little and opened his eyes again. "Don't."

Confused, she shook her head and leaned in closer. "Don't what?"

"Don't love him." He closed his eyes again as she stared at him in shock. She jerked her head around to see if Prince had heard, but he was busy by the stove and apparently had not.

She turned back to Avery, trying to think of a response, but saw he had fallen asleep again. She bit her lip as she placed the cloth back on his forehead. His even breathing suddenly quickened for a moment before settling back. Worried she lay her head on his chest, listening.

She sat up quickly as tears blinded her. A whimper escaped before she could stop it.

"What is it?"

Unable to speak she waved a hand at Avery. Prince hurried over and dropped to his knees, bending to listen for a moment before sitting up with a sigh.

She choked on a sob before turning suddenly at the sound of coughing outside the door. She sprang to her feet and rushed over, jerking the door open just as Bo was reaching for it.

She saw Cain stood behind him and quickly moved out of the way as Bo nodded and they came in.

"Did you find anything?"

Bo looked at her quickly. "What's going on?"

Cain handed her a small packet. "You grind this up and make tea. It's supposed to bring the fever down."

She rushed across the room and busied herself making the tea. "I need more water. And snow." She glanced over at the others. "Cain you're late for work."

He grimaced but nodded. "Come get me if..." He trailed off as he looked at Avery.

She nodded sharply and looked away. "We will."

"I'll go get your water," Bo said, grabbing an empty bucket and following Cain out.

She could hear him asking for details as they went down the stairs. Waiting for water to boil she checked

Avery again. Resting a hand on his chest she could feel the heat radiating from it. "Prince, help me get his shirt off."

Without comment he did, and she busied herself wiping Avery down with cool water over and over again as if she could wipe the sickness out of him.

Bo returned with the bucket full of water and snow and she made him eat and rest.

Near noon, loud bumping sounds coming up the stairs signaled the return of Kei. She met him at the door, wishing she could hug him. She waited impatiently as he removed the ax from his belt and set it by the door. He untied a bulging bag made from an old shirt at his waist and handed it to her. "Workers are digging," he said as he struggled to tip the large bundle of wood strapped to his back onto the floor. "Just outside the city."

Tears started to streak her cheeks as she nodded. "There's a sickness going around."

He looked up at her, worry clouding his face. "I can smell it." He froze. "Avery!"

She stepped out of the way as he raced past her to drop to his friend's side. She carried the bag he'd given her over to the stove and dragged out a large pan. With shaking hands she started putting the skinned and gutted small birds and animals into it, added water, and then shoved it into the side compartment of the stove to bake. She tried not to cry as Bo spoke quietly to Kei, telling him what had happened.

Tears did spring to her eyes when Kei started talking gently to his friend, telling him he had to get better, begging him to wake up.

She prepared another cup of tea and took it to Kei. "Here, see if you can get him to drink some. It's supposed to help with the fever." She left him to go sit with Bo and Prince.

The day passed with agonizing slowness as they sat and listened to Avery's labored breathing. She took turns with Kei wiping him down and trying to get him to drink water and tea. Cain came home early and quietly joined their silent vigil.

She knew Avery wasn't getting any better, but it still shocked her to the core when he just suddenly stopped breathing as she wiped his face.

She stared at his face, resting a hand on his bare chest, waiting for him to take another breath. "Avery," she whispered, patting his cheek lightly. "Avery!"

Kei suddenly appeared at her side, pushing her away as he reached for his friend. "No no no no no no..."

She turned and stared blankly across the room. Her breath came in ragged gasps. She raised her hands to cover her face. This couldn't be happening. He couldn't have died. She couldn't have lost someone else. She'd built herself a new family to replace the one taken from her and now they were dying, too. First Kendric, and now Avery.

Something between a wail and a scream tore itself from her throat as she scrambled to her feet. She pushed past the men milling around Avery's body and stumbled to the far corner, as far as she could get from him.

Leaning her forehead on the rough wood she banged her fist against it as sobs tore out of her. The pain was so good she started hitting the wall over and over again as hard as she could. The pain felt better than the agony that screamed through her, unraveling her from the inside out.

It was so easy to fall apart completely. The sobs, the pain inside, became too much and she slid to her knees and just cried.

Kei's arms wrapped around her and she didn't protest as he pulled her over onto his lap. They were nearly the same height now. He'd grown a little over the winter, but she had more. Somehow, she still fit perfectly against him.

He didn't say anything, merely held her and rocked her and let her cry. When she could finally look up at him she saw lines of tears down his cheeks as well. "Don't die," she choked out quietly. "Don't die, too."

He held her tighter as he dipped his head to rest it against hers. "I won't. We Fey are immune to human sickness." He gently kissed her forehead. "You don't have to worry about me. Understand?"

She nodded as he brushed tears from her cheeks. She sniffled and when she moved to get up he let her. She fumbled in her pocket for a cloth to blow her nose, turning her head to cough.

She looked up at Kei's swift intake of breath and grimaced. "I'm fine. It's just from crying." She sucked in a breath suddenly, as she noticed everyone else was gone. Her eyes went to where Avery had slept and saw only a rumbled blanket. "Kei?" Her voice came out a frantic screech.

He sprang up and put his arms around her again. "He couldn't stay here. You know that."

She nodded and lowered her head as the tears came again. She hadn't really gotten to say goodbye. She sniffled and coughed again.

"You need to lie down."

She grimaced. "I need to check on dinner."

He shook his head vehemently and forced her to bed. "Stay. Rest. I'll finish dinner."

Grimacing again, she nodded. His eyes had started glowing a faint orange. She wasn't about to argue with him. Her own eyes sore and burning from crying, she found she couldn't keep them open no matter how hard she tried. With another cough she rolled over and tried to think of anything other than Avery.

Tossing and turning, she absently heard the others return and snuggled further down into her blanket. She didn't want to talk to them. She awoke slightly when Kei took her hand before passing again into sleep.


When she cracked her crusty eyes open again she groaned and then sat up as coughs suddenly wracked her body.

A hand tentatively touched her thigh and she slapped it away.

"Aro?"

She grimaced over at Kei. "What?"

He sat up, a worry line between his brows. "You're sick."

She glared at him. "I know."

His cheeks flushed as he looked down and she scrambled out of bed, too annoyed to apologize. She quickly saw Cain curled up asleep, everyone else was gone. Panic set in before she realized Prince and Bo must have gone to work and weren't back yet, and Avery...

She choked and started coughing again. Ignoring Kei, she set about her morning chores. Cain woke up, Prince returned, Cain left, Bo returned. So their little world went.

She worked silently, and for the most part everyone else remained quiet as well. Except for her and Bo coughing. At least Bo still was; it was when the cough suddenly disappeared you had to worry.

No one spoke about Avery, about his sudden death. She didn't try to delude herself they wouldn't. They just all needed time to deal with it in their own way.

Sometime after Cain had returned and they had eaten dinner she realized she hadn't coughed for a while. She paused as she washed dishes in one of the buckets and bit her lip. Surely a cough didn't come and go so quickly. But she couldn't be sick like Avery, it couldn't be that fast.

She squeezed her eyes closed, holding in tears, before taking a deep breath and faking a cough. She continued to do so until Prince and Bo both left for work and she curled up in bed. She'd be fine. She had to be. Her men needed her. As Kei joined her she squeezed his hand tightly.

Hopefully she'd wake up in the morning.

She had strange dreams. It took her a long to time to realize she wasn't dreaming at all, but drifting in and out of consciousness. She'd gotten sick then, like Avery had been.

Sometimes she could feel cold on her face and neck. She drank when someone urged her to do so. She wanted to talk to them, to be able to understand what they were saying, but their voices remained distant mutterings. At least the cough stayed away.

She found it odd she didn't mind being sick. It felt like she simply drifted along. Perhaps it was the tea, or just the fever itself. As the fever grew, the voices fell away entirely and became replaced by old familiar nightmares of slavers and the ship and chains. She dreamed of the wreck and their escape, and being thrown into the cold waters. She could feel the water around her, pushing her down, dragging her deeper. The water crushed her, making it hard to breathe as she struggled against it. Prince didn't come to save her and she panicked, thrashing in the water, calling his name. She didn't want to die. She didn't want to be fish food.

"I'm here, Aro."

She relaxed immediately at his voice, but the crushing weight, the inability to breathe still remained. "Help me," she begged him.

"I can't help you this time."

She whimpered at his words and because his voice had started growing more distant. He couldn't help her and she was drifting away.

"Wake up," he told her. "Wake up and Kei will help you. Wake up."

Kei. He wasn't trapped. He had escaped. She fought against the water, struggling to rise above it, to find Kei. Kei lived, he would save her. She just had to get to him. When she finally broke the surface, gasping for breath and opening her eyes, she was surprised to find herself in bed, Prince holding her.

"That's my girl," he whispered, gently stroking her face.

She stared up at his sad face. Why was he so sad? His eyes were red rimmed, glassy, almost as if he were about to cry. She realized despite everything they had been through, all the pain he had endured, she had never seen him cry.

He leaned down, briefly resting his cheek on her forehead and squeezing her tightly before she had the strange sensation of falling.

He turned his head away from her as he sat back. "This had better work," he said sharply.

"We don't have anything to lose do we?" Kei's voice cracked, gruff and angry.

Were they fighting again? The last few months they had been so good, too. Everything started to drift away once more.

"Aro! Stay with me," Kei called to her.

She opened her eyes again. "Strange Fey. I'm right here." His face now filled her view and she saw he had been crying, and recently.

He turned his head. "I need you all to leave now."

She could hear voices answer, but couldn't make out who it was or what they said.

"Now!"

She started under Kei, fear starting to rise within her as she stared up at his blazing red eyes. "Kei?"

He turned back to her, his eyes immediately fading to a golden light as he smiled. "Don't be afraid."

She suddenly was, but she nodded. She trusted Kei, always.

"Do you remember the magic we did together?" His eyes searched hers.

"Fey magic," she answered quietly, no longer afraid. "A magic of the heart and soul. A magic of binding and promise and intent."

He grinned. "Yes. Good memory." His face grew serious. "There are three such bindings. What we did was the first. It was the bond of friendship. I want to do the second with you, Aro. The bond of family. Will you allow me to?"

She stared up at his hopeful eyes, stunned. He wanted to be family? "Yes!"

He let out a deep sigh of relief, briefly closing his eyes. "Thank you." He reached out and pulled up her hands.

She remembered and opened them, palms facing him.

"Good girl." He placed his palms against hers; however instead of keeping them flat together he threaded his fingers through hers. "It's only a little different," he explained as he shifted over her and pulled their linked hands together and placed them at level with their hearts.

"I'll say the words, and you repeat, but change brother for sister. Understand?"

She nodded and sucked in a startled breath as his eyes shifted from golden to orange.

He smiled encouragement. "Ready?"

She nodded again, forcing her eyes to stay open. Happiness and excitement filled her. A knot formed in her belly and her throat grew dry.

"As family I shall bind my heart and soul to yours. Forever beside you I shall stand. Together or apart, always will I be with you. Your Eternal brother I shall ever be."

She smiled at the words as he said them, remembering to keep her eyes locked with his. She repeated the words slowly, struggling to remember them and get them right.

As before their hands grew warm and heat rushed through her whole body. This time she felt a strong tingling sensation too that was not at all unpleasant, and followed the warmth as it traveled.

The little lights came again as well, lighting the area around them, but this time they were much larger and brighter. It seemed there were many more dancing around the two of them. It was hard for her to tell, as she became lost in Kei's glowing eyes.

As the lights settled over her and Kei and then faded away she let out a little sigh. "Did it work again?"

He leaned forward and brushed his lips across her forehead. "Yes, sister. It worked again."

She smiled and let her eyes drift closed. "I'm glad." Her smile grew a little larger as he settled down next to her and took her hand. Drifting off to sleep she realized she could breathe easily again.

# Chapter 21
## On the Road Again

When she opened her eyes she smiled to see Kei sleeping beside her, facing her and holding her hand near his cheek. What surprised her was she could feel a body behind her, a familiar arm across her waist.

She bit her lip, suddenly remembering she had been sick. Sick like Avery, but she hadn't died. Her eyes flitted over Kei's face as she remembered the magic they had done. Had it saved her? She felt perfectly fine, if a little stiff. Her breath caught at the thought he had only done the magic with her to save her life.

"Aro?"

She lifted her eyes to look at Kei. He hadn't moved but was watching her, a small smile on his face. "Did you do it to make me better?" She searched his face, looking for the truth. "Is that why?"

The smile grew a little and he squeezed her hand. "Silly human," he taunted. "I've wanted to do it for a long time. I just didn't know how to ask."

She grinned back at him, the weight of her worry lifting and making her almost giddy. "Thank you, brother." She flushed, a silly happiness washing over her.

He chuckled quietly.

A question occurred to her suddenly. "What's the last one?"

His grin twisted into a smirk. "Ah. Yes. That would be the one for love, for mating." He laughed as her cheeks reddened. "It's similar to marriage. Our version."

"I see." She managed to choke out. "I don't think...um..."

He grinned and squeezed her hand. "Two is enough."

She nodded quickly. Marriage. Mating. She wasn't ready for such things. Even if she had been, unfortunately Kei wasn't the person she thought of that way. "Do the others know?"

He grimaced. "They know I used Fey magic. On you. Only Prince knows what I did."

She nodded again. Since she really didn't know what he did either, she didn't say anything. "Are they angry, that you didn't save Avery?"

He blushed. That she didn't expect. "I said...it wouldn't have worked on him."

"Would it have?" She hated to ask, but she needed to know.

He shook his head. "If we'd shared the first binding, yes. But we didn't. It takes a lot of power to do, I don't have enough to do both bindings one after the other."

"So they know this is the second–"

"No," he interrupted. "I didn't want them to know. Not anything about the bindings."

"Then what did you say?"

"I could use my magic on you because I love you," he admitted, blushing furiously.

She gaped at him and pressed her lips together as laughter sputtered out of her. "You are such an idiot. They believed that?"

He shrugged a shoulder a little. "Yes, they did."

She shook her head, not believing it. She sighed though, as she saw things from their view. She and Kei had always been together. He had gone into a fury because of her, and returned for her. Perhaps it was believable after all. "Well, thank you. For whatever reason you did it."

"I wasn't lying," he said. "I do love you. You're my family."

A smile spread across her face and she didn't try to stop it. "Exactly. I love you, too."

He smiled in return, his eyes slightly glowing with his happiness.

"Are you two done yet?" Prince muttered in her ear. "I'm trying to sleep."

She bit her lip trying to hide a smile as Kei chuckled. "Cranky prince."

"Troublesome child," he replied.

She elbowed him in the ribs, making him grunt in surprise. "I'm not a child."

Kei sat up and she did the same. It was time to get up and start cooking. As she stood it surprised her to see both Bo and Cain starting to get up as well. Everyone had stayed home.

Stretching sore muscles, she headed to the bucket of water and splashed herself awake. When she turned around Bo surprised her by pulling her into a tight hug.

"Glad you're feeling better, pup," he mumbled.

She wasn't quite sure how to respond but hugged him back briefly before smacking his arm. "I'm not a pup!"

Everyone laughed and she glared at them all. "Well I'm not. I'm sixteen now. Legally I can join the army or get married, or...well do whatever I want!"

Bo frowned.

"The laws may differ here," Cain began, clearly grasping at whatever he could.

Prince shook his head. "Actually, in most cities a child it considered legally mature at fourteen."

She swung to glare at him. "And you're just telling me this now?"

His lips twitched.

Clenching her teeth she tried not to laugh and instead turned away. "Cain you're going to be late for work."

The men exchanged glances and she sighed. What hadn't they told her this time? "What now?" She paused as her mind suddenly began to work. "Are we leaving?"

Bo nodded. "Rent here is up for the month in three days. We figured we might as well get moving. Been seeing travelers coming in the last few days, so roads mustn't be too bad." He glanced at the spot where Avery used to sleep. "It's a good time."

She stared at the empty rumpled blankets as well, words catching in her throat. She nodded in response, not trusting herself to speak. She moved over to the stove and set water to boil for tea. "We've a lot to do then."

Preparing for their journey took time. Not only did they have to find and buy supplies, they also had to sell off everything in their room they wouldn't be able to take with them to help pay for said supplies. What exactly they should take and sell caused a few arguments. What made the decision in most cases was the fact they could not afford a horse or mule to carry everything. Anything they took they would be carrying themselves, therefore the less the better.

"Do we need this?"

She looked over and saw Cain holding out a black knit wool sweater. Her breath caught in her throat and she reached and took it, nodding and bowing her head so he wouldn't see the sudden tears in her eyes. "I could use it," she managed to mumble as she turned away, holding it to her chest.

She nearly bumped into Kei and didn't fight him as he took her arm and drew her aside. He stared at the sweater for a moment, his eyes sad.

She raised her eyes to his. "Do you want it?"

He shook his head. "It fits you better."

She smiled a little at his lie, but didn't call him on it.

He held out his hands, a knife in each. "These were his, too. I thought..." He grimaced and winced, struggling for words. "I thought we could each have one. To remember."

Streaks of tears ran slowly down her cheeks as she nodded and Kei handed her one. It was smaller than her others and she was pretty sure she could rig up something to tuck it into her boot. "Thank you," she said softly.

He just nodded and took her hand, squeezing it tightly.

She had assumed she would feel more when they finally set out. Anticipation, excitement...something. Instead there was only relief.

She found it easy to leave behind the horrible room they had called home for so many months. The hardest part was leaving the city, actually walking past the too large area of turned earth a short distance outside the gates. She couldn't stop staring at it as they walked.

Avery had been buried there. He was there. He...

Cain rested a hand on her shoulder. "Do you want to stop?"

Shaking her head vehemently, she quickened her pace instead and forced herself to stare at the dirt road. It took a lot of effort. However, not crying did as well. She had cried enough already. She had to keep going, move on with her life. She wasn't a child anymore.

Luckily the day was clear and crisp. The men chatted about how they hoped they would be lucky and not run into any bad spring storms. It was a risk they all willingly took so they could get moving again.

The roads had become messy with melting snow and mud. She concentrated on not falling on her face. One of her men would have caught her before she did. They had hardly left their old building before she found them surrounding her, protecting her. Even on the sparsely traveled road they did the same.

It didn't really bother her. They had become family. After everything they had been through, all the time they had spent together, they truly were. She didn't mind overly much if they wanted to look out for her. Over the months she had grown stronger, she could take care of herself if she needed to. She would take care of them too, even if it was in her own way

Spring slipped into summer as they journeyed south. The road weaved its way through fields and pastures, gently rolling hills, and expanses of moss and lichen covered rock. Sometimes it cut inland, mostly it ran close to the sea at the edge of a beach or occasionally along the top of high cliffs.

The distance between cities was always at least four days, sometimes a week or more. Occasionally they would walk through ruins, most of them so old and crumbling, barely anything remained. Only one city had fallen within her lifetime.

# Broken Aro

The further south they traveled the news of fighting between southern cities became more common, more detailed.

Pulling her hair back and tying it with a bit of string she looked off toward the mountains in the east. They seemed so far away, and yet were still so very large. Mountains weren't strange to her, they'd surrounded Kingsport, but they had seemed so much smaller. Maybe they had been.

Kei tugged on the ponytail she'd made. "Your hair is getting long."

She smiled a little and nodded. Kei had trimmed it a little a few times over the winter, trying to even out the bad cut her brothers had given her as best he could, however it still hung to just past her shoulders. She certainly couldn't pass for a boy now. She glanced down at herself and frowned. She couldn't really even if she did cut her hair. She'd grown too many curves.

She looked over at Kei and reached over to tug the black wool cap further down over his ears. Soon they would enter another city and the last thing they needed was for him to be recognized as anything other than human. Along with the stories of a lot of fighting south of them, there had also been talk about Fey and the elusive Were.

For the most part people respected and avoided the Were. Easy to do as long you stayed out of places you weren't supposed to be, like their forests. The Fey had become more troublesome. Stories told of wild ones attacking travelers and even the few farmsteads that dotted the fields outside of the city.

She fidgeted as they rested before making the last hike to the city. Judging from the size of it even at this distance, it would be the largest one yet. For some reason she wanted to be safe within its walls.

Damon's words of people invading her mind continued to haunt her. She even dreamed of it, along with a number of other strange things she never remembered. At least these dreams weren't as bad as her regular nightmares. Being in chains and the slaver attack, the beating and near rape, had scarred her. Since the attack she hadn't been comfortable around strange men at all. At least she had finally stopped pulling away from her men. Still, she wanted the safety of the city walls...without all the people. She didn't know if they would try to hurt her, or if they were all even human. She didn't even know if the defenses she had created within her mind would be good enough. All she could do was keep working on them.

She squeezed her eyes tightly closed. Build walls...build walls...

"Aro, what are you–" Prince rested a hand on her shoulder, "Aro!"

Her eyes flew open at the sudden panic in his voice. "What?"

"What are you doing?"

She grimaced. "Trying to keep my head safe. Damon said–"

"Damon?" He looked at her in confusion for a moment. "Ah. The Dragos."

She nodded and shrugged. "I don't believe most of the nonsense he was spouting, about Kei and prophecies and everything, but I thought he had some good advice about protecting myself. I don't want people crawling around in my head."

"I see," Prince said, his voice quiet.

She turned and looked up at him. "You think it's silly."

Surprisingly he shook his head. "No. It is wise of you to so protect yourself."

She grinned and looked away to hide her embarrassment at his praise. "I thought so. Do they come into cities a lot? Fey and Were and Elves? And we just don't see them?"

"More than people know, I imagine," he answered. "It is dangerous for them though. Humans tend to hate them, to kill them if they can. That is why they hide what they truly are. However, if you know what to look for, you can tell who is not human."

Her eyes widened in surprise. "You can?"

Prince nodded and gestured to Kei. "Watch the Fey. Not only do his ears and eyes give him away, but also the way he moves. Fey are rarely very tall, and are often slight of build."

She watched Kei for a while, and understood what Prince meant. He was more graceful than a human. "So it's the same with Dragos?"

"Yes. They too move lightly." He grimaced. "Unfortunately they can take any form, so that is not helpful. But they can't change their eyes, for them, always look for that."

She nodded and bit her lip as she remembered the strange iridescence of them. "And Elves? What do they look like?"

He chuckled. "Elves are beautiful, tall, lithe creatures. Some may be wider of shoulder, but they aren't built like men such as Bo."

She looked over at Bo and his fine array of bulky muscles and nodded.

"Their ears are pointed, more so than that of the Fey. Their eyes come in many colors, but have a brightness to them that's noticeable." He paused. "These traits are not always helpful. The Elves also have magic and can glamor themselves to look more human. So again, you look to their actions."

226

She sighed. He made it sound both easy and hard at the same time. "So what about the Were? In human form I mean."

"They are the most human. Sometimes the color of their eyes will give them away. They range from blues to yellows to amber. Their canine teeth will often be slightly more prominent. Otherwise they look completely human."

"So watch the way they act again," she said with a sigh.

"Yes."

"This conversation has not been particularly helpful, you know," she told him.

He chuckled.

Bo walked over. "Ready to head out?"

She nodded and allowed Prince to help her up. Though his arrogance had lessened somewhat over the months, his manners certainly had not.

They entered the city and allowed the crowd to push them inward. As the markets were their destination and could often be found somewhere along the main street they went with the flow. The money they had saved over the winter had slowly dwindled. She'd heard the men talking they would only have enough left to buy supplies for a few more weeks. She didn't even want to think about what they would do then. Prince had mentioned at the last city they had traveled almost half way to his home. They'd been traveling at least two months already, if not three.

The only reason their coins had lasted so long was due to their own supplements, hunting small animals and birds along the way, catching fish and other sea creatures when the shoreline allowed. Prince would occasionally find edible plants near the road or closer to the sea. They didn't dare try to steal from the crops or pastures. Armed men now regularly patrolled both the road and beyond.

She followed Prince and Bo with Cain and Kei behind her as the crowds grew thicker. She'd never seen so many people out at once before and wondered if it was always like this, or if something had happened. Had the city come under attack? She hoped the crowd was merely due to some sort of celebration. Perhaps it was closer to the summer equinox than she had realized. As the crowd pressed in on them and grew louder and louder she finally understood it had something to do with the Fey.

There had been another attack.

She began to grow worried about Kei and kept looking back to check on him. The city certainly wouldn't be a safe place for him if his true nature became discovered.

The noise of the crowd increased even more. She wished she was taller so she could see what lie up ahead. As it were, she just struggled to keep Prince and Bo in sight.

When someone grabbed her upper arm and jerked her roughly through the crowd she was so shocked she merely squeaked in surprise. Fear wrapped around her as she realized she'd been separated from the others.

Heart beating furiously, she opened her mouth to scream out to them.

The viselike hand on her arm jerked her forward roughly and then again, spinning her about until she suddenly found her face pressed against a chest by an impossibly strong hand on the back of her head. Another arm pinned her against his body, her own arms trapped.

Barely able to breathe she still tried to scream but only a muffled, choked sound emerged, easily drowned out by the noise of the growing crowd. Panicking, she struggled against her abductor, but his arms were like unmoving bars of iron around her. He pushed his way quickly through the crowd, keeping her tight against him, her feet not even touching the ground.

The sounds of the crowd dimmed slightly. As suddenly as he had snatched her, the man flung her away. Her back smacked up against stone hard enough it knocked the breath from her lungs. Her head cracked against the stone, the pain of it bringing tears to her eyes. Glad to be free, she quickly caught her balance, her hands immediately moving for her knives.

"Please, go for your weapons. I'm sure you will do better with them this time."

# Chapter 22
## Secrets

"You!"

He chuckled.

She grimaced, but didn't remove her hands from her knives. "What do you want, Damon?"

"You remembered my name."

She shook her head in annoyance as she looked around, trying to figure out where he had taken her. It seemed to be an alley of some kind, however one not directly off the main thoroughfare. It was strangely empty, yet she could still hear the muted noise of the crowd. "What do you want?"

His smile remained. "I said I would be watching you."

His words sent unexpected shivers up her spine. She remembered, but she hadn't really thought about it. It wasn't her he was interested in. She didn't understand why he had taken *her* from the others. "Have you been?"

"I've been occupied. With other matters." A smile appeared. "However, I am here now. What have you been up to, little one?"

"I don't think it's any of your concern," she snapped. "I would much prefer if you just left me alone." She rubbed at her arm, it continued to throb from the tight grip he'd had on her. "Why did you drag me here?"

He spread his hands. "I did not think your companions would much care for me talking to you."

He certainly had that right. "I don't much care to be talking to you either."

He smiled slightly. "I know. Your thoughts are so full of fear. Are they always so?"

She didn't answer. He took a step closer and she found herself pressing back again the stone wall of a building.

Fear closed around her throat. Was he going into her mind again? She didn't know if the walls she'd tried to build would work, if they even existed.

His fingers brushed across her forehead. "I see you listened to my advice," he murmured. "I'm impressed you managed to create even this. Who showed you how?"

"No one."

"You are an interesting one indeed. First you bond to a Fey, then take his fury, and now somehow build walls in your mind. Did you think your feeble attempt would keep me out?"

"I'd hoped so," she whispered. Apparently it wouldn't. Could she stall him? Certainly her men were looking for her even now. How long would it take them to find her? "Why are you doing this? Why me?"

His fingers traced down her cheek. "That is the interesting thing. Imagine my surprise, coming across you all outside of the city and once again feeling the remnants of Fey magic. On you. Kei is important to me, and you apparently are important to him. I want to know why. Why some puny little human has him taking such risks. Why can you do the things you do? What is special about you?"

She shuddered and turned her head as she tried to sidestep away from him. Her movement angered him. Suddenly his hand pinned her head to the wall. His thumb pressed in at one temple, his fingertips at the other as his palm pressed her head back.

She gasped in pain. Her hands rose to encircle his wrist, trying to pull his hand away. "Stop it!"

"Stop fighting," he said quietly. "It hurts more if you do."

She struggled against him, at the same time trying to keep her mental walls in place. She didn't want him in her mind. She didn't want anyone in there. "Get out!"

"Shh."

Shock froze her for a moment when she was suddenly sucked inward…

She stood upon the battlements of the fortress she had built. Around her, beyond her shining stone, darkness hung and unimportant surface thoughts swirled around. She may have built this massive fortress, but from the outside. She had never actually been within her own mind before.

The darkness wavered. A roar echoed from within.

She straightened and found a bow in her hands. *My bow. From before the city fell.* She smiled. Oh, how she had missed it. *I need to get another one. Sometime soon...*

Something came out of the darkness, distracting her thoughts. It flew around her fortress, a monstrous, horrible, beautiful thing. *It's Damon. Prince had said he could shift forms. This is him as...* She couldn't remember what it was Prince had said the Dragos turned into.

*Dragon.*

She stepped back at the power of the voice that answered her. She raised her bow. *Get out of my head!*

The beast, the dragon, flew closer, circling. *Very impressive. You have done well. For a human. Now, let me in, Arowyn.*

She shook her head, hair flying about in the wind his giant wings made. *Leave me alone! I said no!*

He laughed and then his laughter turned into a wild, terrible roar. It shook the stone she stood on, shook the very air she breathed. Fear froze her in place. *I can't fight this. I don't know how.*

*You're learning. Open a door. Let me in.*

Stubbornly, she shook her head again.

*Then it will hurt.*

The dragon circled again, its wings beating harder. As it neared to make another pass it dove for her, mouth gaping and full of teeth. Damon roared again, shattering her to pieces.

Screaming she flew apart, returning to the real world. She clenched her teeth as he ripped through her mind, circling around and around before attacking her carefully built walls and tearing them apart piece by painful little piece. It burned like searing fire roaring through her head. She wanted to scream but her voice wouldn't work.

Despite the pain she tried to keep him away, to repair the walls that tumbled down under his brutal assault. It wasn't enough. She wasn't quick enough, or strong enough. She didn't know what she should be doing. The pain his destruction caused hurt too much for her to truly concentrate.

It did not take him long to break her.

She whimpered as she suffered him again going through her memories. He muttered little comments as he none to gently rifled through them. Their winter in the city. The sickness.

A choked wail quietly escaped her. She knew what came next. She didn't want to remember.

Avery's death.

*His death was hard on you. Did it hurt you?*

Tears ran down her face as she fought again to force him from her mind. She couldn't take anymore. She didn't want to remember. *And he must not know...*

His mind-voice ripped through her. *What are you hiding?*

He jerked forward the memory of the magic and binding Kei had done to save her.

*I see.*

The black rolling pain began to overwhelm her. *Get out! Get out! Get out!*

*Is that all?*

It wasn't. There were still the complicated feelings she had for Prince. But she would not even think them. She refused to feel them, to even admit them to herself. It helped she couldn't make sense of them and had never had the time to try to sort them out. The past months she had managed to keep them buried within her, to even bury them deeper.

He tore through her recent memories, searching, his presence ripping and shredding and burning its way through her mind. *Stop fighting! What are you hiding? Show—*

His hand ripped away from her as something barreled into them. The shock of his departure startled her. The sting of his nails scratching across her forehead made her gasp, then he disappeared and she started slipping down the wall.

The deserted alley echoed with voices.

She opened her eyes to see Damon on the ground, Kei on top of him.

Kei in a full wild fury, blazing red eyes, talons, teeth and all.

She wanted to call out to him. Whether to stop him or urge him on she wasn't sure. She didn't. Couldn't. All she could do was sit in a daze. Her body shook and shuddered in painful spasms. Her mind roiled in shambles, her walls torn down, her memories raped and raw. She couldn't gather her thoughts enough to think. She only felt the pain.

*Call off your Fey, or he will die.*

She closed her eyes, wishing his voice would just go away. His words slowly sank in and her eyes snapped open. Kei still fought, but Damon now stood.

He didn't have a mark on him.

Prince had told her Dragos were the most powerful creatures in these lands. Kei was strong, but she didn't know if he was strong enough. She couldn't take the chance he wasn't. She couldn't lose him.

"Kei!" He ignored her. She tried to rise and failed. Leaning her head back against the stone behind her she called him again, not only with words, but with her heart, "Kei! Back off!"

He stepped back from Damon, claws clicking at his side. He didn't come to her, but did look over, eyes blazing a furious red.

Hearing the pounding sound of footsteps she turned her head and saw the others running up the alley, Prince in the lead.

She sucked in a deep breath as he dropped to a knee at her side. She didn't want him to worry. She just wanted it to be over. She wanted Damon to leave.

"Are you hurt?"

He cupped her face in his hands, his thumbs wiping away tears she hadn't known she'd shed.

"I'm fine," she lied. She didn't want him to fight Damon. If Kei couldn't hurt the Dragos then Prince certainly wouldn't be able to do anything either.

Her body shuddered again, pain ripping through her head as if the dragon was still inside. Was he? Was he still inside?

Prince froze. He turned to face Damon. "What have you done?"

She rested a hand on his arm as he began to rise. "It's fine."

He cupped her cheek again, wiping away more tears. "No. It is not." He rose in one fluid motion, drawing his sword as he did.

"Prince..."

He ignored her quiet plea, angrily striding forward, pausing only a moment at Kei's side. "See to Arowyn."

Kei came to her and helped her rise. She looked behind him and saw Bo and Cain standing a short distance away, weapons drawn. She didn't blame them for keeping back, not with a Fey in a fury and a Dragos.

She allowed Kei to pull her close. She wasn't afraid of the razor sharp claws that wrapped around her. Kei rested his cheek on her head for a moment and then leaned back. She looked up at him, and her heart started beating even more furiously. His eyes still blazed red, his teeth too long. She wasn't afraid *of* him, but *for* him. What if the city people saw him like this?

She glanced over at Prince. He and Damon had moved further down the alley. They spoke either mind to mind or too quietly for her to hear. Damon looked amused. Prince stood stiff and angry. Rot it, she couldn't deal with both problems at once. However, Prince had at least stopped attacking, for the moment he was safe.

She looked back to Kei. One thing at a time. She rested a hand on his cheek and pushing slightly, forced him to look at her. "Give it to me," she whispered. Kei's back was turned to Bo and Cain, they wouldn't see, not at the moment at least. "Hurry. It's not safe here."

He didn't answer, she wasn't even sure he agreed, before she felt the power of the fury flowing into her. As a test she closed her eyes. The power still came. Good to know. She rested her face against him and allowed him to hold her there while the power continued to quickly drain from him.

His fury swirled around within her, giving her strength, taking some of the pain away. She tried to hold on to some, and succeeded. She directed it through her mind, easing some more of the pain. However the fury enveloped her and threatened to overcome her with its anger and rage.

She sucked in a deep breath, trying to control it. Somehow she managed to regain control, to turn the reckless fury into barely bridled anger.

Kei relaxed against her, the claws around her body receded and disappeared.

"I'm sorry," he whispered in her ear.

The anger began to drain away. She didn't know what he was sorry for. "Silly Fey."

"Your Fey."

"Yes." She smiled slightly at his words and looked up at him. She blinked rapidly a few times. "How are my eyes?"

"Good."

"You should not interfere," Damon said. "It is not your place."

"Nor is it yours," Prince replied.

Aro bit her lip. What were they talking about?

Damon raised a hand at Prince, though his attention had returned to her and Kei.

Something whipped her mind again. The ruins of her walls collapsed further as the dragon suddenly dug deeper, pushing through older memories, learning who she was.

His eye's widened, their strange iridescence whirling with color. "And you are Aro. Are you made of stone?" He laughed, as if he'd made a great joke. He stopped suddenly and leaned forward, regarding her thoughtfully. "Is it possible the son succeeded where the parents did not?" He looked to Kei.

"Dragos," Prince said warningly. "You will stop. Now."

Damon ignored him. He pushed her through her mind again. Her lips trembled at the pain and she closed her eyes tightly.

His strange eyes opened wide and he took a step toward her. "Arowyn Mason."

She looked up at him again. She didn't like the tone of his voice, or the way he'd said her name, like it meant something.

He looked surprised, more than surprised...truly shocked. His gaze traveled around the group. He turned back to her. "Do you know what a Mason does?" He kept talking before she could even answer. "They work with stone."

Kei's arms tightened around her. She had no idea what Damon was talking about. However, the pressure on her mind lessened and she let out a soft sigh of relief. Prince looked back at her, and took a few steps backward toward her.

Damon smiled, clearly pleased, and perhaps a bit amused. "It seems the prophecy spoke not of an artifact at all."

The prophecy again? He truly was insane. Even so, she did not like the way he was looking at her, not at all. Fear skittered up her spine. "What are you talking about?"

"The original prophecy of course. The one Kei's parents were so intent on. 'Find the broken arrow carved of stone, stolen from across the sea. It will heal the Fey and they will rise again.'"

She choked, unable to speak.

"You, my lovely, are Aro Mason. Masons work with stone. You were stolen from across the sea.

Interesting isn't it?" He grew thoughtful. "The only question is whether you are broken or not."

She knew the answer without even having to think about it. Looking up at Kei's brilliant red eyes she saw he did as well and wasn't at all happy about it. She looked back at Damon, afraid he might try to go in her head to find out. "I was, maybe." She looked the boys. "But not anymore."

"Perhaps," Damon agreed. "But that is unimportant. You were when Kei found you. Until recently, you have been. You still fit the prophecy."

"So you say. An old prophecy no one knows anything about."

"The Fey do." He smiled over at Kei. "You have done well, Kei. Very well." He looked back at her. "I wonder how you will do it. It will be interesting, watching you."

She grimaced. "I'd rather you didn't."

He laughed suddenly, the loudness of it startling her it was so unexpected. Kei pulled her closer. The man stood and looked at her again, tilting his head slightly and looking thoughtful. "I wonder..."

"That is enough," Prince said quietly.

Aro snapped her head up to look at him. Prince was furious, nearly trembling with the force of his anger. Why?

She didn't have a chance to ask. Damon laughed and Prince suddenly lunged for him.

"Prince! Don't!" He didn't hear her, he was so furious, perhaps he couldn't. She cursed under her breath. She didn't want him to fight.

Damon laughed as they stepped around the alley in an intricate dance.

She jumped suddenly as Prince's voice rang sharply through the alley.

"You will not!"

"Rot it," she muttered. She winced as the sound sent spikes of pain ripping through her skull again. Kei's power had helped, but her mind remained a painful broken jumble. She motioned Bo and Cain over, only a little surprised they actually came.

Bo carefully looked her over. "How bad is it?"

She forced a fake smile, pushing the anger caused by his worry away. "He was just in my head again. I'm fine."

"So he's the man you saw before," Cain commented.

"Yes, that's Damon." She frowned as she turned back to look at him and Prince. Prince fought, Damon avoided or blocked. He had a sword in his hand now. Where he had that come from?

She closed her eyes for a moment, wishing the pain in her head would go away. She just wanted to find somewhere to go and curl up and sleep for a week. Anger continued to swirl around within her. Damon had hurt her. He could have hurt Kei, he might still hurt Prince.

She wanted the fighting to stop.

Bo stepped forward and to the side, one of his knives drawn. Cain moved the other way, both ready to join the fighting.

"Enough!" She pulled away from Kei. "Damon, leave!"

Damon stiffened. His iridescent eyes whirled as he turned to stare at her incredulously.

"Rot it," she muttered.

Prince lunged but Damon still blocked him easily.

"Little girl, you do not tell me what to do," Damon snarled. "All you creatures are powerless against me." He jabbed his sword in her direction "Pitiful little powerless humans! You are nothing!"

*Gah!* She raised her hands to push her fingers into her temples. She'd only made things worse.

Damon continued to rant, jabbing his sword again. "Even your tame little Fey cannot touch me! Nor can your weak little Elf! Nothing can stand against me! Do you understand? I am a Dragos. You do not tell me what to do!"

Elf? "What?"

Bo and Cain muttered curses.

Prince flung himself recklessly at Damon. "Bastard Dragos! They did not need to know!"

"You should know better." Damon turned on him and his sword flashed. Prince's blade went sailing through the air, clanging against stone before falling to the ground. "Of all of them, you should know to show respect." Damon moved again, so quickly it was difficult to follow his blade.

Prince fell backward to the ground, a hand rising to the slash through his dirty worn shirt.

"Prince!" Not caring about what danger she might be putting herself into, she rushed to drop to her knees by his side.

Damon strode toward them, sheathing his sword. "Your darling Prince is nothing but a weak little Elf. He can't protect you."

She looked over at Prince and reached a hand out to him. He shrugged it away, not looking at her. She didn't know who was telling the truth.

"He's not an Elf," she said in confusion. All of the old stories she'd heard told of their magic and beauty. He looked human, and he certainly didn't have any magic.

Damon swore and before she could react he bent, jerking Prince up and wrapping an arm around him as he flipped him over. "You need to learn to *see*, Arowyn."

Prince struggled against him, cursing loudly, but she knew the strength of the Dragos grip and wasn't surprised when he didn't break free.

"And you," Damon said sharply to Prince. "You need a reminder."

"Stop, please," she begged quietly. She wanted to reach out the short distance and pull Prince away, but didn't dare. Damon was furious enough already.

The Dragos held Prince helpless with one arm and reached up with the other to roughly push his long black hair aside. "Look."

She stared at the mark on the back of Prince's neck. She'd never seen it before. She barely had time to try to figure out what the strange dark markings meant before Damon brushed his fingers over it.

Prince froze and stiffened. "Don't," he pleaded, his voice weak and cracking.

Damon completely ignored him. "This is an Elven rune," he explained to her, his voice suddenly calm. "It keeps his glamor in place. If you remove it..." His fingers dug in, and then he pulled, somehow ripping the mark away. "You see what he truly is."

She stared in shock as Prince cried out in pain and convulsed within Damon's arms. Suddenly he shimmered and Damon moved, dropping him nearly in her lap.

Prince curled up and shuddered on the ground as everyone watched in complete silence.

She wasn't sure what she expected, but nothing really happened. She looked up at Damon, eyebrows raised.

The Dragos grimaced and reached down, turning Prince's head to the side.

Her mouth dropped open at the long pointed ear he revealed. Trying to gather her wits she shook her head vehemently. "It doesn't matter. It doesn't matter what he is."

Both Prince and Damon looked at her in surprise.

"It doesn't." She smiled. "My best friend is a Fey. I'm used to pointed ears." She rested a hand on Prince's shoulder. "Can you stand?"

He nodded slightly and pushed himself up, first to his knees, then to his feet. She scrambled to her feet, a hand out in case he needed assistance. He ignored it.

She looked at him, he seemed mostly the same. She had been expecting more. Yes, his ears were now pointed. They were longer than Kei's. His features remained the same, just a little more perfect. Each line and plane had lost any roughness. His skin however, continued to look pale. Dark rings still smudged beneath his eyes. The dust and dirt of their travels didn't help. Not much had changed. He was still Prince.

His eyes met hers, still their bright sparkling blue. No, they *were* brighter...more blue.

She smiled a little and reached a hand out to him. "It doesn't matter."

"Were you aware," Damon said. "That Elves, like the Were, are mind readers?"

She looked from Damon to Prince and back again. "What?"

"He is weak, yet he can still read your mind."

She looked down at their joined hands.

*I would never hurt you.*

Fear rushed through her and she gasped. Prince's voice, though quiet, had sent echoes of pain through her battered mind. Someone else in her mind...she couldn't...

"No…"

"Every time you touch," Damon continued, "he can wander through your thoughts. Learn your secrets."

She jerked her hand away. Panic rippled through her. She raised a hand to her forehead, her heart pounding away. She couldn't look at Prince. He had been in her mind? All this time...

She closed her eyes and shuddered.

"Aro...," Prince whispered.

She shook her head and took a step backward. She wasn't surprised to feel Kei wrap his arms around her and she turned into them, hiding. She buried her face against Kei, drowning out all the words that came next. All she could think about was how Prince had been in her head, like Damon. He knew her secrets, her thoughts. *He knew...* She squeezed her eyes tightly together as new tears formed.

Kei remained silent, merely holding her tightly while she tried to push away the pain and sort out what was going on.

"Arowyn."

She turned when Prince called her name, though she had trouble meeting his eyes.

He gave her a graceful, formal bow. "I apologize...for my secrets. For hurting you. It has been an honor traveling with you. I wish you well."

She gaped at him and watched in stunned silence as he retrieved his sword and walked stiffly away. "No...wait...I..." She couldn't get her thoughts to form coherent words.

"It is for the best," Damon said.

She jerked her head around to glare at him. "Why would you say that?" Kei pulled her tightly against him again before she could say something else that would get her in trouble.

"Build your walls again," Damon said to her. "You still have much to learn." He looked at Kei, the power of his gaze forcing the Fey to meet his eyes. "Will you continue to protect her? She will need it now, before she grows into her destiny."

Kei held her more tightly, but he nodded.

"Take care of your future queen."

She turned in Kei's arms and pressed her face against him again, squeezing her lips tightly together to keep from telling Damon was an insane monster. Blighting idiot, did Damon really believe all of that? She didn't want to ask. She didn't even want to think about it.

Kei pressed a hand reassuringly against her back. "He's gone."

So was Prince. She hadn't stopped him. Everything had been so confusing. It had all happened so fast. Why had he left so quickly?

"We should get going," Bo said roughly.

She nodded and let Kei guide her back to the main city street. She didn't know what to think. Or to say. Kei kept his arm around her as they walked, later holding her hand as Bo and Cain bought more supplies when they finally found the market. Everyone was quiet, so she didn't feel the need to speak either. It gave her time to try to sort out what had happened.

They left the city before dark and walked down the road toward the next in silence. As the sun began to sink they moved off the road to make a camp for the night.

They didn't have a fire, though they rarely did. Wood was too hard to come by unless they camped near the sea and could scavenge driftwood. Even when they did find wood they hoarded it, making a fire only long enough to cook meals.

The area had grown rocky again and Bo and Cain found a spot somewhat sheltered from the wind. No clouds hung in the sky. At least they didn't have to worry about rain in the night.

After a quick meal of bread and cheese she leaned back against a rock, closing her eyes. Her head still hurt, though not as badly as before. While walking she had started to build up her walls again.

Tears came to her eyes. He'd pulled them apart so thoroughly, it wasn't easy. She worked slowly, making the walls larger, stronger. Horrible Dragos! She hated him. She fought back more tears.

Prince had left. She had let him. She could have run after him. She could have said something. She hadn't. Maybe she was still broken.

No matter how much she tried not to think of him her thoughts kept returning to Prince. She couldn't believe he'd gone. Yet he had been so angry. Perhaps it was for the best as Damon had said. Certainly it would be safer for them, now that he didn't look human anymore. Prince had said once how dangerous it was for an Elf or Were or Fey. Most humans hated them. She didn't really understand that. They'd heard only gossip and stories in their travels here. They'd never come across them on the road or in a city. It seemed to her they left humans alone. Well, except for the Fey. The only one she knew was Kei, and he was different. He hadn't grown up here. The anger rose within her again. It was all Damon's fault. Why couldn't he leave them alone?

She didn't hate Elves. At least not her Elf. She loved him as a brother, perhaps as something more. She still wasn't sure how she felt. However she didn't delude herself they would be together. Ever. He was a prince and an Elf. She groaned. He was an elven prince! Yet...no matter what he was, he had become her friend. Her family.

She opened her eyes and sought out the others in the darkness. "We need to talk," she said quietly.

# Chapter 23
## A Prince is a Prince

"We do," Bo agreed. He turned immediately to Kei. "You knew. About Prince."

She raised her eyebrows. The thought hadn't even occurred to her. Of course Kei would know. If he could smell she was a girl, he'd certainly be able to tell Elf from human.

Kei looked down at the ground. "Yes."

"You didn't say anything," Cain accused.

The Fey fidgeted as he searched for words. "You don't anger an Elf," he said finally. "I learned that much from my parents. Certainly not an elven prince. He didn't want it known who he was, or what." He looked up at them. "We were never in any danger from him. If we had been, I would have said something."

"Is that why you two fight so much?"

"For me, yes." He shook his head. "He is used to the other Fey. I don't think he ever trusted me to be able to control myself."

"I'm more concerned he's been reading our thoughts all this time," Cain said into the silence that followed Kei's words. He shuddered.

"I don't think he really was," she said carefully. They all looked over at her and she continued quickly. "I've felt what it's like, with Damon, when he invades your mind. You feel it, you know he's there when he's prying deep down inside. I never felt anything like that with Prince. I never noticed at all. I don't think he was rummaging around in our private thoughts. Just random ones, like what we're thinking right then. Know what I mean? He didn't do it often either."

Cain grimaced.

Bo nodded his head. "He didn't touch any of us, not more than normal." He looked over at her. "You however..." he left his comment hanging.

Yes, Prince had always been touching her, a hand on her shoulder, holding her hand, curling up next to her every night...

She gasped. "He kept the nightmares away." She looked back and forth between the others to see if they agreed.

"He did," another voice came from the darkness.

She whirled around, fear making her heart beat suddenly faster.

Damon sat leisurely on a rock beside her.

"What are you doing here?"

He smiled slightly as she scrambled to her feet and backed away toward the others. "I've returned to make amends."

*Stay out of my head!*

His lips twisted into a smile. *I do not wish for you to hate me.*

Anger made her cocky and reckless. *A bit late for that isn't it? You hurt me!*

*You're such fragile creatures.* He sighed. *I will try to be more gentle in the future.* He paused. *Though if you would just let me in, we would not have this problem.*

Her eyes narrowed. *Next time try just asking. Perhaps I'll tell you what you want to know. You don't need to be in my head.*

He shrugged. *Perhaps.*

She didn't believe him. Not for a moment.

*I don't need to ask. It's the fighting me that makes it hurt. I can wander through any of your minds, and I do. Remember that. Pick your battles, Arowyn.*

"Very well," Damon said, clapping his hands together once. "I will answer one question from each of you. This will make things right between us."

His sudden declaration put her off guard. What was he up to? She exchanged looks with her men, getting confused shrugs in response.

Cain let out a deep sigh when no one else spoke. "Why did he lie to us?"

Damon gave a short *tsk*. "That is a waste of a question. I'm disappointed in you." At their collective frown he sighed and rubbed his hand over his face. "Humans," he muttered into the air. "Your memories are so short and selective."

He shook his head again before continuing, "He never lied to you. Prince himself answered your question in the past, why he has kept quiet. The answer then being he has many enemies. More so the closer you come to Elven lands. The Elves are not well liked by humans, and for good reason. Humans are considered little better than dogs. They are rarely allowed entrance to Elven lands, and even then, those few are treated like pets. Elves do travel in human lands, usually in at least pairs or more. If not, they conceal themselves with their glamour, their illusions, because they are at least aware of the human's dislike of them." He paused a moment. "In the past, Elves have died because of this hatred, killed by angry mobs or their throats slit in the night."

She paled a little at the thought of Prince getting his throat slit and looked down at her hands. She opened her mouth to ask a question and closed it quickly, remembering she only had one. She had to make it a good one, but for some reason she couldn't think of anything other than the shock and pain on Prince's face when Damon had removed his glamor.

They all sat in silence for a while, digesting what the Dragos had said. Again and again the image of Prince kept coming into her mind. She sighed and sat up straighter. "Elves are supposed to be strong and beautiful and have magic," she said. "That was a statement," she added quickly before Damon could even open his mouth.

He did however, nod.

"So why doesn't he look well? Why haven't we ever seen him use any magic?"

"That is two, but I will answer, seeing as the answer will cover both questions."

She forced a small smile.

"Prince has been gone from Elven lands for a very long time, decades actually. Normally this would not be an issue. Elves take precautions when leaving the lands they are tied to. And yes, they are magically bound to their land. The problem arose when the slavers took from Prince the amulet that kept him connected to his land. Without it, he had no access to its power. Faint though it would be after being gone so long, and him being so far from it. I imagine what remained of the power within him he used to heal from various injuries the slavers did to him."

"He hasn't used magic because he had none to use," Bo stated flatly.

Damon nodded at him and then looked at her. "Quite simply, Prince has been slowly dying."

The words ripped through her, tearing through her heart. She stared at Damon in shock and horror. Prince was dying? How could he be dying? She shook her head, not seeing how the Dragos could be right. He had to be lying.

"I am not lying," Damon said irritably. "Of all the races who live and are magic, the Elves are the only ones that have tied themselves to a particular piece of land. They gain great benefits from this, but also there are consequences."

She closed her eyes, wishing she could ask more questions. Was Prince going to get worse? How long did he have? Would he get better if he made it home?

"Yes, not long, and probably." Damon said flatly.

Her head jerked up as the others looked at him in confusion. He had answered her unspoken questions. *Thank you.*

*I will not make a habit of this.* His voice spoke in her mind. *However I have treated you ill today. I have now made amends. Yes?*

She discovered she could actually agree and silently let him know before turning to the others and sharing the unspoken questions he had answered.

Damon turned to Bo and Kei. "Next question."

Bo sighed and looked over at her, clearly at loss. He thought a moment before slapping his thighs and sitting up straighter. "So then. Since you seem to know what goes on in everyone's head, including Prince's, why has he stayed with us? We have not only been traveling slowly, but stopped for the entire winter. It doesn't make any sense if what you said is true, about his needing to get back home."

Damon's iridescent eyes swirled. "Do you truly wish to know? He will not thank me for answering or you for asking."

Bo looked around at them all, and everyone nodded. Yes, they all had been wondering why Prince stayed with them.

"Very well. It is for the same reason you have all asked only questions about him, the one who you believed had lied and betrayed you, when I offered to answer any question at all."

They all stared at him and then looked around at each other. A blush came to her cheeks that the obvious reason had never crossed her mind.

"We're friends," she said quietly. "Family."

Damon smiled slightly and nodded once.

"Well now I feel stupid," Bo said.

Damon looked to Kei. "Last question."

"What was the prophecy about me?" Kei asked, his eyes faintly glowing.

"Very good," Damon answered, clearly surprised. "I see you are learning, young one. This is good. Prince is not what you should be concerned about. Your future is." He paused a moment, looking at everyone, as if making sure he had their attention. "Your son will make the Queen and he will remain by her side bound to her by three."

Kei frowned, his eyes starting to glow. He shook his head. "I don't understand."

Damon smiled. "You will."

"Wait," Aro interrupted. "How do you know that's even about Kei?"

Damon glanced over at her. "Because his mother was the recorder for the Queen's Seer. For centuries she took note of every prophecy the seer spoke and recorded them, and deciphered them. Dalsia was also the seer's only child. Kei was her only son."

Aro frowned, trying to make sense of it all. "But it doesn't say I'm this queen. Even the prophecy you said is about me doesn't specifically say that. It doesn't make any sense."

"You will understand, in time."

*Or you've got it wrong.* She forced a sweet smile when Damon stiffened for a moment, however he didn't otherwise react.

He rose gracefully.

"I shall be watching, to see how your story continues to unfold."

She rose as well, though no one else did. "You're a lot of trouble," she told him. "But thanks."

He smirked and his eyes sparkled with mischief. "You are most welcome, little queen-to-be." He gave her a short bow and faded into the shadows.

She grimaced after him. "I wish he'd stop with that nonsense." She turned back to the men. "So..."

Bo sighed. "That was...interesting."

"Everyone agree he's talking nonsense about the prophecies?" Everyone grinned and nodded at that, except for Kei, who looked off to side, still lost in thought. She changed the subject quickly. "About Prince, it doesn't really matter, does it?"

"No," Cain answered, a wry smile coming to his lips. "It doesn't."

"The Dragos was right," Bo continued. "We're friends."

"Family," she added with a little smile.

Kei frowned, paying attention again, and his eyes changed from golden to orange. "Prince and I have never gotten along. Mostly because I knew his secret, and he demanded I never share it. I am sorry for that." He lowered his head.

"We understand," Bo said.

Kei shook his head. "There are so many things I do not know. About my people, and our customs and laws. Especially concerning the Elves. It is frustrating." He grimaced. "For all I know he was aware of that and used it to his advantage."

"I wouldn't put it past him," Cain said quietly with a small smile.

Kei caught her watching him and the light in his eyes dropped back down to golden before fading away altogether. "He has protected Aro. Taken care of her. For that alone..." His voice trailed off and he looked away, refusing to finish his thought.

"So we are agreed?" Everyone nodded. She turned back to Kei. "Do you know where he is?"

Kei grimaced. "He left the city, heading south. We can catch up with him tomorrow."

"Good. That is what we'll do," she decided, planting her hands on her hips and daring the men to argue.

Bo laughed. "We had better get some sleep."

# Chapter 24
## Family is Family

She ran, her feet thumping rhythmically along the dirt road. Each step sent a jab of pain through her head and she cursed Damon under her breath. Despite the pain, she kept her pace steady.

They had headed out early, moving quickly through the morning and keeping a watch out for Prince. She had begun to worry they would never find him. The rolling rocky landscape kept him hidden from view until nearly noon. She'd spotted him then, a slowly moving figure walking along a hill far in front of them. She'd run ahead, leaving the others amused behind her.

She ran up another low hill and paused at the top to catch her breath. Seeing him in the dip below brought a smile to her face and she started off again. She slowed as she neared him, thumbs worrying the leather of the straps over her shoulders. What should she say? She had no idea. Of course, she didn't know if he was still angry or not.

All through the night and morning she had thought about Prince, about what she would say, what she wouldn't. Various scenarios played out in her mind. The headache and broken walls in her head didn't make thinking easier. The only thing she knew was she had to get him back. It didn't matter what she had to do or promise.

Dropping her pace to a walk as she neared him, she let out a sigh of relief when he turned and stopped when he saw her. He hadn't ignored her.

He stepped off the road and removed his pack.

As she narrowed the distance between them he stared off to the side, not looking at her. Not a good sign, but she worried more about how worn out he seemed. He looked tired, more than tired, exhausted. That's right, he was dying. She forced such thoughts aside. He wouldn't die, she wouldn't let him.

From somewhere he had gotten a floppy hat that covered his ears. He looked ridiculous. She smothered a laugh. It was easy to do. She didn't know if he was going to tell her leave him alone or not.

Her breath caught as she drew closer. She didn't want him gone from her life. Not yet. She slipped her pack off her shoulders, letting it drop to the ground, as she impulsively darted forward and flung herself into his arms.

She didn't know if he had expected it, or just had really quick reflexes, yet he caught her, swinging her slightly as she clung to him and buried her face against his chest.

Still, he held her tentatively until she thought strongly at him, *I'm sorry!*

His arms tightened around her and he lowered his face to her hair, letting out a deep sigh.

*I hope that is a happy sigh, and not one of annoyance,* she thought carefully in her head.

He let out a deep laugh, the sound of it surprising her enough she raised her head.

His lips were pulled back in a large smile, eyes twinkling in happiness.

She pulled back a little and swatted his arm. "Stupid prince!"

He laughed again and shook his head, a smile still playing on his lips. "Troublesome child."

"I'm not a child," she snapped in mock fury.

He laughed again. She couldn't remember the last time he had laughed so much. She liked to think maybe it was because she had come after him.

He still had an arm around her and she leaned back against him, wrapping her arms around him again and squeezing tight. "Don't leave again," she whispered.

He actually kissed the top of her head. "I won't."

She looked up. "You're back then?"

He hesitated. "The others..."

She smiled. "You're family, silly. Just stop keeping so many secrets. We can't handle the shock!"

He smiled at her jesting tone. "I assure you that was the big one."

"Good. I don't like secrets." She worried her lip. "You should apologize, for not telling us. It will make things better." He frowned and she continued quickly, "Not that you have to mean it, but you should try."

He shook his head as a smile again crossed his face. "Very well."

She beamed up at him and hugged him tightly again before running to retrieve her pack. Taking his hand she tugged him further off the road. "They aren't too far behind. We can wait."

He nodded and followed suit as she sat in a patch of grass.

He glanced over at her after a few moments of silence. "How are you doing?"

She shrugged and fiddled with a few blades of grass. "My head still hurts a bit." When he didn't say anything further she looked over at him. He frowned as he stared off into the distance. "What?"

He shook his head slightly. "I cannot protect you from him."

She smiled a little and shrugged again. "No one can." She made a face. "I don't know why he's doing this to me."

Prince sighed. "He believes in that prophecy."

She snorted. "It's nonsense right? It hardly makes any sense. He probably has it all wrong."

Prince nodded. "So it goes with such things."

"Have you heard this prophecy he mentioned?"

He shook his head. "I've heard of it, but not the exact words."

She glanced over at him. "Do you think..." She paused. "He's not right is he? I'm not going to be queen of...of the Fey." She blushed as she stuttered over the words. "I mean, I'm human. It doesn't make any sense."

"Personally, I don't think so. You are human. I cannot see the Fey following you."

Her relief at his words made her almost giddy and she smiled.

"However," he continued. "I do believe it is you the prophecy mentioned. I would say it is possible you will somehow help the Fey become what they once were. The prophecy does not say you will become the queen." He shrugged as she stared at him. "You are very young, Aro. You have many years ahead of you to do great things. I do truly believe you capable of that."

She ducked her head when his words caused her cheeks to flush. "I just wish he'd leave me alone."

"He believes you will be a queen. They are powerful. Powerful enough to fight a Dragos. He has reason to take interest in you."

She grimaced. "I'm making my walls stronger this time. Maybe eventually I'll be able to keep him out."

He glanced over at her. "What you did...it is impressive."

She laughed. "For a human?"

"Yes," he said, smiling faintly.

"Could you keep him out?"

"If I were stronger. At home..." He shook his head and looked away again. "Even then, not if he really wanted in. It would not be easy for him however." He looked over at her again. "You've left your surface thoughts free. How did you know to do that? I had wondered at that."

She shrugged. "I don't know. It felt right."

He nodded as if her words made perfect sense.

She glanced over at him as she began pulling up grass. "Can you be in my head? Like he was this time? Can you see what I made?"

"Yes."

She paused a moment. "Have you been already?"

He shook his head. "Not within your mind. I...read surface thoughts. That is all."

She nodded she understood. "Can you talk to me, in my head?"

He chuckled. "I could. Yes."

She chewed on her lower lip for a moment. "Could you help me? Teach me how to make my walls stronger. Or better. Whatever."

He regarded her thoughtfully for a while. Was he struggling to think of a nice way to say no? A blush of embarrassment crept across her cheeks.

"You trust me so much." It wasn't a question.

She answered it like it had been, "I do. I trust you with everything."

He shook his head slightly, as if he couldn't believe her words.

Laughing, she leaned over and purposely bumped shoulders with him.

He glanced over at her, a startled look on his face for a moment before he smiled. "Time to go."

She looked toward the road and saw the others approaching. "It is," she agreed, scrambling to her feet much less gracefully than he did. They both pulled their packs back on.

Prince reached over and took her hand. She looked up at him in confusion as he turned to face her, his back to the others. "Thank you," he said quietly. "For not letting me go."

She grinned and shrugged, ducking her head a little. He had sounded so serious she wasn't sure how to respond.

"You mean a great deal to me, Arowyn. Please, never forget that."

"I won't," she said, wincing at little at how shallow her words sounded. He meant so much to her too. She just wasn't sure how to say it.

*I understand.*

She started and glanced up at him before laughing. "I suppose you do."

*Shael.*

Her brows drew together as she cocked her head to the side and stared up at him in confusion. "That I really don't understand," she admitted.

He raised a finger to his lips. *My last secret I give to you, and only you. Keep it safe.*

It took her only a moment before she made the connection. "Your name," she whispered.

He nodded once, solemnly and then winked at her.

She laughed and squeezed his hand.

He turned to face the others again. "Am I forgiven now?"

She nodded, still smiling. "Of course." *I will always forgive you.*

Overall she thought their reunion went well. Kei hung back and glared. Bo and Cain tentatively shook hands and accepted Prince's stilted apology with more grace than she thought possible. She grinned at them all, swatted Kei and tried not to bounce about too happily.

"Let's get moving boys!"

They hesitated, clearly hoping to stop for a break.

She clapped her hands. "Come on! Before our prince keels over and dies." She flashed Prince a wicked grin when he stared at her in shock.

She had forgiven him for keeping his secrets.

Mostly.

# Other Works by Jen Wylie

Flashy Fiction and Other Insane Tales (anthology with Sean Hayden)

Sweet Light (novel)
Dark Madness (novel-coming soon!)

Ring Around the Rosie (short story)
Jump (short story)

Immortal Echoes
-The Forgotten Echo (novella)
-The Untouchable Echo (short story)

Tales of Ever (YA novella series)
-Banished
-Fire Girl
-Shadow Boy
-The Lost Tree
-Dragon Rising
-Sanctuary

# Jen Wylie's Biography

Jen Wylie resides in rural Ontario, Canada with her two boys, Australian shepherd, and a disagreeable amount of wildlife. In a cosmic twist of fate she dislikes the snow and cold.

Before settling down to raise a family, she attained a BA from Queens University and worked in retail and sales.

Thanks to her mother she acquired a love of books at an early age and began writing in public school. She constantly has stories floating around in her head, and finds it amazing most people don't. Jennifer writes various forms of fantasy, both novels and short stories.

Find out more about Jen at www.jenniferwylie.ca and follow her on twitter @jen_wylie